She was determined to stand her ground.

"I don't work weekends, Mr. Lindstrom," Lei said, no longer hesitant or nervous. "I'm sorry." When it came to her children, she couldn't be pushed. She would never allow the twins to feel neglected.

Paul was amused by the steel in her voice. So the shy and submissive Miss Howe could say no when she really wanted to. He liked that. "Fair enough," he said. "We'll get started Monday."

He gazed at her profile—the firm jaw, the straight shoulders. He wanted to massage the nape of her neck or curl a lock of that glorious chestnut hair around his finger. But coming on strong would be counterproductive. She would freeze up so solidly it would take him days to thaw her. There was no denying the spark between them. What he wanted would come to him if he played his cards right....

Dear Reader,

Happy New Year, and many thanks for the notes and letters you've sent to the authors and editors of Silhouette **Special Edition** over the past twelve months. Although we seldom have time to write individual responses, I'd like to take this opportunity to let you know how much we value all your comments. Your praise and plaudits warm our hearts and give our efforts meaning; your questions and suggestions keep us on our toes as we continually strive to make each of our six monthly Silhouette **Special Edition** novels a truly significant romance-reading event.

Our authors and editors believe you deserve writing of the highest caliber, satisfying novelistic scope, and a profound emotional experience with each book you read. Your letters tell us that you've come to trust Silhouette **Special Edition** to deliver romance fiction of that quality, depth, and sensitivity time and time again. With the advent of the new year, we're renewing a pledge: to do our very best, month after month, edition after edition, to continue bringing you "romance you can believe in."

On behalf of all the authors and editors of Silhouette **Special Edition**,

Thanks again and best wishes,

Leslie Kazanjian,
Senior Editor

P.S. This month, ask your bookseller for *The Forever Rose*, a new historical novel by one of your Silhouette **Special Edition** favorites, Curtiss Ann Matlock—the author has promised "family ties" to her next two contemporary novels, coming this year from Silhouette **Special Edition**!

BROOKE HASTINGS
Reluctant Mistress

Silhouette Special Edition

Published by Silhouette Books New York

America's Publisher of Contemporary Romance

Author's Note

Last summer, I noticed a tiny onyx hand around the neck of a friend who'd been raised in Hawaii. She told me it was a good luck charm, adding that, yes, she did believe in it. When you grow up in the islands, she said, the inexplicable and intangible are a fact of daily life. This book is the result.
Thanks, Susan.

For Pam,
who owns the *puuhonua*
up on Warren Avenue.
Thanks for listening.

SILHOUETTE BOOKS
300 East 42nd St., New York, N.Y. 10017

BROOKE HASTINGS

is a transplanted Easterner who now lives in California with her husband and two children. A full-time writer, she won the Romance Writers of America's Golden Medallion Award for her Silhouette Romance, *Winner Take All*. Brooke especially enjoys doing the background research for her books and finds it a real challenge to come up with new plot twists and unique characters for her stories.

Hawaiian Pronunciation Guide

Each vowel is usually pronounced separately, as follows:

> *a* as in *above* (in some words, as in father)
>
> *e* as in *send* (in some words, as in weigh)
>
> *i* as in *magazine*
>
> *o* as in *no*
>
> *u* as in *tube*

Dipthongs, however, are slurred together; for example, *ao* and *au* as in *cow*, *ai* as in *eye*, and *ei* as in *jay*.

The next-to-last syllable (or vowel) is stressed (for example, *aloha* = a-LO-ha; *hookipa* = ho-o-KI-pa). This would be the first syllable of two-syllable words (*mana* = MA-na) and the final syllable of words that end in dipthongs (*makai* = ma-KEYE).

See glossary at the back of the book.

Prologue

Niihau, Hawaii

Leilani hadn't asked about the future, though the wizened woman pouring water into a glass had more than once foretold it. Her name was Liliha, and she was a *kahuna nui*, a high priestess and healer in the ancient Hawaiian religion. Born in a small village on Kauai over eighty years before, Liliha came from a long line of priests. Her father had taught her his magic while she was still a girl, just as his father had taught him, but there the lessons had stopped. The old ways had fallen into disrepute after that.

In time, though, attitudes had changed. Pastors and *kahunas* prayed side by side nowadays. People in need of help had been known to consult both.

Liliha, who was Lei's grandmother, was considered one of the most powerful *kahunas* in Hawaii *nei*, as feared as she was revered. She carried the glass to the kitchen table and sat down. Using her thumbnail, she scraped ginger into the water to ward off any mischievous spirits that might be nearby. A shiver ran down Lei's spine. She'd witnessed this ritual twice before. Both times, Liliha's visions had been cryptic and confusing, her words of advice ambiguous and frightening. Both times, disaster had struck.

She addressed the old woman in Hawaiian, speaking the lyrical, fluent dialect unique to Niihau—the Mystery Island, the Forbidden Island. "I asked for advice, Grandmother, not for knowledge of the future. You're the cleverest person I know. How can I convince Marshall to change his mind?"

Liliha ignored the question, her eyes fixed on the glass. The water gradually became clear as the ginger settled to the bottom. The future was supposed to become clear along with it. If Liliha had any interest in Marshall Canning, the Honolulu-based developer Lei worked for, it didn't show.

She shifted uneasily in her chair, too respectful to interrupt again. Two weeks ago, while clearing some land for a housing complex south of Waikane on Oahu, Marshall's men had uncovered an ancient burial ground and ruined *heiau*, or temple, on the site. Native groups considered the area sacred and wanted development there stopped. Marshall sympathized with their feelings but was worried about his wallet. He'd offered to transfer everything to another site, but he wasn't willing to turn a substantial part of his land into a shrine and sacrifice his profits in the process.

Muttering to herself, Liliha pulled a silver coin out of her pocket and placed it beneath the glass. Her *unihipili* or low self—what psychologists would have called her unconscious—evidently wasn't cooperating in this mystical rite, and the coin was meant as an inducement, or at least an attention getter. Lei didn't know how or why, but the ancient ways worked. Her grandmother had second sight. She'd cured people when modern medicine had failed to.

Another minute went by. Too tense to hold her tongue, Lei finally murmured, "Perhaps the future is too unsettled to see. Everyone is being so stubborn. Still, there must be some approach I haven't thought of, some compromise—"

"Just like your mother," the old woman said with a shake of her head. "A *haole*." Despite her sharp tone, she looked more resigned than disapproving.

A *haole*. A Caucasian. Lei didn't know what Liliha meant, unless it was that her mother, Ella, had worked for and married a white man, Lei's father, Creighton Howe, and Liliha thought she would do the same. "But I've told you, Marshall thinks of me as the daughter he never had. There's nothing romantic between us."

Liliha waved her hand dismissively. "Forget Marshall Canning. He has nothing to do with this." She pursed her lips. "You with a *haole*. I never thought I would see it. You said you would give yourself only to a *kanaka*, and I believed you. There are so few of us left. Our blood runs thinner with each new generation." She sighed. "Still, fate is fate. It's not your fault."

Crystal ball or not, the idea of Lei marrying a *haole* was ridiculous. She preferred *kanakas*, men who were at least part Hawaiian, for their looks, their sensibilities and their gentleness. "Excuse me, Grandmother, but if your glass shows me with a *haole* husband, it must be wrong. If I ever—"

"Husband?" The old woman gazed into the water again. "I see no husband, only a lover. The vision is clear. It will be soon."

Lei simply stared at her. That was impossible. Her niece and nephew came first in her life. It had taken them years to get over the loss of their parents. The day she took a lover would be the day she found someone worthy of being their father, someone she loved and wanted to marry.

Even so, Liliha's prediction unnerved her. The old woman had been right far too often. "But how can that be? I have no interest in men. The twins are too young. I'm far too busy. There must be another explanation. Maybe the man in the glass is a friend, or someone I'll meet when..."

Her voice trailed off. There was another possibility—a chilling, brutal one. Twice before, Liliha had predicted her future. Twice before, the visions had preceded violence. She shivered with horror. "You said I would give myself. This man . . . Are you sure he doesn't just—take me?"

"You mean rape you?" Liliha cackled, openly amused by the question. "Not this one. He won't have to. He's a handsome devil—for a *haole*, that is. Yellow hair, blue eyes, strong and tall. . . ." She smiled slyly. "You'll offer yourself, my girl. He won't even have to ask you."

Lei relaxed a little, telling herself that nobody she knew fit that description even remotely. Besides, one didn't turn into a seductress after twenty-five years of being the opposite. The old woman wasn't omniscient. She'd been known to make mistakes.

"He sounds like one of those Californians who come here with the pro surfing tour," she said. "I'm afraid they're not my type. Couldn't you conjure me up someone more appealing?"

Liliha's eyes twinkled. She was as earthy as she was shrewd and quick. "My powers don't extend to conjuring, only to seeing what's in front of my nose. He's a man, not a beach boy. Strong. Passionate. Experienced in the ways of the world."

"He sounds tempting," Lei said with a smile, "maybe even tempting enough to lead a backward girl like *me* down the garden path into vice and ruin." If he was even half the man Liliha claimed, she looked forward to meeting him.

"So you're still the innocent." Liliha rolled her eyes at the idea. "It's the bad influence of your father's missionary forebears, Leilani. We Hawaiians have more sense. We know that pleasure's not a sin."

There was only one way to parry the old woman's gibes— by playing along. "Pleasure, eh? And what does your glass tell you about this *haole*'s talents in the bedroom? Will bells peal? Will the earth move?"

Liliha grinned. "I should chase you out of the kitchen for mocking me, but maybe the spirits want me to answer." She stared into the glass again.

Lei leaned back in her chair, watching absently as the old woman's smile faded and a look of intense concentration stole over her face. It was all very well to trade quips about some fanciful *haole* lover, but that wouldn't resolve the dispute at Waikane. Liliha had to help her.

A sudden, thready gasp yanked her attention back to her grandmother's face. The old woman's eyes were riveted on the water, glazed with distress. Lei's heart began to pound wildly. She knew that look. She'd seen it twice before. After the first time, her father had died. After the second, she'd lost her brother and his wife.

"What's wrong?" she asked. "What do you see?"

"I see . . ." Liliha hesitated, reluctant to answer.

"What, Grandmother?" It was something awful. The air felt heavy with doom. "Tell me!"

Liliha pushed away the glass. Avoiding Lei's eyes, she muttered, "I saw suffering."

"From what? Who was suffering? Was it me?"

"I don't know. I couldn't tell."

Lei didn't believe her. She was too evasive, too upset. "That's what you said the other two times. You spoke of pain and anguish, and you said the visions were too cloudy to tell anything more, but you were trying to spare us, weren't you?" She raised her chin, as stubborn as she was frightened. "Nothing's worse than nameless fear, Grandmother. Nothing's worse than not knowing. Tell me what you saw."

"You have a strong will, my girl. Maybe too strong." Liliha's expression softened. She wasn't a warm woman, but she loved her family, especially Leilani. There was profound sadness in her eyes as she said slowly, "All right, since you insist. There were two visions. You were in both."

"And the first?" Lei prodded. "What was I doing?"

Liliha sighed, then answered in a near whisper, "Your hands were clenched. Your body was rigid. You were in great pain. You wanted to escape but didn't. And in the second..." She paused. "Fear and anguish. The pain was in your mind this time. It was even worse."

Lei told herself that suffering was nothing new to her. She'd survived it before and would do so again. "And was I alone in these visions? Did you see who caused the pain?"

The old woman nodded. "It was the *haole*. He wasn't in the visions, but I could feel his *mana.*" His vital force. "It was very powerful."

This whole conversation had revolved around some mysterious stranger who would turn her life upside down, so who else could it have been? The prophecy could have been far worse—it could have concerned her mother or the twins. "There are worse things than an unhappy love affair," she said. "Besides, the future you see in your glass isn't always fixed. You've told me that it can be changed sometimes."

"It's not just an unhappy love affair. It might drain away your life, crush your soul." Liliha leaned forward, urgent and grave now. "The *haole* will cause you pain. It's your fate. In my vision, the more you resisted, the worse it was, but maybe if you do what he wants..." She shuddered. "Don't fight him, child. Don't defy destiny. For once in your life, bend to someone else's will."

Something inside Lei rebelled. This was twentieth-century America, not ancient Hawaii. A man couldn't dominate a woman by the sheer force of his *mana*, and any female who sacrificed her free will on the altar of fate was either a fool or a coward. Liliha must have misinterpreted what she'd seen.

Still, the old woman believed what she'd said, and Lei didn't want her to worry. "Very well, Grandmother. I'll do what this man wants."

"You won't," Liliha replied. "I'm not a fool. I can see the defiance in your eyes. Your father's blood runs too strongly in your veins, making you think mortals can challenge the gods." She took Lei's hand and squeezed it, startling her. The old woman rarely embraced her. "You'll fight, child, but you'll lose. Come to me afterward. Maybe I'll be able to help you.''

"Yes. I will.'' That much was true. Lei had always turned to her family for comfort and strength.

Liliha released her hand and straightened. The session was over, the subject closed. Relieved, Lei reminded her about the problem that had brought her to Niihau. "About the Waikane project, Grandmother... There are protests every day—just marching and speeches, but feelings run high on the issue and these things have a way of getting out of hand. Marshall threatened to—''

"Forget him. He won't matter.''

"Do you mean that someone else will decide what happens? The courts or the politicians?''

The old woman shrugged. "When I looked into the glass, I saw you and then the *haole*. I felt the presence of my people and my ancestors, but there was no aura of Canning. Maybe he'll leave Hawaii, or sell his land... or die.''

Liliha was indifferent to Marshall's fate, but Lei wasn't. He was as generous personally as he was tough in business, hiring her when she was only twenty, encouraging her to finish college and never complaining when she missed work because of the twins. The world seemed to be shifting under her feet. A lover she didn't want, a man she loved suddenly vanishing... She didn't want to think about such things. She didn't want to believe they could happen.

She pushed the possibility from her mind. Her grandmother might be a *kahuna nui*, but she was also old and frail, as fallible as anyone else. She'd made a mistake. She must have.

Chapter One

Paul Lindstrom was sitting in the first-class section of a 747, wondering why he felt drawn to a place that by all rights he should have wanted to avoid. He barely paid any attention when a flight attendant tried to flirt with him. She wasn't his type.

No one was anymore, not since Karen had left. He still missed her at times, but the thought of marrying her had given him the chills. Maybe he wanted the impossible—to fall so deeply in love that even moving to the suburbs and becoming an expert on lawn care and diaper rash looked good. With Karen, it hadn't. It had felt all wrong.

At the moment, his only commitment was to lower his golf score. With the office in its annual January lull, he'd been able to play several times a week. He'd enjoyed the respite, but a couple of hot deals were shimmering on the horizon, and he expected to enjoy those, too. The last thing he should have wanted was to chase off to Hawaii and what sounded like a complicated, trying assignment, but for some reason he did.

Maybe it was the challenge. He had a rare talent for getting trouble-plagued projects back on track, something that had earned him a fancy title and the chance to open a San Francisco branch of the Los Angeles-based company he worked for. He'd even been invited to invest in one of the company's projects last year. For a kid who'd left home at seventeen and lived in a banged up car while he looked for a job and a place to live, that was heady stuff.

He glanced at his boss, who was snoring softly in the next seat. A few years before, when Everett had reached seventy, he'd turned the presidency of his company over to his son and moved to Northern California. He was still the chairman, though, keeping a close eye on the bottom line and approving or rejecting each possible project.

Paul admired him enormously, both personally and professionally. It was typical of Everett Canning that he would drop everything in order to help someone who needed him, in this case his brother, Marshall. A developer in Honolulu, Marshall was in the hospital recovering from a heart attack. He'd asked Everett to take over a large, troubled project until he got back on his feet, and Everett had agreed immediately. Then he'd called Paul and asked if he minded being loaned out for a couple of months.

Paul owed Everett more than he could repay. He wouldn't have refused even if he'd wanted to. It was just odd that he hadn't wanted to.

Lei always went to the airport with Marshall to meet people from out of state. They enjoyed being greeted with the traditional lei and kiss on the cheek, and as a part-Hawaiian, she was perfect for the job. Marshall always told her that nobody looked as good in a muumuu as she did, but the flattery wasn't necessary. She enjoyed welcoming visitors.

Today, though, the duty was a sad one. The man by her side wasn't Marshall Canning, but Cliff Whitney, who handled the financial end of Marshall's business. Marshall was in St. Francis Medical Center recovering from a heart attack. Though the doctors had labeled it relatively mild, it still had come as a shock. Despite the cigars he constantly smoked, he'd never had a chest pain in his life.

Lei looked out the window. She and Cliff had come to meet Marshall's brother, Everett, who was flying in from San Francisco to help however he could. In two years with the company, Cliff had become the closest thing Marshall had to a right-hand man, but he was no developer, no deal maker. Marshall was too much of a loner to have trained anyone to take his place.

A jumbo jet was moving slowly into place by the gate. "There they are," Lei said. "I only hope we recognize him." She'd never seen Everett in person, but there was a picture of him and his family on Marshall's desk.

Cliff smiled. "Me, too. I wouldn't want you to kiss the wrong guy."

"You wouldn't want me to give the wrong guy this lei." She was holding two of them, one made of fragrant plumeria, the other of rare Niihau shells. She and Cliff had bought it at Marshall's request, a precious and special gift for a man who was doing them a special favor. Love had brought Everett to Hawaii, not business. Both brothers were developers, but there was no legal tie between Canning Enterprises of Hawaii and Canning Construction and Development of California.

"Umm." Cliff touched the shell lei reverently. "My wife would love to own something like this. I wish I could afford to buy her one for our twenty-fifth anniversary."

Between a new car, a huge mortgage and four children in private schools, it was no wonder that Cliff was always broke. "Maybe Marshall will. I'll drop him a hint as soon as he's better."

"Assuming he ever is." Cliff stared into the jetway, watching the first passengers emerge. "I still can't believe he had a heart attack. I thought he was immortal—never seriously sick and able to juggle five different deals without forgetting a single detail. I don't care what the doctors say—this is scaring the hell out of me."

Lei didn't reply. She was every bit as scared as Cliff but reluctant to say so aloud, as if giving voice to the thought would make it come true. She couldn't forget the previous Saturday, and her grandmother's disturbing prophecy: *"Forget Marshall Canning. He won't matter."*

A moderate heart attack wouldn't be enough to cause that. Marshall was supposed to return to work in a few months. Maybe something else was going to happen.

Cliff touched her arm and pointed into the tunnel. "There he is. He's wearing a yellow shirt and tan pants."

The jetway was dim, so it took Lei a moment to spot him. He was holding a large flight bag, and was engrossed in conversation with the man to his left. "Who's he talking to? Marshall didn't say he was bringing anyone with him."

"Another passenger, probably. A businessman, judging by that fancy attaché case he's carrying. Check out the pinstripes, Lei. Talk about looking like a *malihini*!'

He did look like a newcomer, or maybe like a lawyer on his way to court. Someone who'd done business here before would have realized it was a Friday, when even executives at the old-line *haole* firms wore colorful aloha shirts to work. It was Honolulu's way of asserting its unique identity.

She and Cliff inched forward, stationing themselves near the front of the crowd. She got a clearer look at Everett's companion as he emerged from the tunnel. Blond, sun-streaked hair. Easily over six feet. Thirtyish, broad shouldered and athletic looking—not an ounce of flab in sight. Tanned and handsome, maybe even handsome enough to draw stares from passing women, although not from Lei. As she'd told her grandmother, she preferred *kanakas*.

Her grandmother. The thought brought her up short. She recognized this *haole* visitor. He was the man in Liliha's glass. The descriptions matched exactly, except that she couldn't see the color of his eyes.

Cliff smiled and waved. "Over here, Mr. Canning! Welcome to Hawaii, sir."

The men turned when they heard Canning's name. The stranger's eyes, she saw, were blue. The color drained from her face.

Paul dropped several steps behind Everett and sized up the people who had come to meet them. The man was dressed in a brightly printed shirt and dark pants instead of a suit, but he had the confident air of a high-level executive. Casual clothing or not, he was probably someone important.

The girl was younger and very lovely—everything a man wanted to find waiting for him in a tropical paradise. She was slender and tall, probably around five-foot-ten. Her eyes were a warm dark brown, gently rounded and spaced exotically wide apart. The rest of her features were more classic—soft, full lips, a delicate nose and high cheekbones set in a perfect oval frame. She had long, wavy chestnut hair and beautiful skin, so smooth and dewy that he found himself wanting to touch it. It was lighter than one would have expected in a pure Polynesian, so probably she was a mixture. Lots of people here were.

She was beautiful enough to be a model hired by Marshall Canning to give his brother a proper Hawaiian greeting, but Paul had the feeling she was an employee. Only one thing puzzled him. For a moment or two, she'd stared at him in utter shock. Then she'd forced a smile onto her face and looked straight through him, as if she was pretending he didn't exist.

Lei was certainly trying, but she wasn't succeeding. She was acutely aware that the man behind Everett was studying her in the most elemental male way. He was the man in Liliha's vision. There was no doubt of it.

She wanted him to stop looking at her. She wanted him to stop desiring her. Most of all, she wanted him to go away, to thank Everett for an enjoyable conversation on the plane and then excuse himself, never to be seen again.

Everett set down his flight bag and held out his hand to Cliff. "I'm Everett Canning, Marshall's brother."

"Cliff Whitney, Mr. Canning—the company's controller." They shook hands. "Thank you for coming. I spoke to your brother on the phone this morning and he sounded a bit better—a little stronger and more cheerful."

"Thank God for that." Everett smiled at Lei. "You must be Leilani Howe. We missed each other when my wife and I came here three years ago. You were visiting your family on the island that's privately owned. Niihau, isn't it?"

"Yes, Mr. Canning." She stepped forward and raised her arms. "Aloha and *mahalo*."

He grasped her wrists and gently pulled them down. "You're giving those to the wrong fellow, Miss Howe. Lindy? Where the hell did he...?" He looked around, spotting his companion a few yards behind him. "There you are. Come over here and let me introduce you."

Lindy. Lei's smile faltered. She knew that nickname well, and not just in reference to the famous aviator. One of the local papers followed San Francisco society news religiously, regularly reprinting excerpts from the city's premier gossip column. She'd seen the phrase dozens of times in print—"Canning Veep Lindy Lindstrom..." The man with Everett was no casual acquaintance from his flight, but one of his employees. He wasn't going to go away, not anytime soon.

Paul walked forward. So Leilani did work for Marshall Canning. That meant she'd be working with *him* soon, a thought that made this mission infinitely more appealing.

Everett clapped him on the back. "Mr. Whitney, Miss Howe... This is Paul Lindstrom, who runs my office in San Francisco. I'll be filling in for him at home while he handles your problems here in Hawaii. I just hope I can get him to leave once my brother recovers.''

Whitney looked startled while Leilani stiffened and struggled to smile. For the life of him, Paul couldn't figure out what her problem was. He wondered if he reminded her of someone she preferred to forget.

Whitney shook his hand a little tentatively. ''I have to admit I didn't expect this. Marshall didn't mention you were coming.''

''Marshall didn't know,'' Everett said. ''I didn't want to tell him over the phone, just hours after he'd had a heart attack. I'll explain things when I see him.'' He paused. ''I'm seventy-two years old, Cliff. I don't pick things up as fast as I used to or have the patience and energy I once did. Lindy is the best troubleshooter I've ever seen. He's straightened out screwed-up projects from Seattle to San Diego. He isn't familiar with Hawaii, so you'll have to brief him thoroughly, but once he has a feel for the situation, he'll do twice the job for you that I could. That's a promise.''

''In that case, we appreciate your coming,'' Cliff said to Paul. ''God knows we could use some help.'' He looked at Lei and grinned broadly. ''You're holding those things in a death grip, Lei. Greet the man before you pulverize them. I'm sure he won't bite you.''

Lei hadn't realized she was clutching the leis so tightly. Embarrassed, she looped them over Lindstrom's head, taking care not to touch his crisp, clean hair. Given how jumpy she was, he probably thought she was *pupule*—crazy. She had to get a grip on herself. She had to get used to his existence.

She caught the spicy scent of his after-shave as she settled the leis around his neck. Ignoring the unsettling tingle in her wrists, she told herself that anyone with half a brain would be delighted to see him. If he was as good as Everett said, he was exactly what they needed.

She fanned out the leis so they rested properly against his chest, then hesitated. If she didn't kiss him hello, Cliff would never let her hear the end of it. He loved to tease her, probably because she was so closemouthed. That was typical of ethnic Hawaiians, but she was private even for a Hawaiian. She wasn't sure why, but she found it hard to talk about herself.

She couldn't bring herself to meet Lindstrom's eyes, so she looked at his mouth. He was smiling. Obviously he was amused. Like Cliff, he was waiting to see what she would do.

He was so tall that she had to stand on tiptoes to reach his cheek. She wobbled precariously, then blushed. Nothing like this had ever happened to her before. She was usually graceful and steady.

Having no choice, she rested her hands on his shoulders to balance herself. Then she kissed him firmly, letting her lips linger on his cheek so Cliff couldn't tease her about rushing. "Aloha, Mr. Lindstrom, and *mahalo*." Glad it was over, she released him and took a step backward, almost stumbling over her feet in the process. She wanted to sink through the floor.

Paul set down his attaché case. He knew he'd received the exact same greeting as countless other visitors to these islands, but there was nothing routine about his response to it. His throat was tight and his heart was racing, as if he'd spent the past five minutes making love to this woman. It was a little like being hit by a truck, only infinitely more pleasurable.

Perfume filled his nostrils, either from the flowers or from Lei herself, he wasn't sure. His cheek felt hot where her lips had touched it. He could still feel the light brush of her fingers on his shoulders and chest as she nervously adjusted the two leis. And he'd thought nobody was his type anymore! Leilani Howe sure as hell was.

He studied her, taking in her flushed face and lowered eyes. She was enchanting, captivating. Maybe it was the spell of the tropics, but he didn't care that he was in a crowded airport with his boss looking on, or that he and Lei barely knew each other. He wanted her to think of him as a man, not as a business associate.

"Miss Howe." He tucked a finger under her chin. She started at the unexpected contact but didn't recoil. Instead she gazed at him with those enormous brown eyes of hers and waited. Encouraged by the glazed confusion he saw, he kept his finger under her chin for a moment longer. Her skin was as soft and sweet as he'd imagined it would be.

He smiled his warmest, gentlest smile. "You keep using the word *mahalo*. I don't know what it means."

"It means thank you. *Mahalo* for your *kokua*. For your help." Her eyes slid downward again. "We use those two words often in Hawaii." She pronounced the name of the state with a little catch in the middle: Hawai'i.

"You're very welcome." He was experienced enough to know when a woman was attracted to him, and this one definitely was. A few months in Hawaii looked better all the time.

A lock of her hair had fallen across her cheek, so he tucked it gently behind her ear. The flush on her face deepened. "I like the way you greet people here. Beats the heck out of the way women do it in Beverly Hills."

Lei didn't want to know how women greeted people in Beverly Hills. She wanted Paul Lindstrom to stop being so charming—to stop smiling at her in a way that could have melted hardened lava and touching her as if she were as delicate as an orchid. He was affecting her in a devastating way, making her feel agitated and hot and frightened. Liliha's prophecy—and her prediction of pain and fear—hung over her head like a sword. She didn't answer.

"I can see that you're dying of curiosity. It goes something like this." He put his hands on her shoulders. "'Lindy, darling! How are you? It's been much too long!'"

His voice was a breathless falsetto, as phony as it was honeyed. Lei smiled despite herself—even Eddie Murphy couldn't have done a funnier female impersonation.

"Then they kiss the air on each side of your cheek, like this." He demonstrated, complete with smacking noises.

She was still smiling when he released her. "I've seen that in the movies. I thought they were exaggerating."

"No way. It's one of the reasons I prefer San Francisco." There was a devilish glint in his eye. "Ask me what they do in San Francisco, Miss Howe."

"Maybe some other time, Mr. Lindstrom." She took a wary step backward. She knew better than to encourage him.

"A wise move, my dear," Everett drawled. "The women he has in mind throw their arms around him and kiss him on the mouth, not necessarily platonically. Especially the bored, married ones." He picked up his flight bag. "I didn't bring any other luggage, so I'll catch a cab straight to the hospital. I'll come downtown afterward. In the meantime, why don't you settle Lindy in the company apartment and introduce him around?"

"Let us run you up there—"

"No thanks, Cliff. I want to get going. I won't relax until I've seen my brother for myself." He paused and smiled. "And Lindy—a modest piece of advice."

Paul cocked an eyebrow at him. "What's that, Everett?"

"Leave Miss Howe alone. She's not in your league." Still smiling, he waved jauntily and sauntered away.

It wasn't advice Paul planned to take, but Everett was probably right. Lei looked so mortified he could have kicked his boss clear to the next island for embarrassing her. Things went from bad to worse when Cliff coughed to cover his laughter and excused himself to retrieve his car, leaving the two of them alone.

"We should get your bags," she finally said, watching Cliff walk away.

"Right." They started toward the baggage claim area, Lei walking briskly and stiffly.

An awkward silence fell. Paul was nettled that things had deteriorated so quickly. Sometimes he thought Everett enjoyed making his life difficult, teasing him in front of people he'd have to work with and terrifying a woman he was obviously interested in.

He grimaced. Getting annoyed wasn't going to help. "I want you to know one thing, Miss Howe," he said solemnly. "Remember those married women Everett mentioned? I've never kissed any of them back."

Once again, Lei was amused despite herself. Did he expect her to congratulate him on his high morals? Praise him for refusing to take part in adultery? She glanced at him, saw the boyish grin on his face, and smiled helplessly. He'd only been joking. Some of the tension left her body.

Two of his suitcases had come through by the time they reached the carousel, but he made no move to leave. Bags kept emerging and the carousel kept turning, but whatever he was waiting for didn't appear. He got grimmer and grimmer, until Lei finally asked him what was missing.

"My golf clubs," he said. "Custom-made. They cost me a fortune."

Unless she missed her guess, so had his imported luggage, his leather attaché case and his perfectly tailored suit. Obviously he had money, but not so much of it that losing an expensive set of golf clubs didn't bother him.

Fortunately they probably weren't lost. "Your airline usually brings golf clubs directly inside, just to be on the safe side. Their office is right over there. If you want to check, I'll wait with your bags."

He returned a minute later with the clubs, smiling in relief. Marshall loved to play golf, so Lei knew about the local courses. She described Marshall's favorites as she and Lindstrom made their way outside.

Cliff had thrown some cartons of files in his trunk for a meeting later that day, so there wasn't enough room for the clubs. Lindstrom wedged them in front, then opened the back door and waited for Lei to precede him into the car.

It took her a few minutes to realize that he could just as easily have put the clubs in back and himself in front. She wasn't naive enough to think he'd arranged things that way by chance. Most women would have been either annoyed or flattered, but Lei was simply uneasy. The closer he came, the more attracted to him she was, and she didn't want to be. She wanted to find him ugly and boring, so she could dismiss Liliha's prophecy as an awful mistake.

He rested his arm along the back of the seat and turned to face her. She told herself he was only getting comfortable, not coming on to her, but there was less than a foot of space between them and his hand was only inches from her neck. She knew it was silly to feel threatened, but she still edged closer to the door. The trip couldn't end soon enough.

"If we have the time, I'd like to do some sight-seeing," he said to Cliff. "I know there's more to Oahu than warehouses. I definitely saw blue and green from the plane."

Cliff laughed. "Office buildings. Shopping centers. Condos and hotels. If you want beauty, you'll have to drive into the country." He glanced at the clock. It was one-thirty. "I have a meeting at two, but Lei can probably take you. She's the best tour guide in the office."

Lei didn't want to be alone with Lindstrom, but fortunately she had an excuse to put him off. "Mr. Canning—Everett, that is—said he'd stop by the office later. We might miss him if we go out this afternoon."

Lindstrom smiled as if he could see right through her. "How about tomorrow, then?"

Her grandmother had described her as willful, but that wasn't really true. On the contrary, she hated to argue and was quick to give in to people's demands. There were only two areas where she couldn't be pushed, Hawaii and her children. Time and again, she'd fought with all her heart to preserve the beauty of her beloved islands, and she would have cut off her hands before allowing the twins to feel lonely or afraid.

"Tomorrow is Saturday," she said. She wasn't hesitant or nervous now, just determined to stand her ground. "I don't work weekends, Mr. Lindstrom. I'm sorry."

Paul was amused by the steel in her voice. So the shy and submissive Miss Howe could say no when she really wanted to. He liked that. "Fair enough," he said. "We'll do it Monday."

He gazed at her profile—the firm jaw, the straight shoulders, the sternly set mouth. He wanted to massage her nape or curl a lock of that glorious chestnut hair around his finger, but he didn't. Coming on too strong would be counterproductive. She would freeze up so solidly it would take him days to thaw her out. What he wanted would come to him in time if he played his cards right. There was no denying the spark between the two of them.

"On the other hand," he continued, "we *are* in the middle of a crisis. I might need your help this weekend—to explain something or dig something out of the files, for example."

She crumbled so completely that he would have been ashamed of himself if he hadn't really meant it.

"Of course I'll be available. My number is on Marshall's Rolodex." She paused. "The easiest time for me to come is after nine at night. If you need me, just call."

"Actually, I'll probably spend the weekend looking at paperwork," he admitted. "Marshall told Everett it was endless."

"The project has a long history. I'll give you the material I put together for Everett. It should provide a good overview."

Paul nodded and loosened his tie. The car was air-conditioned, but he was used to San Francisco and felt uncomfortably warm. He unbuttoned the top few buttons of his shirt, and then, feeling a little foolish with all those flowers and shells around his neck, pulled off the leis and tossed them onto the seat.

A horrified look crossed Lei's face. She controlled it very quickly, but Paul still knew he'd committed a grievous faux pas. "What?" he said. "Is it bad luck to take them off? An insult to my hosts?"

There was a burst of laughter from the front seat. "It's probably both, Mr. Lindstrom, but—"

"People call me 'Lindy.'"

"'Lindy,' then. You see those shells you just pitched onto the seat? Those are from Niihau, where Lei's family lives. They're extremely rare—worth thousands of dollars. A very valuable gift for a highly esteemed and much appreciated visitor." Cliff stopped for a red light, then looked back over his shoulder and added with a grin, "I'm speaking of Everett, of course."

"Who presumably would have had the sense to be more careful with them." Paul wasn't used to making such stupid mistakes. Chagrined, he picked up the leis and put them back on. "I'll give the shells to Everett when I see him," he said to Lei, "but if you don't mind, I'll keep the flowers. And please—forgive my ignorance. I made the mistake of thinking Hawaii was just like the States—"

"We *are* one of the United States, Mr. Lindstrom," she interrupted. "It would be better to say that you thought Hawaii was just like the mainland."

He rarely blushed, but he did so now. Then he shook his head in dismay. "From bad to worse, huh? You want to ship me back to San Francisco?"

Lei smiled at the pained expression on his face. She hadn't taken offense at his slip, though some in Hawaii would have. She simply hadn't been able to resist correcting him. "I don't think so," she said. At least he was willing to listen and learn. "You Californians are an ignorant bunch, but we'll do our best to educate you."

"I'll look forward to it," Paul said. He'd always enjoyed a challenge. Learning about Hawaii was going to give him a run for his money—and so was Leilani Howe.

Chapter Two

Canning Enterprises was located in Emerald Plaza, a forty-story office and apartment tower on Bishop Street in Honolulu's compact commercial district. The "Big Five" *haole* firms that had once dominated Hawaii's economy were just down the street, and major government offices were a short walk away. Cliff parked in the building's garage, pulling into a space by the elevators. Marshall Canning had put together the *hui*, or investment group, that had financed Emerald Plaza and still held a major interest in the project. The benefits included a pair of prime parking spaces, a small but choice office and a corner penthouse apartment.

They went directly upstairs. The apartment hadn't been used in weeks, so it was hot and a little musty. They hadn't aired it out because they'd expected only Everett, who was staying at Marshall's house.

It was two by then, and Cliff was late for his meeting. He wasn't concerned about that; Hawaiians didn't believe in enslaving themselves to the clock.

"I'll get Mr. Lindstrom settled, then show him around the office," Lei said. "We can brief him when you get back."

Cliff nodded. "Fine. I shouldn't be too long—two hours at the most." He shook hands with Lindstrom, then let himself out of the apartment.

Now that she and Lindstrom were alone, Lei was downright nervous. "If you'll come with me..." she said. They picked up the luggage and started down the hall, Lei leading the way. She could feel him studying her, assessing his chances. He barely knew her, but he wanted to take her to bed. That was typical of men. It was all physical with them, at least at first.

A part of her wanted to give up and get it over with. Maybe Liliha was right. Maybe the force of his spirit—his *mana*—was so strong that she would surrender without a peep.

She led him into the master suite, which was furnished with pieces made of precious Hawaiian koa wood. She stared at the king-size bed. A *haole* lover. Was this where it would happen? Would he take her on this enormous bed?

"I'm sorry it's so hot in here," she mumbled. "I'll turn on the air-conditioning."

She walked briskly into the living room, set the thermostat at sixty-eight and opened the drapes. Windows ran along both exterior walls, providing a sweeping view of the island. Directly ahead of her, the ornate and lovely Iolani Palace sat in a verdant park surrounded by busy city streets. The Koolau Mountains rose like undulating green velvet on her left, while the Pacific was visible to her right, a soothing, seemingly endless expanse of azure.

Lindstrom crossed the room and joined her by the window. "Maybe you should leave them closed. I'll never be able to work with a view that beautiful in front of me."

She felt a tug of empathy. It was only natural to like someone who praised her islands. Flustered, she withdrew into the safety of tour-guide formality. "We call this way *makai*, toward the sea," she said, pointing at the ocean, "and that way Diamond Head, because it's toward—"

"Diamond Head Crater," he finished. "I thumbed through a guidebook during the flight over. It mentioned the names for directions. There's also *moka* and *eewa*, right?"

He'd butchered the two words, so obviously he'd skipped the section on Hawaiian pronounciation. "Yes, but they're pronounced 'MOW-kah' and 'EH-vah,' Mr. Lindstrom." *Mauka* meant toward the central mountains; *Ewa* referred to a town west of Pearl Harbor.

"I was always lousy at languages, and why don't you make that 'Paul'?" he replied.

Lei found it odd that he would ask her to call him 'Paul' rather than 'Lindy,' but she didn't comment. She wasn't going to use either. "You won't have any trouble with Hawaiian. The rules for pronouncing it are simple. There are only a few words you'll come across in day-to-day conversation. If your own guidebook doesn't have a good glossary, you can use one of ours."

She walked over to a wide, floor-to-ceiling bookcase. "We have a wonderful collection of Hawaiiana here—history, business, natural science.... It will be hard to work effectively in Hawaii unless you're familiar with our history and culture, so you may want to do some background reading." She removed a thick volume from one of the shelves. "This is a good basic history."

She recommended book after book, but Paul was too preoccupied to absorb what she was saying. Nobody called him 'Paul' except for his mother and Everett's daughter, Melissa, so why had he asked Lei to? He only tolerated it because it reminded him of things it was important not to forget—in his mother's case, the years before he'd left home, and in Melissa's, the fact that he couldn't always have the things he wanted.

He'd started calling himself 'Lindy' when he was eighteen, feeling that it represented someone different and better than the raw-boned, ignorant adolescent who'd run away to Los Angeles the year before. On Lei's lips, though, 'Lindy' would have sounded all wrong—too brittle and informal. She seemed to belong to another world, an ancient and ethereal one that existed only in Hawaii. The more he saw of that world, the more he wanted to enter it.

She was removing yet another book from the shelf when she checked herself and smiled ruefully. "I get carried away when it comes to Hawaii. It's the professor's daughter in me, I guess. You'll do well to read even half of these." She put the book away. "Would you like to see the rest of the apartment?"

Anything that kept Paul alone with Lei was fine with him. "Sure. Where does your father teach?"

"He taught anthropology at the University of Hawaii in Manoa. He's gone now. His books are on the shelf—his name was Creighton Howe." She walked into the dining room. She'd said as much about her father as she was comfortable saying. "Marshall likes to hold lunch meetings in here. It's efficient and convenient." She continued through to the kitchen, turning down the thermostats on the freezer and refrigerator. "The cleaning service comes in three times a week. They'll do whatever you like—wash and iron your clothes, pick up and deliver your dry cleaning, even shop for you if you give them a list of what you want. Please don't hesitate to take advantage of them. We want you to be comfortable here."

Paul knew he wouldn't be asked to pay for any of these amenities. "Everett was right. A few months of this and I'll be spoiled so rotten I won't want to leave."

"You'll be working very hard for us. It's the least we can do." She led him across the hallway into a small office. He always stood a little too close—close enough to touch her, close enough to be a threat. "You can access our computer system from this terminal. Cliff will give you a personal access code and a list of the current passwords.''

He nodded and smiled, the same warm smile he'd directed her way before. She felt a nervous flutter in the pit of her stomach. Thank God they were almost finished. ''There's just one more room—another bedroom. If you'll come with me?'' She turned around.

''You're very efficient,'' he said as they walked down the hall. ''I'm beginning to think you don't need me at all—that you could straighten out the Waikane project by yourself.''

''Thank you, but I couldn't. I'm not very good at politics—at least, not at the compromise sort of politics.''

''Really? And what sort are you good at?''

''Talking to people about something I believe in. I've been accused of nagging them half to death at times.''

Laughing, he thanked her for the warning and opened the door to the final bedroom. As he glanced around inside, she murmured, ''I think I've covered everything, so unless you have a question...''

''At the moment, all I want to know is...'' He looked at her plaintively. ''Do I have to keep wearing these leis?''

She fought down a smile. Like most mainland men, he probably felt unmasculine in them. ''I'll take the shell lei for Everett if you'd like.'' She took a jewelry case out of her purse and flipped it open. ''You might want to put the flowers in the refrigerator so you can enjoy them later on.''

''I'll do that.'' He handed her the shells and walked off toward the kitchen.

When he rejoined her in the foyer, she noticed that he'd buttoned his shirt and straightened his tie. If he'd been someone else—not the *haole* from Liliha's glass—she would have told him it was proper to dress less formally here and suggested places to shop, but the topic seemed too personal. It was none of her business what he wore.

They left the apartment and rode downstairs. Canning Enterprises was on the twelfth floor, directly across from a door reading Canning-Davis Property Management. "Another of Marshall's companies?" Paul asked.

Lei was more relaxed now that the intimacy of the quiet apartment was behind them. "It used to be. He started the firm in the early fifties with his brother-in-law, Charles Davis, and several minor investors. About five years ago, just after I came to work here, Charles died, and his son John decided he wanted to run the company."

She paused, thinking that if Marshall's brother trusted Paul Lindstrom, then so could she. "Marshall didn't have the stomach for a fight. His wife had died a few months before, and he was still grief-stricken. He sold John a controlling interest and kept the rest of his stock as an investment. John's done very well with the firm. He and Marshall get along fine now. In fact, John got his fiancée a job as our receptionist. You'll meet her in a moment. Her name is Amy Farrell."

They walked into Canning Enterprises. Paul took a quick look around. The reception room was small, containing little more than a wooden desk, coffee and end tables made of glass and bamboo and twin love seats upholstered in a bright print that would have been considered gaudy in San Francisco but seemed exactly right for Hawaii. There were no windows to provide a view, but the tropical plants sitting in large containers along the walls helped make up for it.

Lei introduced him to Amy Farrell and explained why he'd come to Hawaii. Davis was obviously a rich man, he thought, because Amy had a diamond the size of a small rock on her finger.

She excused herself to answer the phone, assured the caller that Marshall was feeling better and turned back to Lei. "Grace went to the hospital with Marshall's mail and messages. He absolutely insisted. We can't figure out how he plans to talk the nurses into letting him work."

"By threatening to check himself out if they don't?"

Amy grinned. "Could be. Bernice Kapakala called. She wants to talk to you about setting up another meeting on

Waikane. I told her you'd get back to her. And my Great Aunt Meg phoned to find out how Marshall was. When I told her that Everett was flying in from California today, she said you should bring him to their fiftieth anniversary party next Saturday night—that everyone will want to see him again." She glanced at Paul. "Under the circumstances, I'm sure she'll want Mr. Lindstrom to come, too. Why don't I have her send invitations to both of them?"

"If you're talking about a week from tomorrow, I doubt Everett will still be here," Paul said. "I'd love to come, though." Getting to know people, especially prominent, influential ones, might help him with his job.

"Good. Auntie Meg throws wonderful parties. You'll have a terrific time." She jotted his name on a piece of paper, checking with him to make sure she'd spelled it right. "Is there anything you need me to do, Lei?"

She thought for a moment. "Mr. Lindstrom will need a car. Could you have Jerry Hayakawa send one over?"

"Any special make?"

Lei looked at Paul. "He's a GM dealer, but if you'd prefer us to lease you a Mercedes or a BMW—"

"I drive a Cutlass at home. That'll be fine."

She'd figured him for the luxury- or sports-car type, but nodded matter-of-factly. "A Cutlass, then. Mr. Lindstrom is staying upstairs, Amy, so he'll need a set of keys and a sticker for the garage. He can use Marshall's space. And could you phone Mr. Chambers at the bank and have him issue another company credit card?"

"I have plenty of credit cards," Paul said to Lei. "You don't have to go to the trouble—"

"It's no trouble. You should have it on Monday. One more thing, Amy. There's no food in the apartment, so could you call Chang's Market and ask them to put together an assortment of staples? I can pick them up—"

"I can do my own shopping, Lei. Really. Just tell me where the nearest store is."

"It's no trouble," she repeated. "I'll run over there before I leave work."

"It's a waste of breath to argue," Amy said. "Offering *hookipa*—hospitality—is a matter of honor with Hawaiians, and Lei is Hawaiian to the core."

"So my looks and charm have nothing to do with it. She would put herself out for anyone in my position."

"Yes, Mr. Lindstrom, I would." Lei was so poker-faced that Paul wondered if she'd realized he was teasing. "Would you like to see the office now?"

"Just see it? You're not going to offer to give it to me?"

"*Hookipa* doesn't extend quite that far." She opened the door nearest the hallway. "This is my office."

He was hoping to learn more about her from the room, but it was completely impersonal. There were no family pictures or knickknacks around, only some posters of Hawaiian scenery that might or might not have had some special meaning for her. They walked through the conference room next door into the corner office Marshall used. Photos covered almost every inch of wall space, and community service awards and objets d'art were scattered on the chests and tables.

"You'll be working in here," she said. "Marshall's secretary is next door. That's Grace Pepperman, the woman Amy mentioned when we came in. She's very efficient. She's been working for Marshall forever."

"Knows where all the bodies are buried?" he drawled.

"Unfortunately not." She gave him a quick, sly grin. "Otherwise she would have warned him about that ancient burial ground at Waikane, wouldn't she?"

He laughed, but didn't reply. So the lady had a sense of humor, after all. He was so enchanted by her that he started wondering how he could talk her into having dinner with him. Maybe he could tell her he was dying for a home-cooked meal and throw himself on her mercy. Or pretend to be overwhelmed by everything he had to learn and plead for a working dinner to help him get started.

They passed by Cliff Whitney's office and entered a large room containing file cabinets, office machines and several desks. Lei introduced Paul to the two employees there, a young bookkeeper, Fred Madeiros, and a middle-aged clerk-typist, Eileen Fujimoto. The remaining two desks, she remarked, were used by Marshall's assistants, both of whom were out in the field at the moment.

As they returned to the reception room, she added, "Their names are Ned Beecham and Mack MacKenzie. You'll probably meet them this afternoon—they check in most days to tell us how things are going."

"Up at Waikane, you mean?"

"That's where Ned is, but Mack is managing the construction of a shopping center *mauka* of Pearl Harbor. As far as Waikane is concerned..." She paused. "Our general contractor, Bob Lum, is careful and reliable, but you know contractors. You have to keep after them. Marshall was supervising Waikane himself originally—it was different from anything he'd built before and he was very nervous about it. When he was hospitalized, Ned came back from the Big Island to take over. He was working on a condo project at the time. One of Marshall's partners is handling that now."

"Tell me about Ned. How's he doing at Waikane?"

Lei knew it was important to be honest. "Okay, I guess, but his field is sales and promotion, not construction. Mack would have been better, but the shopping center is scheduled to open in April and we couldn't pull him away. He's one of the best project managers on the island and one of the few people Marshall delegates responsibility to."

Paul knew from personal experience that problems cropped up constantly during the rush to finish construction. If Mack was capable of resolving them, he was worth his weight in gold. "I'll look forward to meeting them. About Waikane... All I know is what Marshall told Everett—that he planned to build affordable housing on the site, but a burial ground and religious ruins turned up where nobody thought they existed and now you've got protests and possible legal action on your hands." He nodded at the coffee maker on top of a cabinet in the corner. "I could use some more background, but first, could I get a cup of that coffee?"

Lei was embarrassed he'd had to ask. "I'm sorry. I should have offered you some when we came in. Please—sit down." She crossed the room. "Let me get you something to eat. We have Danish, cheese and crackers and fruit."

"I didn't know women did things like that anymore. Is that another example of *ho-o*...what was that word again?"

"*Hookipa*, and yes, it is." She smiled. "It's not a male-female thing. If I were your guest, you would do the same for me. How do you like your coffee?"

"Black, and a Danish sounds great." Paul made himself comfortable on a love seat. With her long hair and ankle-length dress, Lei was the most graceful, feminine woman he'd ever seen. It delighted him simply to watch her.

As always, Lei could feel the warmth of his gaze. There were women, she knew, who could cut men dead with the coldness of their eyes or the harshness of their tongues, but she wasn't one of them. Besides, Lindstrom was here to help them. He'd done nothing she could really object to, so it was unthinkable to be anything but gracious. The vision in Liliha's glass was irrelevant.

She heated a Danish in the microwave and poured him a cup of coffee. "If you don't mind, I'd like to wait till Cliff gets back to discuss the project," she said, setting the snack in front of him. "I thought I'd introduce you to the lawyer who handles most of our permit work first. He's just downstairs. Why don't you unwind while I check to see if he's in and return Mrs. Kapakala's phone call?"

Paul nodded, sipping his coffee gratefully as Lei disappeared into her office. It was different from anything he'd tasted before—lighter but sharper.

Amy assured the latest in a steady stream of callers that Marshall was on the mend and hung up. She was good on the phone—well-spoken and charming. "That's Kona coffee, from Kona on the Big Island," she said. "Do you like it?"

"I'm not sure." He took another sip. "I'd make it stronger, I think. I'm one of those guys who thinks coffee should have the consistency of unrefined petroleum."

"In that case, I'll pick up another coffee maker and brew you your own supply."

"If this is more Hawaiian *hookini*—"

"That's *hookipa*, and don't argue."

"I wasn't going to. I'm getting to like the idea." He took a bite of the Danish, which was moist, buttery and oozing with apples. "This is terrific. So tell me, where's the nearest gym?"

She laughed. "To work off the calories?"

"Exactly." The girl was sharp.

"Thirtieth floor. Just show them your apartment key."

Paul wanted to get a feel for things, and Amy Farrell seemed like a good place to begin. "I should warn you," he said, "that I have a reputation for being curious to the point of nosiness at times. I don't enjoy prying, really, but it's hard to deal with sticky situations unless you know all the facts." He smiled. "So tell me about John Davis. Lei says you're engaged. How did you meet?"

She didn't look offended, merely amused. "We're third cousins. I've been in love with him for as long as I can remember, but he's six years older than I am, so it took him a while to notice me. We started seeing each other two and a half years ago, after I finished college. Maybe you know it— Pomona in Southern California."

"Sure. Good school." Pomona was small, prestigious and expensive. In addition to everything else, Amy probably had money. "Lei mentioned that John got you this job. I have to wonder... Why is a well-educated, wealthy girl like you working as a receptionist?"

"You do come right out with things, don't you?" she asked with a grin. "I'd been out of school for a month and

I was trying to figure out what to do with my life. The receptionist here had just gotten married and moved to Maui, and John thought I should work here for a while and see how I liked the development business."

"And Marshall agreed."

"Yes. He said he would teach me whatever he could—that he would give me extra responsibilities besides making coffee and answering the phone."

"And did he?"

"Not really. At first I thought it was personal—that he didn't trust me...." She looked downward. "It's a long story. I probably shouldn't—"

"If you're referring to the dispute over control of the management company, Lei already told me about it. Obviously she realizes that I can't be effective unless people are honest with me." He settled back in his seat. "You were saying you thought Marshall didn't trust you. Is there any reason he shouldn't?"

"Only that John holds minor interests in several of the properties he controls. John would like to get into development, but he's smart enough to know it's better to be Marshall's partner than his competitor. I think Marshall understands that now, but he's too used to doing everything by himself to be a good teacher. You have to pick things up on your own."

Paul understood now why there'd been nobody here to step in when Marshall had taken ill. When it came to business, Everett was the only man Marshall respected enough to trust completely. He'd probably have to learn about Waikane from the ground up. It wasn't a challenge. It was a trial by fire.

Chapter Three

Lei had never slammed down a phone in her life, but after speaking with Bernice Kapakala, she was irked enough to come close. Paul Lindstrom had been here only a few hours, but Bernice already knew all about him. Her source of information was her chatterbox of a cousin, Rose, a nurse at St. Francis Medical Center. Rose claimed she'd heard Everett and Marshall talking by chance that afternoon, but she'd relayed the conversation to Bernice in such detail that it must have taken some zealous eavesdropping. She'd even told Bernice about what had happened between Lei and Paul at the airport. Bernice thought it was simply hilarious.

None of that had anything to do with the reason she'd called, though. She'd heard that Everett Canning was coming to Hawaii to take over at Waikane and wanted to ask Lei what she knew about him. As the leader of Hawaii Ohana, a native rights group, Bernice was in the forefront of the fight to prevent the desecration of the sacred lands there.

Now that Paul had replaced Everett as the man in charge, her interest, and the group's, had shifted to him.

Lei pushed back her chair. She was smack in the middle of this mess, both professionally and emotionally, and she was beginning to hate it. Everyone expected the moon. No one would compromise. It was incredibly frustrating.

She told herself to forget it—just to do her job, which was to act as a neutral liaison between the community and Marshall Canning, and let Paul cope with the mess. The problem was, she wasn't neutral and everyone knew it. She agreed with Hawaii Ohana. Sacred places had to be respected.

Bernice wanted her to talk to Paul—to make Hawaii Ohana's case as strongly as she could. She was willing, but she and Bernice differed in one important respect. She felt human remains shouldn't be disturbed. Hawaii Ohana believed that nothing should be, not even a single rock from a single one of those widely scattered ruins.

In any event, Paul wasn't a free agent. He would have to clear his actions with Marshall first. And if he was as good as Everett said, he would get all the facts before he decided what to do.

He was reading the latest issue of *Hawaii Business* when she walked back into the reception room. "If you want to look at previous issues, they're in a bookcase in the large office," she said.

He tossed the magazine onto the coffee table. "I'll do that. Are you ready to go?"

She nodded, explaining as they rode downstairs that the law firm they were about to visit, Bissell, Jennings and Slakey, was one of two that Marshall kept on retainer. They specialized in the technical aspects of real estate, while the other firm, Nakamura and Associates, handled the areas that were primarily political.

Ross Slakey was waiting for them in his office. He spent the next hour educating Paul on development in Hawaii— the applicable laws, the pertinent government agencies, the dozens of permits required, the political maneuvering. Then, putting some books and documents into a carton, he asked if Paul had any questions.

"Just one," Paul said. "Can Marshall be legally stopped from proceeding with the Waikane project?"

Ross shrugged. "Not by the courts. We've got all the necessary permits, even a waiver that allows us to remove and rebury human remains if they should be found. Nobody thought we'd need it, which is probably why they issued it in the first place. Still, you know politicians. What they giveth, they can taketh away, even if it requires special legislation to do it."

"And is that likely to happen?"

"Politics is Nick Nakamura's field, not mine, but my personal opinion is no. We're talking about housing for working people, not a hotel for rich tourists. Until the ruins turned up, Canning was the good guy in this soap opera. No other developer would have touched the project. There wasn't enough money in it."

"We haven't briefed Mr. Lindstrom on the details yet," Lei said. "We were waiting for Cliff to get back from a meeting. He should be upstairs by now. Can you join us?"

Ross said he'd be glad to. Everyone was having coffee in the conference room when they returned—Cliff, Everett, Grace and Ned. They made small talk about Marshall's progress, then chatted about a case Ross had won recently. Eventually Amy came in with keys to the apartment, the office and the Cutlass. Paul shoved them into his pocket and suggested that they get down to work.

The Waikane site, Ross told him, had originally been agricultural land owned by a family trust. A year and a half ago, the trust had sold it to a foreign developer named Matsuo Fujimoto, who had secured approval to build a golf course there. Environmentalists had been quick to object, saying Ohau had too many golf courses already, while agriculture was becoming an endangered activity on the island.

Fujimoto had ignored them and started clearing the land, but only weeks later, some business problems had forced him to raise a large amount of cash in a hurry. Faced with increasingly vehement opposition to his golf course, he'd decided to abandon the project and sell out. Potential buyers were gun-shy due to the protests by then, so he'd set the price relatively low.

Returning the area to agriculture wasn't practical. Most of the banana and papaya trees were gone by then, and the tenants who'd farmed there had moved on. "And that's where I got involved," Lei said. "Affordable housing is in pitifully short supply on this island. Given the lower price, I thought Marshall could build quality apartments on the site and still make a modest profit. But he had to move quickly, before some other developer got over his cold feet and bought the land for condos or a hotel."

"I'll never figure out how she talked him into it," Everett said with a chuckle. "My brother's raised money for half the charities in town, Lindy, but he's never mixed business with philanthropy before."

Lei smiled. "It wasn't easy. I had to appeal to everything from his vanity to his love of a challenge."

"And nag him half to death?" Paul teased, and then almost groaned at his choice of words. For a guy who almost never made a slip, he'd been incredibly tactless lately. "I'm sorry—that didn't come out right. I was thinking of what you said upstairs—"

"I know. It's okay." Every time Paul put his foot in his mouth, Lei warmed to him a little more. "I did keep after him. In a way, I saw it as my job to get him to undertake the project." She paused. "In the old days developers could do pretty much what they pleased here, but community, environmental and native groups are more powerful now. Marshall wasn't used to that. He kept running into problems with them. My family background gave me ties to those groups, so he hired me to do community and media relations for him. My job is to make sure that everyone understands each other—to stop problems before they start."

"If you want the truth, Lindy, he was looking for a public relations fix and he wound up with a girl who leads him around by the nose." Everett patted her hand. "Don't scowl at me, Lei. You've been good for him. He probably would have had a heart attack years ago if you hadn't taken him in hand."

Marshall *had* mellowed over the years, but Lei ascribed the change more to his wife's death than to her. Loneliness and the knowledge of his own mortality could soften a man. "If that's true, I'm glad," she said, "but nothing I said or did could influence him about Waikane. He was determined to ignore the protests and move ahead. By Wednesday I'd given up trying to change his mind and was begging him just to let things cool off for a while—to keep everyone off the disputed part of the property." Her eyes welled with tears. "I wish to God he'd listened. Maybe he wouldn't be in the hospital right now. Maybe Bobby Lum wouldn't be, either."

Everett sighed. "Grace told me about that while we were riding back from the hospital. Thank God the boy is all right." He turned to Paul. "Marsh blew up at Lei for pestering him that day and stormed off to Waikane. Bobby Lum is the general contractor's youngest son. He's also Marshall's godson. He was pulling out a tree stump when a rope snapped and he lost control of his tractor. It swerved and flipped over. If there hadn't been a hospital just down the coast, he might have died from internal injuries. Marsh charged back to the office as soon as Bobby was out of surgery, muttering that it was sabotage. He was so upset he went home early. Half an hour later he collapsed."

"And could it have been?" Paul asked.

"Sabotage?" Everett glanced around the table. "Opinions, anyone?"

Cliff smiled wanly. "Lei thinks it happened because some crazy old *kahuna*—some native priest—put a curse on that stretch of land, but personally—"

"I never said that. I just mentioned he'd been out there chanting prayers. He was asking for help, not putting curses on anyone, and he certainly isn't crazy."

"Personally," Cliff continued evenly, "I think it was an accident, and so does Bob Lum. The hillside is fairly steep there, and his son wasn't as experienced as he probably should have been. When the rope snapped, the tractor got away from him and rolled over. Fortunately he's a strong, healthy kid, and he's doing very well."

Paul nodded and asked Ned Beecham, "Have there been any further incidents?"

"No, but we've kept the men away from the disputed area. Unofficially, that is. Bob sent them farther up the coast, but in another week or so there'll be nothing else left to clear. Then they'll have to go back there."

"Unless we decide to leave that area alone," Lei said.

Ross Slakey, the attorney, shook his head. "With all due respect to you and your friends, Lei, you can't expect Marshall to scale down a project that, in essence, he's already losing money on. He's tying up cash that could earn him a better return elsewhere. And a third of this project belongs to other investors whose money he's ethically and legally obligated to protect."

"Not to mention what it would cost him to commission a new design, reapply for permits and renegotiate with his contractors," Paul said.

Lei's heart sank. Paul Lindstrom was just like Marshall, concerned first and foremost with the bottom line. "That doesn't mean it's not feasible," she said. "You could at least look at the alternatives."

"Lindy wouldn't be my best troubleshooter if he didn't examine every possible option," Everett replied. "Give him some time, Lei. He just got here a few hours ago."

"I'm sorry if I sounded impatient." She was afraid she'd sounded like a total shrew. "I know you'll do everything you can, Mr. Lindstrom."

Paul doubted she really meant it. On the contrary, she probably thought he'd ram this project down the throats of her friends with no consideration for their feelings. "I can see that this issue means a lot to you, Lei. There may be options no one has thought of. If there are, I'll find them. That's a promise. Okay?"

"Okay. *Mahalo*." She stood. When he spoke to her that way, she believed him. He radiated such a compelling mixture of confidence, dynamism and sensuality that the impact left her spellbound. "It's almost five. I want to get you some maps from the auto club before it closes. It's right near the grocery store. Can I take the Cutlass?"

He handed her the keys. "I'll meet you by the elevator in the garage and help you carry everything upstairs. How does five-thirty sound?"

"Fine. Don't forget to have Cliff show you the computer system. Good night, everyone. I'll see you on Monday."

Paul followed her with his eyes as she crossed the room and closed the door, then said, "She's really something. I can see how she wrapped Marshall around her little finger."

Everett chuckled. "Now, Lindy, I told you at the airport—"

"It was just an observation, Everett. Both of us know that I never let anything interfere with business." Grace and Cliff smiled knowingly, but Paul paid no attention to them. He was attracted to Lei and it showed, but they would learn soon enough that he meant what he'd said.

"Has anyone explored the possibility of obtaining some sort of financial relief?" he asked. "A land buy-back by the state, or enough of a tax abatement to make a smaller project financially viable?"

"There was no point exploring it," Cliff said. "Marshall had already refused to change his plans."

Ross cleared his throat. "Uh, actually, Cliff, I talked to Nick Nakamura the day before Marshall's heart attack, and he *had* put out some feelers in that area. The results weren't encouraging. You know politicians. If there's extra money around, they'd rather rebate it to the taxpayers and buy themselves some extra votes."

Paul wanted to hear more about those discussions. He asked Grace to schedule a meeting with Nick as soon as possible, thanked everyone for coming and turned to Cliff. "Run through the computer system with me, and then I'll let you get out of here."

Everyone filed out of the conference room, Everett and Paul walking side by side. "I thought I'd go back to the hospital for a while and then have dinner," Everett said. "Do you want to meet me somewhere?"

Paul shook his head. "Thanks, but I have a lot to learn and very little time to learn it in. I should get started." He also hoped to talk Lei into eating with him, but he didn't admit it. Everett would never have let him hear the end of it.

He and Cliff had been working at the computer for half an hour when Mack Mackenzie showed up. Paul finished up with Cliff, then talked to Mack about the shopping center project for a while. He figured that Lei would fetch him from the office when she didn't find him in the garage, but she never showed up.

It was six by the time he made it downstairs. A Cutlass was parked in Marshall's space, but there was no sign of Lei. He quashed his disappointment. Obviously she'd carried the groceries upstairs herself, then left. He returned to the office for the carton Ross had given him, then continued up to the apartment.

There wasn't a grocery bag in sight when he walked into the kitchen. Puzzled, he opened the refrigerator. It was filled with food, including a barbecued chicken in a foil take-out bag and plastic containers filled with various salads. The pantry had been stocked, as well.

He went into the office next. Several maps were sitting on the desk, the car keys on top of them. He thought about driving out to Waikane in the morning, but decided to wait till Monday. Why go alone when he could go with Lei?

His stomach growled. It was past eight in California, and he was hungry. Rumpled, sticky and stiff, too. He returned to the kitchen for a piece of chicken, then took a shower. He was in the bedroom getting dressed when he heard the front door open. He tucked in his shirt and went to see who it was, thinking that even a cleaning man would be welcome company. The apartment was a lot quieter than a hotel, and he felt isolated and a little lonely.

He brightened when he saw Lei, who was holding a large carton and closing the door with her foot. He strode over and took the box from her. "What's...? Oh. The files. I'd forgotten all about them."

Lei had, too, until she'd unpacked the groceries and was halfway to the bus stop. Paul had changed out of his suit, she noticed. She tried not to stare, but couldn't help it. He was barefoot, dressed only in faded jeans that hugged his hips and thighs and a T-shirt that matched his eyes. She could see the muscles in his legs and chest and the fine blond hairs on his arms. He was handsome in casual clothing, very handsome.

A flush rose up her neck as she shifted her gaze to the carton. "This should get you started. If you need more information, you can check the computer files or the original paperwork. It's in the top drawer of the horizontal file cabinet in Grace's office. I should really get going now."

Paul wasn't going to let her leave, not after the way she'd inspected him. It was the damnedest mixture of interest and shyness he'd ever come across, and it had left him aching to touch her. One way or another, he was going to keep her a while longer. "I'm afraid I'll need a few more minutes of your time," he said. "I'd like you to brief me on what's in these files." He started down the hall.

Lei followed him into the den. It had been an order, not a request, but a perfectly reasonable one. He was the boss now, and she couldn't refuse to stay here just because he made her nervous.

He seated himself in the middle of the couch and set the box on the coffee table. She walked halfway into the room. "Did you see the maps and keys on the desk?" she asked.

"Yeah. Thanks. And thanks for putting the groceries away."

"You're welcome. They have a wonderful take-out counter at Chang's. I thought you might be too tired to go out, so I bought you salads and a barbecued chicken—"

"I already had a piece. It was terrific. You thought of everything, Lei. I really appreciate it." He patted the couch. "Come sit down. It won't take long."

Since he was smack in the middle of the sofa, she couldn't join him without practically touching him. She perched herself on the edge like a bird poised for flight and clenched her hands together in her lap. "What would you like me to do, Mr. Lindstrom?"

He pushed the box along the table until it was directly in front of her. "Tell me what's in the folders. A sentence or two each will do it." A smile spread over his face. "And relax, Lei. It's not a test. I'm not going to grade you when you're done."

She took out a folder, feeling awkward and apprehensive, trying to think of a suitably witty reply. Nothing would come. She'd learned to hold her own over the years, but Paul Lindstrom made her feel sixteen again.

She compensated by adopting a brisk, businesslike tone. "This contains some background material—copies of newspaper and magazine articles about the original golf course project, the protests and Matsuo Fujimoto." She set the folder down and took out the next one. "This contains articles running from when Marshall bought the land to the present."

Paul picked up the first folder and flipped through it. Lei appealed to him to an extent he'd forgotten was possible, but he was trying not to show it. She was attracted to him, but for some reason she was also scared to death of him. "This will be very helpful," he said. "You must have spent a lot of time in the library yesterday."

"Yes. The next folder—"

"The more I know about the history of a project, the more effective I generally am. You have to figure people out—get a sense of what makes them tick and learn what will motivate them to do what you want." He paused, wondering how to put her at ease. Unfortunately, promising not to jump her probably wouldn't work. "On the mainland, I always knew who the major players were before I went in, but Hawaii is totally new to me. Between the politicians and the bureaucrats..." He scanned the top article in the folder. "I'd like to have everyone straight by Monday, but these names make my eyes glaze over. What's this one? Councilman WAY-lee-hee?"

Her lips twitched. "That's Wye-LEH-heh, Mr. Lindstrom, the city council planning chairman, and he won't take kindly to your mispronouncing his name. He doesn't like mainland *haoles* to begin with."

"*Haoles?*"

"Caucasians."

"But I'm a Swede, not a WASP. Doesn't that count as ethnic?"

Her smile lasted a fraction longer this time. "I'm afraid not. If I were you, I'd study up on Hawaiian pronunciation and make sure I got his name right."

"I told you, I'm lousy at languages. Maybe you could make me a set of flash cards. Drill me every morning."

"If you think it would help." Her tone said it was hopeless. "This next folder contains papers pertaining to the Land Use Commission's redistricting of the project site."

"Sounds scintillating. I can't wait to look at it." He yawned and stretched. "Is it okay if I put my feet up on the table?"

Lei giggled; she couldn't help it. His struggles with Hawaiian were funny, but not as funny as a man his age and size asking permission for something like a hopeful little boy. "Only if they're very, very clean," she said.

"They are." He raised a foot to demonstrate. "See? I just showered."

She could tell that. His hair was still damp. "In that case, you have my blessing."

He stretched out his legs and yawned again. Obviously he was tired, and probably a lot more interested in sleep than in her. Reassured, she took out the next folder. "I'm afraid I might put you to sleep. If you think redistricting is boring..."

"I know. The rest of the stuff isn't exactly Michener's *Hawaii*." He laced his hands together behind his neck, his eyelids drooping a little. "If I nod off, just poke me."

If he fell asleep, she was going to leave, but she didn't argue. She continued telling him what was in the files, only gradually becoming aware of a change in the way he was looking at her. His eyes grew gentler and more intense. Warm, lazy desire seemed to emanate from his body. She responded by adopting a more formal tone and making her descriptions as brief as she possibly could.

Paul never even noticed. Between too little sleep and not enough food, he was a little spaced-out. He only knew that he loved looking at Lei and didn't want her to leave.

She set the final folder on the table, as nervous by then as when she'd first come in. "That's it, Mr. Lindstrom. If you have any questions, please call me. Have a nice—"

"It's a big apartment, Lei. Empty, lonely and thousands of miles from home." He stretched and yawned. "I hate eating alone. Stay a little longer. Please."

"I'm sorry. I can't." She started to get up.

He caught her by the wrist to stop her. "Sure you can. You're just afraid to." His voice was husky and persuasive. "For some reason, I make you uncomfortable. Tell me why."

Lei stared into her lap. What was she going to say? That if she stayed here, she might take leave of her senses and throw herself at him? That if she let him too close, she would suffer for it? It sounded crazy. It *was* crazy.

"Lei?" He rubbed the inside of her wrist with his thumb, tracing slow, teasing circles on her flesh. The caress left her warm and a little breathless, exciting her and alarming her at the same time. She wasn't used to this sort of thing. "Just half an hour, okay?" He released her wrist. "We'll talk. Nothing else. I promise."

She shook her head. "I can't. Really, I have to go."

"Why? You don't want to. I know you don't."

He was wrong. He'd made her desire him, but she wasn't enjoying it. Not a single cell of her wanted to stay. "It's late. I have a long bus ride home. My children will start wondering what's happened to me."

There was an awkward silence. Tension seemed to fill the room. "Your children?" he finally said.

He sounded confused, even shaken. She turned her head, watching in bewilderment as he swung his legs off the coffee table and sat up. His eyes weren't warm and seductive anymore, just distracted.

"I have twins," she explained. "A boy and a girl."

"Twins." He ran his hand absently through his hair. "I see. If I'd known that, I wouldn't have kept you so long. I hope it wasn't too much of an inconvenience."

She'd never seen a man cool down so fast. She was no psychologist, but she'd read something about Madonna complexes once and wondered if this was an example—if her status as a mother had put her into a different category in his mind. Off-limits—*kapu*—rather than available. Someone to be respected and protected rather than desired.

A little bemused, she said, "It wasn't. I called my sitter before I went for the groceries and told her I'd be late, but I didn't expect to be this late."

"I'm sorry. I wish you'd said something sooner." He paused. "Is that why you don't work weekends? Because of your kids?"

"Yes. Marshall's always been great about that. I attend a lot of evening meetings as part of my job, so he lets me come in late and leave a little early. Basically I work while they're in school. I hope that's okay."

"Of course. It's only fair." He stood up, a concerned look on his face. "It's dark outside. I want you to drive the Cutlass home. You'll get there faster and it's safer than taking the bus."

Lei was tired, and driving beat taking a bus that stopped every few blocks, but she didn't want to leave Paul without a car. "Suppose you want to go somewhere? You'll get stir-crazy all alone in the apartment for the whole weekend."

"I won't have time for anything more than a walk around the block. There's too much to learn."

She started to refuse again, then checked herself. She'd promised to take the kids shopping in the morning. She could drive the car home, return it in the morning and catch a bus to the Ala Moana Center from a few blocks away. "Then thank you, Mr. Lindstrom. I'll bring it back tomorrow and leave the keys with the garage attendant."

Paul told her to keep it, but he didn't argue when she insisted on bringing it back. He simply wished her a polite good-night and walked her to the door. He was still adjusting to the idea that someone who'd been introduced to him as "Miss Howe" could be the mother of twins.

Curious about her background, he sat down at the computer and accessed the personnel files. Martha Leilani Howe was twenty-five years old. Her children, Jessica Anne Howe and Jason Michael Howe, were eight.

Good Lord—eight! he thought, stunned. She'd been a child herself when they'd been born. She was listed as single, not divorced or widowed, so presumably she'd never been married.

There were no previous jobs listed. She'd finished high school at eighteen and graduated from the University of Hawaii six years later. He doubted she could have managed that without help, perhaps from her family, but it still couldn't have been easy. Single motherhood never was.

He knew that from personal experience. His mother had kept him housed and fed, but she'd also taken shortcuts that sickened him in order to afford luxuries she didn't need, leaving him alone all night at times. He'd long since forgiven her, but he hadn't forgotten the pain.

There wasn't a doubt in his mind that Lei was different, and he admired her for that. She'd been sixteen and pregnant once, with a boyfriend who'd probably taken off, but she'd turned her life around. It explained a lot, such as why she was so wary of men.

He switched off the computer, telling himself to forget her. A woman like Lei would be looking for a commitment, but he was lousy husband and father material. Besides, how much time would they have together? She'd be exhausted half the time, overwrought the other half and overworked every minute. She'd drag him to zoos and aquariums. He'd wind up trapped at soccer games and music recitals. That wasn't for him.

He walked into the kitchen, opened the refrigerator and took out the chicken and a couple of salads.

Chapter Four

It was Lei's rotten luck that both her children should have decided by the age of six that they cared about their appearance. She no longer bothered to compete for a bathroom in the morning; she simply got up early. Then all she had to do was feed them, promise them they didn't look grotesque and drag them away from the mirror in time to get to school before the opening bell.

After that, the commute downtown was practically a vacation. She went by bus because a monthly bus pass was cheaper than driving and parking a car. The cost of things was never far from her mind.

That was part of the reason she'd pressed Marshall so hard about Waikane—because she knew firsthand how important affordable housing was. Her modest home in Manoa cost her a fortune every month simply because it was located in a desirable area. No one had forced her to keep it after Tom and Cindy had died, of course, but she hadn't wanted to uproot the twins from their friends and school.

Besides, she never could have found another sitter like Mrs. Keala, a warm but firm widow who lived down the street with her son and his family and loved the twins almost like her own.

All in all, Lei was lucky. Between her salary and the twins' survivors' benefits, the bills got paid on time every month with money left over for extras like music and karate lessons. The only thing she didn't do was save. Every spare dollar went for plane tickets.

There were no phones on Niihau, and after a month or two she'd start longing for the sound of her mother's voice. Sometimes Ella came to Oahu, but usually Lei went to Niihau, flying to Kauai and taking the private boat. Liliha refused to leave there, so it was the only way Lei could see her.

Although the twins had no blood ties to Ella or Liliha—Tom had been Lei's father's son by his first wife, a Frenchwoman—she always took them along. Her relatives on Niihau were the only family they knew. Cindy's parents called occasionally from Boston and always sent birthday and Christmas presents, but they'd been able to visit Hawaii only once.

Having been to Niihau for Christmas, it would be a while before Lei could go again, but the island was very much on her mind as she rode to work Monday morning. Although she hadn't heard from Paul all weekend, she'd thought of him constantly. She'd jumped every time the phone rang, sure he was calling to summon her downtown, convinced she would wind up on a couch with him again, nervous, aroused and miserably uncomfortable. She could have used some time on Niihau, surrounded by love and far from the phone.

Amy was sorting through the mail when she arrived at the office. She helped herself to coffee and asked how Amy's weekend had been.

"John and I picked out china, crystal and silver patterns. I thought it was fun. He thought it was two days at hard labor. And yours?"

Lei crossed to Amy's desk. "I took the kids shopping and deluded myself into thinking Generra and Guess were bargains because they were on sale. Marshall phoned. He claims the hospital is making him sicker, but the doctors don't agree. They're keeping him awhile longer. There were lots of calls from reporters, too. They all want interviews with Mr. Lindstrom." She nodded at Paul's door, which was closed. "Is he in yet?"

Amy pretended to be baffled. They were good friends, but Lei was as reserved with Amy as with everyone else. And as Cliff did, Amy couldn't resist teasing her at times. "Mr. Lindstrom? Oh! You mean Lindy." She smiled slyly. "That's what everyone else in the office calls him, Lei."

"Do they? How fascinating! Is he here, Amy?"

She ignored the question. "They do. *I* do. Of course, he doesn't look at me the way he looks at you. If he did, I might be tempted to stray."

"You wouldn't!" She'd loved John Davis forever.

"No, not really. Well, maybe a little, given what a hunk he is. He's a nice guy, too. Everyone thinks so."

"Did I say he wasn't?" Lei asked.

"Nope. You just look like you want to run in the opposite direction whenever he smiles at you." Amy looked her up and down. "Is that why you braided your hair and dressed like a banker? To intimidate the helpless man?"

Lei was wearing a green silk blouse and a black skirt, hose and pumps, a more formal outfit than usual but one Amy had seen a few times before. "It would take a lot more than a French braid to intimidate Paul Lindstrom," she said. "He's about as helpless as an armored tank."

"True. I should have said 'discourage.'"

"Same thing." Amy was right, though. She'd wanted to look cool and serious. "Is he here or isn't he?"

"He is. Nick Nakamura is with him. Do you want me to buzz you when Nick leaves?"

"Please." Lei took her mail and carried it into her office.

She received such a constant stream of notices about hearings, programs and lectures that sometimes she felt as if her life were one long meeting. Only one invitation in the current batch was a must, a seminar about Waikane sponsored by an environmental group. She noted it on her calendar, then tossed her purse into the bottom drawer of her desk.

She resisted the urge to kick something when the clasp popped open and everything spilled out. She hadn't worn the bag in weeks, so she'd forgotten the clasp was loose. The phone buzzed as she was stuffing everything back inside. It wasn't Amy telling her Nick had left, but a call from a reporter who covered Hawaii business for a paper in Hilo. He'd heard about Paul's arrival and wanted an interview, but unlike all the other reporters, he was interested in the condo project on the Big Island rather than in Waikane.

"Mr. Lindstrom isn't involved with that, Fred," she said. "Harry Topping is taking over for the time being."

The reporter snickered. "Come on, Lei. Harry couldn't build a tree house, much less a condominium."

She laughed. "But he could sell lava to Pele." The door opened and Paul strolled in. His smile hello was brief and impersonal, but she had the same reaction she always did—a racing pulse, a rush of warmth, a burst of anxiety. She nodded hello and returned to her call. "I'll find out if Mr. Lindstrom has any comment on the subject. If he does, I'll ask him to call you."

"Have him call me anyway. Our readers are interested in Waikane, too. Ancient ruins, a mysterious accident, a sudden heart attack . . . What can I say? It sells papers."

"I'll bet it does. I'm glad we're keeping you folks entertained." She said goodbye and hung up the phone.

Paul sat down in the chair beside her desk. "Good morning. You'll find out if I have any comment on what subject?"

"The Kohala condo project. The one on the Big Island. That was a reporter from the *Hilo Sentinel*, Fred Wong. He wants to speak to you about Waikane, too."

"And he'd already heard I was here? News travels fast in Hawaii."

"Very fast. Reporters were calling me all weekend."

He grinned. "Better you than me. So other than that, how was your weekend?"

"Fine. And yours?" She was astonished by how normal this conversation was. There was no tension, no disturbing erotic byplay.

"It was okay. You were right about going stir-crazy, though. Everett came by for dinner on Saturday, but I was still so restless by Sunday that I drove down to the Ala Moana Center to look around. I found the row of automatic teller machines and got some cash, then checked out the food court. It's a take-out paradise. I went shopping, too. Bought myself a couple of aloha shirts."

She looked at him skeptically. He was dressed just as formally as on Friday, in a dark suit, blue shirt and striped tie. "You didn't. You're kidding me."

"I certainly did. I read about Aloha Friday in one of my guidebooks. I'm a great believer in adopting the customs of the indigenous population." He leaned back and stretched out his legs. "I worked hard this weekend, Lei. Listen to this. Kaneohe. Wahiawa. Kamehameha." He beamed at her like a little kid who'd just mastered the alphabet. "Well?"

Much to her amazement, he'd pronounced them all correctly. "I'm dazzled. You're not lousy at languages, after all."

"Yes, I am, but I compensate for my lack of talent with maniacal persistence." He picked up her letters and flipped through them. "Do you actually go to all these meetings?"

"I will to the extent that you want me to, and to the extent that I have the time."

"Use your own judgment. You know what's important better than I do." He tossed them back on her desk. "About the reporters who've been calling... I want to meet with Marshall before I talk to the media. Everett expects him to be released from the hospital by Wednesday, so set up a briefing for Friday morning. We can hold it upstairs. Make sure there's plenty to eat. Reporters are more tractable when they're well fed.''

If Lei had ever doubted that Paul meant to keep things professional, she didn't now. Though polite, he was also every inch the boss—crisp, decisive and commanding. She would have obeyed him without question except for one thing. His plans were going to cause problems.

''But your position makes you an important figure here,'' she said. ''The media will want to meet you as soon as possible. Why don't you hold the briefing tomorrow morning?''

''To tell them it's too early to tell them anything?'' He shook his head. ''Friday at ten, Lei. No sooner.''

''They won't like that. They'll write stories implying you're arrogant and uncooperative. It would be better—''

He cut her off. ''I said Friday at ten. Stop arguing and set it up.''

''Yes, Mr. Lindstrom.'' She knew when to cut her losses. ''Will there be anything else?''

He stared at her for a moment, then slowly smiled. ''Did an arctic front move in, or is it just my imagination?''

''I'm sorry if I sounded curt. I'll take care of it right away. Is there anything else you'd like me to do?''

''Do *you* think I'm arrogant and uncooperative?''

''My job is to give you my opinions and follow your orders,'' she answered respectfully. ''It's not my place to comment on your personality.''

''In other words, yes. And I thought you were docile and shy when I met you on Friday!'' He sighed. ''From what Nick tells me, even a seasoned diplomat would have trouble negotiating a compromise on Waikane. He says it's as explosive as it is complicated. One wrong move and I could screw things up royally. I'm not inviting the press around until I know what the hell I'm talking about.''

"Nick said that?" She'd thought everyone was simply being stubborn.

"Repeatedly. He said that groups that usually cooperate could wind up at each other's throats, that there could be ethnic and class conflict over the issue. You don't need that kind of ugliness here."

Lei fiddled with her pen. Nick had a sixth sense about politics that only a fool would have ignored. Somehow she had to placate the media without putting Paul on the spot. "Would you be willing to write out a statement explaining who you are, why you're here and how you plan to proceed? I could attach it to the news release announcing the briefing. It would give reporters something to write about."

"Sure. Give Grace your media list and ask her to fax everything out. I want you to go to Waikane with me this morning. It's time I had a look around."

"Fine, Mr. Lindstrom. And *mahalo*."

He stood up. "One more thing, Lei."

"Yes?"

"Quit calling me that. It's getting on my nerves."

She couldn't resist. "Yes, sir."

"Real cute." He rolled his eyes and strode away.

Smiling, she turned on her computer and got down to work.

They left for Waikane a few hours later. Lei drove, taking the shore route so Paul could sightsee. She made a comment now and then, but there was too much traffic to chat. She didn't want to lose her concentration and rear-end some tourist who'd jammed on his brakes to gawk at the beauty of a white sand beach, the spectacular way the sea met the shore at the bottom of a rocky cliff, or the mist-shrouded Koolaus, cool, green and lovely in the distance.

They reached the construction site to find about a dozen demonstrators at the side of the road. It was lunchtime, so the only sounds Paul heard were the protesters' chants and the whoosh of passing traffic. The area was very rural. There was only an occasional house and few businesses other than farms.

"That's Hawaii Ohana—it means Hawaii Family—a native rights group, and the Windward Conservation League, an environmental group," Lei said as they got out of the car. "Do you want to meet them or avoid them?"

Nick had told him that Hawaii Ohana wanted housing except on the sacred lands, while the WCL wanted the entire area returned to agriculture. "I'll meet them," he said.

They walked over. The land here wasn't pretty, but scarred and barren. Tree stumps still covered the area considered sacred. Paul noticed a casually dressed man making sketches about ten yards *mauka* on the other side of the unlocked fence—an artist of some sort, he assumed.

Lei introduced Paul to the protesters, joking with some and embracing others. Her closeness to these people worried him. He couldn't have her running to them with a report every time he made a move.

He told them as much about himself as he could, stressing that his first priority was to study the situation and learn his way around. Afterward he asked for their opinions and comments. Lei said very little, but she seemed impressed by the way he handled himself. He was pleased by that; he was still intensely attracted to her and wanted her to like him. As for the rest of what he wanted, he'd decided not to pursue it. Whenever he weakened, he thought about having a pair of eight-year-olds as chaperons, and recovered immediately. Temporarily, anyway.

Eventually the man who'd been sketching joined the group. He was a tall Polynesian about the same age as Paul. "David Kapakala, Paul Lindstrom," Lei said. "David, Mr. Lindstrom is—"

"My mother mentioned him." They shook hands. "You're Everett Canning's hotshot assistant from San Francisco, right?"

Although Paul didn't care for the mocking edge in Kapakala's tone, he answered pleasantly, "I work for him, yes. Is your mother the Bernice Kapakala I've heard so much about?"

He nodded. "For weeks now, she's been nagging me to come out here and look around, but I've been too busy." He held up his sketchbook. "I'm an architect. I was on my way to Laie to meet with a client, so I decided to stop off. I thought I'd soak up the mood, wait for some inspiration and see what I came up with."

"And?"

"It would be a challenge to work on the project. I'd do it in my spare time if I had any. What I do have is a nervous boss breathing down my neck, pushing me to turn out designs for expensive homes."

"So your field is houses." Paul didn't add the obvious, that a major development was a far cry from a single-family home.

"At the moment. People love my houses. They stand in line to hire me. But I can design any damn thing you can name, Lindstrom, because I happen to be brilliant."

Kapakala was as arrogant as hell, but Paul didn't mind that. Arrogance was fine as long as there was talent to back it up. "I hope I'll get the chance to look at some of your work," he said.

"Lei knows my houses. She can take you to see some of them. So what do you think of the plans for this project?"

"I haven't looked at them yet." He'd wanted to visit the site before he met with the architect.

"You're really on top of things, aren't you?" Kapakala drawled.

"I try to be, yes." He'd be damned if he was going to explain himself. The man was beginning to irritate him.

Lei took a step forward. "Try to behave yourself, David. Mr. Lindstrom's only been here since Friday. He's been reading through files all weekend."

"Well, if he likes the design, he has as much taste as your boss does. Exactly none, that is. It's flat. Boring. Utilitarian." He looked at Paul. "A site this beautiful deserves passion and grace. Graham Smith—the architect—wouldn't know an original idea if it hit him in the face. He's an uptight *haole* who's so hung up on costs and benefits that he's forgotten about human emotion. Like you, maybe, Mr. Lindstrom from the mainland."

Paul felt like kicking the guy's butt by then, but managed to smile coolly. "Not like me, Mr. Kapakala. I'm all for projects with passion and grace—as long as I can bring them in on time and on budget."

"That's my specialty, Lindstrom." He smiled at Lei. "You bringing your thrifty friend to my mother's meeting on Wednesday night?"

"I am if you haven't alienated him past the point where he's willing to be in the same room with you. I swear, David, you get ruder every time I see you."

"It's all your fault, darlin'. I'd be a lot sweeter tempered if you'd have dinner with me once in a while." He winked at her and strode away.

Lei waited a moment, then said apologetically, "He *is* brilliant. I tried to get Marshall to use him, but Marshall can't stand him. I guess you can't, either."

"He could be worse. At least he's got good taste in dinner companions." Paul looked around at the group. "Thank you for talking to me. I hope you'll be patient while I get my bearings and confer with Mr. Canning. Maybe we can come up with a compromise everyone can live with."

An elderly Hawaiian at the rear of the group spoke up. He was a striking man, with a shock of curly white hair and an aloha shirt printed with a bold brown-and-black kapa design. "Such modesty!" he said with a smile.

The man started forward then, taking it as his due when everyone made way for him like the Red Sea parting for Moses. "There's no 'confer,' no 'we.' There's just you. You get what you want, I think. Even from Marshall Canning."

Paul was too polite to argue. "I hope you're right, sir, because what I want is to resolve this dispute."

"Then come with me." The old man took Lei's arm and added, "I've seen you walk only on the burial area, child, never on the *heiau*. Why have you avoided it?"

"I haven't," she replied. "It's far away. I just never got around to going there."

"Or maybe you feared what you would feel. You're sensitive to such things, Leilani, like your grandmother." The old man touched Paul's shoulder. "I'm a *kahuna*, but not like her grandmother. She's powerful, that sly old woman." He chuckled. "Even I fear her. She heals with her mind, so maybe she can kill with it, too. The *anana*, we call it. The death prayer. Just as well that she stays on Niihau."

Paul considered the native religion a mixture of self-delusion and superstition, but he knew better than to show it. As the three of them walked *mauka*, he noticed the strain on Lei's face and wondered if she'd taken the old man seriously. With a so-called priestess for a grandmother, you never know.

"You must understand, my son," the *kahuna* added softly, "that the land is sacred. The burial ground doesn't make it so. Neither does the *heiau*—the temple. It was sacred, so it was used for sacred purposes. The *heiau* that once stood here must be very old for the stones to have been scattered and buried as they were. As old, perhaps, as the first of my people to reach this place. Nothing can be disturbed."

Paul nodded. "I respect your point of view, sir." That much was true. The old man was undoubtedly sincere. To him, development equaled desecration.

They walked across the burial ground. A tingle ran down Lei's spine. She could feel the goodness, the purity and the peace of this place. Her emotions welled up and she clutched the *kahuna*'s arm, finding it difficult to keep her composure in the joyful presence of her *kupuna*, her ancestors.

What she didn't expect—couldn't have known—was that the feeling would persist even after they reached the area where the temple had once stood. It had happened only once before, at an ancient, extremely sacred *heiau* on the Big Island. She looked at the *kahuna* a little wildly. They hadn't walked straight inland, but to their left. He'd deliberately led her to this spot. "Is it like this everywhere?"

"It's strongest here. It's the most sacred spot, I think. Do you understand now?"

"Yes, Mr. Leinau." She was too shaken to say anything more. She could only stand and absorb the aura of the place. Bernice had been right. The land belonged to everyone. Buildings had no place here. Development had to stop.

Paul watched them impassively. The rocks that had been scooped up and scattered about by the preliminary grading looked like any other rocks to him. The area was probably of interest to archaeologists, but its sanctity existed only in the minds of Lei, the *kahuna* and other believers. Stones were stones, dirt was dirt and land was land.

"Close your eyes and open your heart," the old priest said to him. "You're a good man, but your senses have been clouded by civilization. You've been educated to think—and taught not to feel."

Paul honestly tried. He closed his eyes and reached for the mysterious and transcendent, but nothing happened. "I'm sorry, sir. Maybe Mr. Kapakala was right about me. I didn't feel a thing."

"Each of us feels in his own way. David walked on this land and saw a wonderful vision. Leilani felt great emotion, great joy. I myself have seen warriors here." The *kahuna* smiled. "You must return sometime and try again."

Paul said that he would, but he didn't expect to succeed. He didn't believe in the supernatural and never would. As for the *kahuna*'s beliefs, as much as he respected them, they were just one factor in a complicated equation.

Lei drove him to the work site next. He asked a couple of questions, answered several more and left satisfied that things were going well. "Is there a restaurant around here?" he asked afterward. "I'm starving."

"There's one a few miles up the road." It was the first thing she'd said since they'd left the *heiau*.

"Then let's have lunch there." He didn't care if the food was good or bad as long as it filled him up.

She nodded her agreement. Given the strength of her feelings, he knew that sooner or later she was going to press him about the ruins, but he didn't want to argue with her over lunch. As soon as they reached the restaurant, he asked her to tell him about the meetings she'd attended regarding Waikane. She was miles away at first, but her distraction gradually faded as they continued their conversation.

By the end of the meal, they were talking so easily that he felt he could raise the subject of her loyalty without offending her. "Walking across that land seemed to affect you deeply," he said. "Your emotions are really involved in this, aren't they?"

She looked at the table. It was something he'd grown used to—her habit of avoiding his eyes whenever she felt uncomfortable. "Yes, I am. Those are my ancestors."

"I understand that, and I want to help, but sometimes in this business . . ." He grimaced. She was so sweet and guileless. What was she going to think about the way he operated? "You have a problem with no obvious solution here. I'll have to work all the angles, maybe even shade the truth a bit now and then. It's something I'm pretty good at. For example, I once told a city that a company was our partner when it wasn't yet, because I knew it would get us a zoning change that would convince that company to commit to us. I can't have people talking about what I'm really up to. It's a recipe for having things explode in my face."

It took Lei a moment to understand where Paul was headed, and once she did, she couldn't decide whether to reassure him or scold him. In the end, she did a little of both. "You have my complete loyalty," she said coolly. "I never discuss what happens in the office."

"That's all I wanted to hear. I'm sorry I had to ask, but you're close to people who oppose the project. I was afraid you'd tell them something you shouldn't, or let something slip without meaning to."

In other words, Lei thought, he'd taken her for either a snitch or a fool. "I'm careful about what I say. I'd never pass on confidential information." She realized it wasn't strictly true, and reddened. "Except to my mother and grandmother, that is, and they're on Niihau. They have an interest in the outside world, but they don't get involved in it."

"Then there's no problem." He called over the waitress and handed her a credit card, then cupped his mug and gazed at it with an unreadable expression on his face.

He was so quiet, so enigmatic. She wondered what he was thinking. Maybe that she was touchy and excitable. Argumentative, too, given their disagreement over the news briefing this morning. She should have been calmer just now, more diplomatic before.

She toyed with her napkin. He'd probably had reason to question her loyalty, given her friendship with the protesters and her emotional response to the land. It hadn't been personal. He'd only been doing his job, making sure he could trust her.

"Paul?" she finally murmured.

He looked up, then smiled. "'Paul,' huh? Does that mean you're not annoyed with me anymore?"

"I wasn't annoyed. I thought *you* were. I just wanted you to know... I overreacted and I'm sorry. You had every right to question me."

"I wasn't annoyed, either. I was thinking that I'd misjudged you. I assumed you were naive and easy to maneuver, but you're not. You're bright, determined and nobody's fool. I'll have to watch out for you."

"Watch out for me?" She didn't know what he meant. "In what way?"

"Both of us know you're going to lobby me hard about Waikane. You're just waiting for the right moment, and then *wham*. I'd better be ready." The waitress brought the charge slip to the table; he signed it and took the receipt. "I have a meeting with Graham Smith this afternoon. We should probably go."

"We can take the Pali Highway back. It's faster, and Marshall's house is right on the way. I'll show you where it is."

They walked to the car in silence. The more Lei thought about what he'd said, the more upset she got. She wasn't the way he'd described. She didn't want him to think she was. It would hurt both their ability to work together and the cause she cared so deeply about.

She put the key in the ignition, then clutched her purse in her lap and turned to face him, nervous for the first time all afternoon. "About what you said in the restaurant ... I'm not like that—so hard and manipulative. I try to be—"

"Hard and manipulative?" He sounded astonished. "*You?* I don't think that at all."

"But you said you'd have to watch out for me."

"You warned me that you're a bulldog when you think something is important. You're smart and you do your homework. That's a dangerous combination, Lei. You're probably as persuasive as hell."

He smiled the way he'd smiled at her on Friday—warmly, admiringly. Her heart sped up and her palms got damp. She couldn't cope with that look—not now. She'd been through an emotional wringer at the site.

"You're other dangerous things, too," he said softly, "like gentle, beautiful and desirable. Yeah. I'd better watch out for you, all right."

Thoroughly flustered, she blurted the first thing that came to mind. "But I'm the mother of twins, Paul."

The smile turned into a boyish grin. "I know. It's enough to make me wish I were cut out for fatherhood. I'm probably not, though." He pushed up the center armrest and took away her purse, placing it on the seat between them. "I don't know whether that's a weapon or a security blanket, but you won't need either one. Relax and tell me what's on your mind. I promise not to bite your head off."

"I just..." She glanced down for a minute. "I know you want to learn all you can about the project before you form an opinion, but once you have... You might not have felt the things I did at the site, but they do exist. When you grow up in Hawaii, you learn that something doesn't have to be visible or rational to be real. I hope you'll keep an open mind about it. That's all."

"The issue isn't how open my mind is. It's whether Marshall will give me any independent authority." He buckled his seat belt. "Everett isn't optimistic. He says Marshall feels he's done more than his share just by getting involved in this project. He's in no mood to make concessions."

"I know. I keep hoping he'll change his mind." Lei started the car and pulled into traffic. Her thoughts were on Paul. Did he respect her? Trust her? Even like her?

The traffic got so heavy as she drove south that her attention shifted to the road. Cars kept stopping abruptly or darting from lane to lane. Then, just after she'd turned onto the Pali Highway, a van cut in front of her and zipped onto the shoulder. She braked so hard that her purse flew off the seat and she and Paul were thrown forward and then back again.

"Are you all right?" she asked.

"I'm fine. It's as bad as California here." He bent down. "Don't worry—I'll pick everything up."

The clasp on her purse had unsnapped again. She looked at the floor by Paul's feet. Everything had spilled out. *Everything.*

He started tossing things back inside. Her wallet. Her checkbook. Her brush. Her pills. She wanted to crawl under the seat. In this day and age, everyone knew what that sort of plastic compact contained.

I'm a very good girl, she wanted to tell him. *A devoted, loving mother. I don't sleep around. In fact, I don't do anything at all. My periods were like a week in hell at times. That's what I got the pills for.*

She couldn't get a word out. It was too embarrassing, too personal. She just sat with her hands on the wheel and her eyes on the road, squirming with humiliation, sure he thought she was a tramp.

Chapter Five

Paul hated to admit it, but David Kapakala was right about Graham Smith's design. It *was* flat and utilitarian. It *did* lack passion and grace. On the other hand, it was competent, practical and relatively easy to build.

Still, had it been Paul's project, he would have hired someone like Kapakala and told him to design a complex that swept across the landscape, taking advantage of the wonderful view. He'd have needed a height variance and some help from the government, but that didn't worry him. The old *kahuna* was right. He usually got what he wanted.

Unfortunately, though, beginning all over would have cost more money than Marshall was willing to spend. When Paul arrived at Marshall's house on Wednesday, he was looking for a little maneuvering room, not total control.

Everett, Lei and Cliff were sitting around Marshall's bed, the three of them reminding Paul of courtiers attending an ailing king. He was surprised to see a dirty ashtray on the night table. A man who'd had a heart attack should have had more sense than to smoke. Still, Marshall looked pretty good. A little pale and drawn, but alert and well groomed.

Paul shook his hand, then pulled over a chair and sat down. Tuesday's newspaper was sitting under the ashtray, folded to an article about Paul's arrival and plans. According to Everett, Marshall hadn't been pleased about it.

"I've talked to a lot of people this week and scheduled meetings with several more," Paul began. He named them— city council members, people from the city planning commission and the Hawaii Housing Authority, union leaders. "It won't be easy, but I'd like to take a shot at restructuring the project or scaling it down so that—"

"The project stays the way it is," Marshall interrupted. "You're here to keep things moving, not to hold meetings and issue news releases."

Everett sighed. "Hear Lindy out, Marsh. He's good at solving complicated problems. The best I've ever seen."

"You bring some *malihini* out here from the mainland and you think he can wring concessions out of people I've already spoken to? People I've known and worked with for years?" Marshall waved his hand. "I'm sorry, but there's no way."

"Is there any harm in letting me try?" Paul asked.

"Not to you, maybe. It's not your money. Do you have any idea what my monthly carrying costs are?"

Paul rattled off the figures, silencing him for the moment. "It'll take another few weeks to finish clearing the land. In the meantime, my talking to people won't cost you anything. If I can find a way to protect the burial ground while producing the same level of profit—"

"No damn way exists. If it did, I would have found it. I had to bust my butt just to get the city to pay a fair share of the infrastructure costs, so they're not going to hand you a blank check to save a bunch of bones."

Lei leaned forward a little. "But Marshall, he's worked miracles on the mainland. In Seattle—"

"This happens to be Hawaii, Lei. We have our own problems and our own rules."

Paul checked the urge to insist that one place was pretty much like another. It would only make Marshall more irascible. "The dispute has focused attention on the project, sir. There's opposition, but there's also support that didn't exist before. The politicians—"

"Will give you maybes, possiblys and I'll-think-about-its, and then do exactly nothing. The delays will cost me a fortune. Your job here is to keep things moving until I'm out of this house. I have nothing more to say."

Paul ignored the statement and listed specifics, mentioning every way he could think of to modify the project without losing money. Marshall shot them all down, saying he'd asked for that and been refused, that Hawaii didn't work that way, that it wasn't cost-effective. Frustrated, Paul finally asked what the sense of his even being here was.

"You're here because Ned Beecham can't keep a project on schedule and you can," Marshall replied. "Cancel your meetings and get out to the work site. I want every inch of that land cleared by next Friday."

Paul looked at Everett. "You really want me to stay?"

"He's my brother, Lindy. Humor me. It's only for a few months."

A few months in a hornet's nest, Paul thought, but nodded resignedly. "All right. Friday will be pushing things, but I'll try. If there's nothing more to discuss . . ."

He started to get up, but Everett waved him back down. "Marsh, Lindy has no legal standing in all this. I want you to sign some sort of document directing him to act on your behalf. Have your lawyer draft something."

"Whatever. Talk to Ross about it." He yawned and gestured toward the door. "I'm going to have to throw you all out. I can hardly stay awake."

Everyone trooped out of the bedroom, gathering in the living room to talk. Lei looked so downcast that Paul wanted to take her in his arms and comfort her. He didn't, though, because there was no point tempting himself with something he couldn't have.

"I'm sorry," he said. "I was hoping he'd let me explore the possibility of a compromise, but I can't disobey a direct order. I just don't have any leeway here."

Everett strolled to the piano and leaned casually against it. A calculating gleam entered his eye. "Maybe I can get you some. I think I should have a talk with Ross."

Paul understood what he was saying. "You mean the right sort of contract would give me more authority than Marshall intends. You think you can talk Ross into it?"

"Maybe. Situations change. People who said no to something a month ago might say yes tomorrow. Ross is bound to realize that it's in everyone's interest to give you a freer hand." He paused, looking troubled. "My brother can be mulish, Lindy, but he's not usually totally unreasonable. Believe me—he's not himself. He was anxious about this project to begin with, and then he got hit with the dispute over the ruins, Bobby Lum's accident and a heart attack, one right after the other. He's afraid things will unravel and cost him a bundle, and it's made him dig in his heels."

He thought for another moment. "He'll come to his senses sooner or later, and in the meantime, I have to protect him however I can. Let's hope Ross will be willing to buy you some time. Marsh has no patience for fine print. He tells Ross what he wants and signs what Ross comes up with. How about it? Will you give it a try?"

Paul shrugged. "You're the boss, Everett. I'll do whatever you want as long as it doesn't land me in jail."

"If it does," Everett said with a laugh, "I promise to bail you out. Go on back to the office. I'll put in a call to Ross this afternoon. I want this settled before I fly out tomorrow morning."

"You and me both. I'll talk to you later." Paul looked at Lei. He'd driven here himself, coming directly from lunch with a union leader, while she'd come with Cliff. "Ride back with me, okay?"

"Sure." Lei assumed he had business to discuss but wouldn't have time to speak to her in the office. He'd been so busy for the past two days that they'd seen each other only in passing.

In the car, though, he started telling her about the meetings he'd attended, driving as though he had all the time in the world instead of a schedule that was booked solid. People had been friendly but wary of getting involved, he said. Unwilling to commit themselves but careful to leave the door open for future negotiations.

Since she'd worried he didn't trust her or even like her, she wondered why he was confiding in her. Maybe he simply felt like talking. If so, she was flattered he would choose her as a sounding board.

She realized as they rode up the elevator that she wasn't nervous or anxious anymore. She was still very aware of him, but it no longer frightened her. Her embarrassment over the pills seemed silly now; he'd probably barely noticed them. As for Liliha's prophecy, it couldn't have been right. He wasn't looking for an affair and neither was she. Nothing would happen.

Paul held a brief staff meeting when they got back, finding that everyone in the office thought Everett's plan was a stroke of genius. For all Marshall's toughness in business, he was generous personally, and his employees were intensely loyal. Grace, especially, adored him, because he'd paid for cosmetic surgery for her little grandson when the insurance company wouldn't. If it would help to keep him in the dark for a while about Paul's activities, they were willing to do it.

As the session broke up, Paul remarked to Lei, "About Bernice's meeting tonight—it never hurts to talk to people. I just hope they understand that I'm not putting them off when I say I can't make them any promises."

"They'll probably be hostile at first, but all you can do is try." She paused. "Why don't I pick you up? You're pretty much on my way, and Bernice's house is on a curvy back road that can be hard to find at night, especially for a green *malihini* like you."

He laughed. "I think I could manage to get there, but I'm not going to turn you down. It will give us a chance to compare notes afterward."

"A quarter of eight in front of the building?"

"Sounds good." He checked his watch. "I've got a meeting at city hall. Amy, if Everett calls about Ross, just take a message. I'll be back by five." Watching him stride away, Lei told herself that if she could have bottled and sold whatever energized him, she would have made a fortune.

She left work when she usually did, around four, but Everett hadn't called yet. Her stomach was in knots by then. She'd never been much good at waiting.

As always, the twins rushed up for kisses when she walked in the door. She worried about spending enough time with them, not the "quality time" the experts went on about, but ordinary time spent snacking, doing chores or watching TV. It was worst on the evenings when she had to go out, so she cooked their favorite dinners and played with them until it was time to leave. Like most kids, they could sense guilt the way a shark senses blood and always took full advantage of it. That particular evening, they talked her into letting them stay up late for a special on TV.

Although she got downtown early, Paul was already waiting. He made a thumbs-up sign when he saw her, and she smiled in relief. He would work things out. He had to. Somewhere along the line, she'd come to place an enormous amount of faith in him.

He told her that Everett and Ross had agreed he should be put in charge of the Waikane project and authorized to do whatever was necessary to keep development there on track, including holding meetings and news conferences in order to reduce community opposition. Marshall understood the value of manipulating public opinion, so he was sure to agree to at least that much. Much more to the point, the wording in the contract was vague enough to permit Paul to negotiate changes in the existing project if he thought there was no other way to get the site developed. Any agreements he reached would be subject to Marshall's approval, of course, so Ross's sleight of pen wasn't really unethical. It was just . . . expedient. A matter of semantics and judgment.

"Naturally," Paul said with a wink, "I think the dispute over the burial ground will have to be resolved before we can start building out there. Judicial or legislative enjoinment is inevitable."

Lei now believed that the *heiau* was just as sacred and inviolable, but she didn't want to antagonize Paul by asking for too much too soon. "Then the project will just have to be modified," she said lightly.

He sobered. "I'll do my best, Lei. I don't know if I'll succeed."

"Don't tell me you've actually failed at something!" she teased.

"As a matter of fact, I have. People won't always compromise. Not every problem has a solution."

She was speechless for a moment. He radiated such confidence that she'd assumed he'd accomplished everything he'd ever set out to. "And Waikane?" she finally murmured.

"It's a challenge, but I think I can help. Of course, I always think that." He smiled. "I've only been wrong twice."

He told her about his two failures, a resort in Phoenix and a visionary complex on the San Francisco waterfront. Both had gotten mired in local politics. So might Waikane, he admitted.

The thought of failure left her a little subdued. Bernice noticed it the minute she opened the door. "What's wrong?" she asked. "You look upset."

"It's been one of those days, I guess. Work, the kids . . . You know how it is. This is Paul Lindstrom, Bernice. Paul, Bernice Kapakala."

"Get yourself something to eat, dear." Bernice took Paul's arm. "I'll introduce Mr. Lindstrom around."

Lei made her way to the coffee and cake. She was reaching for a cup when David Kapakala strolled over. "So your *haole* friend showed up," he drawled. "I thought maybe he wouldn't. Hostile crowd and all that."

"He wants to help. Give him a chance." She poured herself some coffee and carried it to the couch, in no mood to listen to David's sarcasm.

He tagged along behind her and sat down next to her. "Actually, I made some calls to the mainland. Checked him out. He's got a hell of a reputation. A regular California *kahuna*. I think I could work with the guy."

She raised her eyebrows. "You mean you'll try not to be obnoxious tonight?"

"I won't say a word. I'm just here to watch, darlin'." He grinned at her. "Let's settle back and enjoy the show."

"It's a serious meeting, David, not some sort of—"

"Take my word for it, Lei. I've heard about how Lindstrom operates. It's going to be a show."

In a way, he was right. Paul started with his speech about how he couldn't make any promises, then asked question after question about people he'd met or heard about, trying to get a sense of where they stood and what might induce them to compromise. The unspoken message was clear. He wouldn't have asked so many questions if he hadn't thought he could make a difference.

The audience started out being suspicious, even antagonistic, and wound up eagerly volunteering information. Lei could hardly believe it. They didn't give their trust easily, especially not to *haoles* from the mainland, but they trusted Paul Lindstrom. It was a question of emotion, not logic. He had an amazing ability to reach people's hearts.

She was exhilarated but quiet afterward, awed by his performance but too reserved to say so. They talked nonstop on the way home, discussing various community leaders and public officials. Where Marshall thought of her as a daughter, Paul treated her as an equal. She felt important, respected.

The lobby was locked by the time they arrived, so she drove into the garage and stopped by the elevator. Paul opened the door but didn't get out right away. "Thanks for the ride and the company. Tonight was helpful. I'm finally getting a feel for things."

"I'm glad." She lowered her eyes, longing to compliment him but unable to get a word out. "Good night, Paul."

"Good night. I'll see you in the morning." He turned to leave.

When it came right down to it, she couldn't let him go without saying something. "Paul?"

He looked over his shoulder. "Hmm?"

"Just..." She hesitated, shy and a little flustered. "I've never seen them respond that way to an outsider before. But when you spoke, even when you just listened, the sincerity and—and decency just shone out of you. I think...I think maybe you're a gift that's been sent from the mainland to help us."

Paul settled back in his seat. No woman had ever looked at him the way Lei just had—with a gratitude and admiration approaching hero worship shining out of her eyes. The more time they spent together, the harder it was to keep his distance, and that look didn't help. He had the feeling that if he'd taken her in his arms, she would have given herself without reservation. The temptation to find out for sure was almost overwhelming. Almost.

He took a deep breath and reminded himself about her kids. As a single mother, she'd have heavy responsibilities and more than her share of problems. He couldn't just ignore that. He'd have to listen and try to help. But right now, he owed every bit of his time and energy to Everett, Marshall and Waikane. The only relationship he could handle was a relaxing, undemanding one, and Lei couldn't provide it.

He smiled at her. "That's one of the nicest things anyone's ever said to me, but it's not true. I'm more of a hustler than a saint. I do want to help, but mostly because it's a challenge. The land doesn't have the same meaning for me as it does for you and your friends."

"I know that. It doesn't matter." Her eyes were so wide and gentle, they took his breath away. "You give yourself too little credit, Paul. You're a good man. You want to do what's right. I think it makes you uncomfortable to admit it because it isn't fashionable or sophisticated."

"Maybe you're right. Goodness isn't especially prized in my line of work." He was so aroused he found it hard to talk naturally. Either he left now or he took her upstairs. "Good night, Lei. I'll see you tomorrow."

Lei's heart was racing and her face was flushed, but she didn't let that worry her. Paul hadn't tried to touch her. He didn't even look as if he wanted to. She murmured goodnight, then watched him walk away.

He was at the capitol all day Thursday, so the next time she saw him was at the news conference on Friday. He wore a brightly printed aloha shirt that made him look like a *kamaaina*, a native, but Hawaii had seldom seen his like before.

His opening remarks were brief. His job, he said, was to keep the Waikane project on schedule. Off the record, he admitted that he hoped to negotiate a compromise, adding that the obstacles, including his boss, were formidable.

What astonished her was what followed. Reporters were notoriously cynical, but he gradually won them over. He wound up interviewing *them* as much as the other way around, gaining the same sorts of insights as on Wednesday, but from an entirely different perspective.

The question-and-answer session was off-the-record, but it would color the way the story was reported. Paul had impressed them. They wanted him to succeed. Anyone who spoke to them, read their words in newspapers and magazines, or listened to them on the radio or TV would sense it.

As they rode back downstairs, Lei drawled, "Mr. Lindstrom, I believe you could sell saltwater to sailors. Hawaiians haven't been this impressed with anyone since Captain Cook landed, and they thought he was a god. I can't wait to see you in action tomorrow night at the Greenwoods' anniversary party. Everyone who's anyone will be there. Fresh grist for your mill."

"You mean I'm going to have to work?" He looked desolate.

"Every single minute, but don't worry. I'll stick like glue and make sure you meet all the right people."

"You mean you'll watch me every moment and make sure I don't have any fun," he grumbled.

She laughed. "So suspicious! I suppose the least I can do is chauffeur you. The Greenwoods live on a narrow road off Kahala Avenue. Their house can be hard—"

"For a dumb *malihini* like me to find at night. I know." Paul also knew that it was out of her way, but he didn't object. He enjoyed her company, even if it left him damn frustrated at times. "Six thirty out front?"

"Perfect," Lei said. And it was. He was exciting to work with and fascinating to talk to. She looked forward to spending the evening with him.

Chapter Six

Lei had known Paul would look good in a dinner jacket. After all, he'd looked good in everything else she'd ever seen him in, from a pin-striped suit to an aloha shirt. "That outfit can't possibly be rented," she said as he got into the car. "It fits too well. I'll bet it's from some fancy San Francisco men's shop like Wilkes-Bashford. And I'll bet you never leave home without it."

"Maybe you'd buy the Golden Gate Bridge from a guy in a checkered sports coat, too." He fastened his seat belt. "I asked my secretary to pull it out of my closet, where it was gathering dust, and air-express it to Honolulu. Everyone said Hawaii was informal. I didn't think I'd need it here."

"'Gathering dust,' my foot. You probably wore it at least twice a week at home." She gave him a cheeky grin and pulled away from the curb. She'd had a wonderful day with the kids and was in a breezy, exuberant mood. "I used to read about you in Phil Clark's society column. You were always at operas or ballets or charity balls. He always referred to you as 'Canning Veep Lindy Lindstrom,' and your girlfriends always had names like Buffy or Tracy or Candice. Very upper crust, that crowd you ran around with."

He laughed. "I don't know which of those calumnies to refute first. I didn't wear a dinner jacket more than once a week at home, and the crowd may have been upper crust, but I'm definitely not. I don't know anyone named Buffy, but I do know a Pat, a Nancy and a Barbara. They weren't girlfriends, though, only dates."

"There's a difference?" she asked.

"Sure there's a difference. A date is someone you go out with once or twice, usually to some benefit you only attend because you're thinking of doing a deal with one of the other people there. A girlfriend is longer term."

"Someone you take out three whole times, I suppose."

He thought it over. "Six or seven, maybe. I'm not sure. I haven't had one in a while. A girlfriend, that is, not a date."

"You mean nobody will go out with you more than five times?" Her eyes widened in mock astonishment. "How perfectly extraordinary, Paul! A straight, single man in San Francisco and the women won't have you!" She paused. "What's *wrong* with you, anyway?"

Paul did a mental double take. Lei had never gotten so personal before, not to mention so sassy. It was provocative and challenging and he loved every minute of it.

She looked sensational, too. She was wearing an ankle-length black sheath with rhinestone straps, and she'd let her hair down, sweeping it back from her face with a pair of rhinestone clips. She always wore a gold chain around her neck, tucked into her blouse, but now he saw that there was a tiny onyx hand on the end of it. For some reason, he found it incredibly provocative. He'd planned to spend the evening talking to people about Waikane, but for once, business was going to take a back seat to pleasure. He wasn't about to accompany a woman this captivating to a party and then ignore her.

"Nothing's wrong with me," he said. "The problem is with you women."

"Really!" She rolled her eyes.

He rested his arm along the back of the seat. "Really. At the age of thirty, some wild hormonal change takes place in the female body that turns women who were once completely rational into total lunatics. They stop thinking about success in their careers and start dreaming about kids in suburban houses. They stop ranting about their need for independence and start nagging you to set a wedding date."

"So you're one of those, are you!" She wrinkled her nose in disapproval. "Well, I can't say I'm surprised."

"One of what?" he asked.

"Men who are afraid of commitment."

"That's another thing about women," he grumbled. "You're always psychoanalyzing men. And what's that crack about not being surprised supposed to mean?"

Lei glanced at him. He was grinning at her, obviously enjoying their verbal skirmish. She hesitated, then decided that any man who slandered women that way was asking for it. "You and Karen Douglas. That was the tip-off, right there."

"That I'm afraid of commitment?"

"Exactly. Phil Grant always used to write about 'Canning Veep Lindy Lindstrom' and 'Wells Fargo exec Karen Douglas.' And then it was suddenly Karen Douglas and George Somebody, and this whole parade of Buffys, Tracys and Candices began. I suppose Karen was ready to settle down and you weren't, so she found someone else. Sounds like a typical case of male arrested development to me."

"Just a damn minute," he said with a laugh. "For three years the woman told me she needed space. That her career came first. That marriage was an obsolete institution and that children would cramp her style. I took her at her word. We had a great relationship. Then she turned thirty, and bam! Suddenly she was reading the surburban listings in the real estate section and consulting articles about raising perfect children. Is it *my* fault she suddenly went crazy?"

"There's nothing crazy about a person stretching and growing. You should try it some time. You might like it."

Paul could have told her that he was stretching and growing even as they spoke, but he held his tongue. She clammed up whenever he got too familiar, and he wanted to keep her talking. "So the man is always wrong. Some woman changes her mind about what she wants and if he doesn't go along, he's a louse with a bad case of arrested development."

"Not a louse." The look she gave him reeked of pity. "A poor, misguided creature adrift on an isolated sea, unable to connect and unite with another human being—"

"I'll have you know that I've connected and united with any number of other human beings in my time, Miss Howe."

She burst out laughing. "I'll just bet you have. Candice and Tracy and—"

"Untrue. Utter slander."

"Pat, Nancy and Barbara, then."

"Nope. Nobody since Karen. I go out because it's good for business. Everett usually picks up the tab. On the whole, I'd rather play golf and make deals."

"And you haven't had time to do either one here. Poor Paul!" She paused. "Cheer up, though. You'll be able to remedy those deficiencies tonight. You might even find a woman you like."

"All in a single night?" He whistled softly, pretending to be amazed. "Amy wasn't kidding when she said her aunt threw terrific parties."

"Not *that* terrific," Lei said with a smile. "I should have said you could make a start. Stick close and I'll introduce you to fascinating women, men who live and breathe deals, and members of the best golf clubs on Oahu. I'm sure you'll be able to take things from there."

"I could, but why should I work that hard? The least you can do is find me a fascinating woman with millions to invest, a handicap under eight and no interest in babies."

Lei didn't know anyone like that, but said she would do her best. Then she told Paul about some of the people he would meet, from the old-line bankers, attorneys and Big Five executives who comprised the *haole* elite to the businessmen and politicians, many of them local-Asian, who ran Hawaii today. She wasn't surprised when he'd heard of almost all of them. Obviously he'd done his homework.

"I only met most of these people after I went to work for Marshall," she remarked. "I'm sort of his bodyguard. He takes me along to rescue him in case he gets cornered by some widow on the prowl for a second husband."

"Obviously another example of a man who can't make a commitment," Paul said.

"On the contrary, he was so devoted to his late wife that he's sure nobody can take her place."

"Umm. Sure. It's a good line, anyway."

"What a cynic you are! He adored her. Even John Davis says so. Personally, I think he'd be less lonely if he remarried, but he won't hear of it." She pulled into the Greenwoods' long private driveway. "Besides, if it were a line, he'd have as many girlfriends—excuse me, dates, which he'd have the honesty to admit weren't strictly business at all—as you do, and he doesn't."

Paul winced. "Pardon me while I lick my wounds. You're sure as hell frisky tonight. What kind of pill did you ingest before you picked me up?"

Lei smiled, savoring the memories. "I had the nicest day, Paul. When I saw the sunshine this morning, I decided to take the kids to the beach. Usually we go to Ala Moana because it's quieter than most places, but Jason wanted to surf and the North Shore is best for that. I learned as a kid and I've been teaching him and Jessie. He's great at it. And then, this afternoon, they had a piano recital. Both of them are so musical—I was so proud of them." Tom had been musical, too, she thought wistfully. Whenever she heard the twins play, it was as though a part of him were still alive.

She suddenly realized she'd been running on at the mouth. "I'm sorry. I probably sound like one of those annoying women who think they invented motherhood."

Trotting around with a pair of eight-year-olds had never been Paul's idea of a good time, but much to his surprise, he wouldn't have minded spending the day with Lei. There was something warm and appealing about the things she'd done. Of course, most anything was better than plowing through books and reports. "Don't apologize," he said. "You're entitled to be proud. You're obviously a wonderful mother."

"I hope so. I try to be." She pulled in behind a long line of cars parked along one side of the driveway. "If you look down there, you can see the house through the trees."

The place was huge, surrounded by flowering trees and vines and set back from a placid stretch of sea. Paul helped Lei out of the car and offered his arm. She clutched it gratefully, murmuring, "Between my heels and the pitch of this driveway... If it starts raining again, I'll probably slip and break my neck." It had rained on and off since Thursday, and was clouding up again. She tightened her grip as they started walking. "I hope I'm not cutting off your circulation."

"Actually, I kind of like this—having a helpless female cling to me for support. I won't let you fall." He felt strong and chivalrous, like a medieval knight. It didn't matter that Lei was over six feet tall in her heels and probably no more helpless than an Amazon. "Another example of my arrested development, no doubt."

She smiled at his dry tone. "It's not your fault, really. After all, San Francisco is known for its steep hills. Who can blame you for becoming addicted to clinging women?"

She was right about the hills but wrong about the women. Not a single one of them had made him feel the way she did. He'd told himself that the pleasures of being with her were worth the frustration of going home alone, but his body wasn't buying it. The next few hours were going to be more difficult than he'd realized.

A gentleman would have warned her not to trust him, but he hated the thought of the barriers that would immediately spring up. "Not a chance," he said. "The women in San Francisco are too liberated to cling."

If so, Lei thought, it was definitely their loss. She liked being with Paul—liked his intelligence, his sense of humor and his air of confidence. She liked the way he treated her, as someone whose company he enjoyed rather than as a potential sexual conquest. She was even beginning to like the flush of arousal she felt whenever he smiled at her or said something a little provocative. It had been years since she'd felt so feminine and desirable.

She wasn't naive, though. He was a man, she was a woman and the occasion was extremely romantic. But she'd come in her own car and had control over the situation. Everything would be fine as long as she kept her head.

A security man at the bottom of the drive directed them to a large lanai in back of the house. Hundreds of people were gathered in the room, which was roofed but otherwise open. It was decorated with dozens of hanging baskets containing bright, fragrant flowers and Japanese lanterns that cast a warm, romantic glow. A pair of staircases on the *makai* side of the lanai led down to flatlands containing a pool and tennis court. A large tent had been set up on the shorefront beyond.

Cocktails and hors d'ouevres were being served as a band played a medley of old Beatles' hits. Lei and Paul went through the reception line, then circulated. They worked as a team, Paul whispering questions into Lei's ear every now and then, Lei whispering back information about someone's business interests or family and political connections. Having seen him at work before, she wasn't surprised when he managed to introduce productive topics into conversations that began with social chitchat. As always, he was charming and impressive.

They were standing with two other couples, the men Warren Greenwood's colleagues from his days at the Big Five firm of Alexander & Baldwin, when a classmate of Lei's from college waved to her from several yards away. Paul didn't seem to need her at the moment, so she started over to meet the woman. He immediately slid his arm around her waist and pulled her back. She gave her friend a smiling shrug. They could talk to each other later.

Without looking at her, still speaking just as fluently, he cupped the curve of her waist and moved his fingers lightly back and forth, over and over again. The caress was so subtle that it took her several seconds to recognize how sensual it was. Once she did, a pulsing warmth suffused her body. He seemed so involved in the conversation that she wondered if he even realized what he was doing.

She got her answer a moment later, when he rubbed the side of her rib cage with his thumb, moving it slowly but firmly up and down, coming unnervingly close to her breast. Though his touch was gentle, it was also far too erotic not to be deliberate. She felt it everywhere—in the tingling at the backs of her wrists and knees, and in the sudden tightening of her nipples, in the moist heat between her legs. Within moments, her heart was pounding out of control.

He slid his hand downward and gently but possessively massaged her hip. She swallowed hard. Once she would have been frightened or annoyed, but now she was just aroused. And that was dangerous.

When she started to move away, he tightened his grip to keep her where she was. Short of making a scene, there was nothing she could do, and she'd never made a scene in her life. She stopped resisting and stood docilely by his side, waiting with a mixture of confusion and anticipation. His fingers had stilled for the moment, but maybe he would start caressing her again. She blushed, chagrined to find herself picturing it graphically.

The reality was even more inflaming than the fantasy. He moved his hand a fraction and pressed lightly with his thumb, finding and rubbing the top of her hipbone. She trembled as his palm inched downward. There was nothing indecent about the way he was touching her—not yet—but it was more intimate than what she was used to. It excited her in a way she'd never experienced before. She was out of her depth and she knew it, torn between wanting him to stop and aching for him to continue.

It was dark in the lanai, but hardly pitch-black. She wondered if anyone would notice what he was doing, notice how she was responding. But no one seemed to.

Paul kept talking. He also kept touching her, drawing her close and caressing her with undetectable strokes of his thumb. She looked at him a little dazedly. He looked back. His eyes were warm and amused. She had the feeling he was only inches from smiling. Then he turned his attention back to the Greenwoods' friends.

Though she blushed even harder, she also came to her senses. It would serve him right, she thought darkly, if she did the exact same thing to him as he was doing to her—slid her hand under the back of his jacket and fondled his backside. Except that he probably would have loved it.

Fortunately cocktail party conversations never lasted more than a few minutes. One of the men excused himself to say hello to someone else and the group dispersed. "Where to next?" Paul asked.

He looked as innocent as a newborn babe. She could cheerfully have kicked him. "A dark, quiet corner," she muttered. "I have a few choice things to say to you."

He grinned at her. "I'm in *pilikia nui*, huh?"

"You're darn right you're in big trouble, and don't think you can get around me by talking in Hawaiian." She softened though, just a little. It pleased her enormously when he made an effort to fit in. Besides, maybe she'd unwittingly encouraged him by teasing him so much.

They stopped near one of the staircases. "You're beautiful and captivating and your perfume is driving me crazy," he said. "And that dress—I'd like to buy you diamonds to wear with that dress. They'd look like fire against your skin. The champagne went to my head, I guess, and I—''

"No, it didn't." She found it hard to yell at a man who gave her such lovely compliments. Besides, it wasn't in her nature to get truly angry. "You only had a few sips. You knew exactly what you were doing."

"Okay, then. *You* went to my head. I weakened, Lei. I admit it. I couldn't stop thinking about touching you. I kept wondering how you'd react—if you felt even half the electricity that I did." He captured a strand of her hair and gave it a playful tug. "You did. You're not afraid of me anymore. That's good."

He was right. She wasn't. Just exasperated and, though she wasn't going to admit it, rather amused. "And to think I believed you when you said you preferred golf and deals to women! Talk about a good line!"

"But it wasn't. I just hadn't met *you* yet."

She couldn't tell whether he was joking or serious, but it didn't matter. "I'm flattered, but if you do anything like that again, you'll have to find your own way home."

"If you're worried about my aversion to kids, don't be." He smiled. "Your twins sound terrific. We'll work around them."

The man was as dense as lead. "I don't want to work around them. They come first in my life."

"I understand that. I don't mind doing things with them as long as we can be alone sometimes." He caressed her shoulder, massaging it with a gentle, erotic touch. "Stop fighting it, Lei. It's inevitable."

Inevitable. She paled and looked away, remembering Liliha's words about destiny and fate, stunned that Paul should have spoken in the exact same terms. Then, lifting her chin a little, she told herself that his opinion was no more infallible than a vision in a glass of water. There was a surefire way to turn him off. All she had to do was use it. "So that's why you were talking about diamonds! This is very sudden, Paul. I never expected you to propose."

He was taken aback. "Uh, Lei—"

"Really, I never imagined you were in the market for a wife and family. I'll certainly consider it, but your credentials aren't impressive. For one thing, your record on commitment—"

He laughed and held up his hands, aware now that she was joking. "All right. You win. Just don't psychoanalyze me anymore. I'll be good. I swear it."

"Why do I have the feeling that you're not taking me seriously?" she asked with a sigh.

"I am. Really."

"I hope so. I'd like to stay here and enjoy myself, but if I have to keep telling you—"

"You won't." He sobered. "I can't pretend to like it, but I do understand that we're coming from different places. I'm sorry I let myself forget it. I don't want you to be uncomfortable."

Lei was satisfied that he meant it. He was a bit of a wolf, but he was also decent and fair. She gave him a forgiving smile and took his arm. "Back to work, then. There's the mayor. Have you met him yet?"

Paul shook his head, almost wishing Lei would punish him for stepping out of line instead of being so sweet and understanding that he wanted to take her in his arms all over again. Sulking and coldness would have made her easier to resist.

He resigned himself to frustration and let her lead him over to the mayor. He'd been a louse to make a pass at her. He deserved to suffer for it. But the way she'd blushed and trembled when he'd caressed her... The dazed desire in her eyes when she'd gazed at him... He took a deep breath. He'd go nuts if he thought about things like that, but there was no way on earth he could help it.

Chapter Seven

Eventually the band left and a string quartet took its place. Several waiters rolled a crimson carpet down the center of the lanai, and a minister arrived. Music filled the air and a hush descended over the crowd.

Paul wasn't sentimental, but the ceremony that followed touched him deeply. For fifty years, the Greenwoods had been blissfully happy and very much in love. Very few people found that in life. He would have liked to be one of them, but he wasn't sure he had the capacity for that kind of love and devotion.

Beside him, Lei dabbed at her eyes with a tissue. "That was beautiful. They're such a perfect couple. They have it all." She stuffed the tissue into her purse. "I envy them. Isn't that an awful way to feel?"

"Nobody has it all." Paul took her arm and escorted her downstairs. "They probably have a butler who robs them blind or pets who aren't housebroken or indolent children."

"I don't know about the butler or the pets, but their sons are very successful—an A & B executive and a doctor."

"A grandchild who writes satanic rock music, then."

She sniffed and giggled. "I'm afraid not. One grandson's in medical school and the other's studying filmmaking. Their granddaughter owns a clothing shop. Of course, Kim is . . ." Her voice trailed off.

Paul wondered why she'd stopped. "She's what?"

"Nothing. I shouldn't have said anything."

Reading between the lines, he figured the woman was a total bitch. They walked into the tent and found their way to their table. He realized he'd have a chance to find out, because they'd been seated with the Greenwoods' grandchildren and various other relatives, including Amy Farrell and John Davis, whom he'd met a couple of times in the office.

Dinner was served at a leisurely pace, the band playing almost continuously. Paul asked Lei to dance the first number, but only because it would have been impolite not to. He wanted to keep the promise he'd made, and holding her in his arms wasn't going to help.

Given what had happened earlier, he expected her to be tense and stiff, but she followed his lead as if they'd danced together hundreds of times in the past. He spent the entire time resisting the urge to pull her closer. He didn't ask her to dance again.

She had plenty of other partners, though, most of them older men who were friends of Marshall's. Paul stuck to the other women at his table, a few of whom reminded him of why golf and deals had appealed to him more than women lately. They were too aggressive for his taste, especially Kim Greenwood. Sooner or later, he was going to run out of polite ways to say no to her.

By dessert he'd decided to avoid her, but she outmaneuvered him, intercepting him as he walked off the floor with Amy. "Waltz with me, Lindy. I need someone who won't step on my toes."

"How do you know it's going to be a waltz?" he asked.

She smiled coyly. "Because I told them to play one."

He could smell the Scotch on her breath as he led her onto the floor. "You've only danced with Lei once," she said, twining her arms around his neck. "How come?"

"She's a great dancer. I didn't want to monopolize her." He put Kim's arms back where they belonged.

"Or maybe you're afraid Marshall's pals will notice and report back to him. I mean, she *is* his exclusive property."

A remark like that didn't deserve a reply. Paul said nothing. "Surely you've heard the rumors!" Kim prodded.

Again he didn't answer. "So proper and stiff," she said with a giggle, moving lasciviously against him. "Are you like that in bed, Lindy?"

He backed away from her. "Tell me more about your store."

"You'd love the underwear I sell. I have some on right now. Would you like to see it?"

For the sixth time, he reminded himself that he was her grandparents' guest and should try to be polite. Besides, she was stinking drunk. "If I'm ever in the market for that kind of thing, I'll stop by your store."

"Do that," she purred. "I'll take you into the back room and give you a private showing."

He was beginning to think the dance would never end, when, miraculously, Lei appeared with Kim's cousin Tom, the film student. Tom mumbled that he needed Kim's help and dragged her away, leaving Lei and Paul standing awkwardly in the middle of the floor. He smiled and took her in his arms. She was warm, soft and incredibly graceful.

"You owe me one," she said. "For engineering your rescue, that is."

He laughed softly. "Was it that obvious?"

"Umm. You looked absolutely grim. What on earth was she saying?"

He wasn't about to repeat the part about Marshall. "Let's put it this way. It was the closest I've come to being sexually harassed. Whatever you want, you've got."

Lei didn't even have to think about it. "During the past hour, I've been jostled, pushed and tripped repeatedly. You, on the other hand, dance passably well, no doubt due to all those charity balls you've attended." In fact, she'd never had a better partner. "Dance the next dance with me, Paul. Tom is showing a film he made about his grandparents after that, and then we'll go back to work."

A wise man would have refused, but Paul was too captivated to be sensible. The next number was a pulsating tango that they hammed up outrageously and enjoyed enormously. They were doubled over with laughter afterward.

Tom's film, a skillfully edited mixture of old movies, family photographs and new interviews, filled everyone with nostalgia and joy. Suddenly a party that had been pleasant but impersonal became an emotional and intimate celebration of love and life. The warm mood made it that much easier for Paul to get to know everyone.

Lei took him from table to table, watching admiringly as again and again, polite hellos gave way to genuine interest. She left his side only once, to waltz with a dear friend of Marshall's. Although she told herself she was doing her job, the truth was that she couldn't tear herself away. When Paul asked her to dance to a fast-paced rock number, she jumped at the chance. They danced often after that, but never to anything slow or romantic. If she'd ever had a better time, she couldn't remember it.

Neither could Paul. He stopped caring about how busy he was and how many responsibilities Lei had. He only knew that he wanted to be with her. And nothing he'd promised precluded his gently trying to win her.

The last table they stopped at was the Greenwoods'. Paul had met them on the reception line but hadn't had a chance to talk to them since. "I've been watching you work the room," Warren said. "Very impressive. Join us for a while." He asked a waiter to bring a couple of chairs over.

A short, middle-aged man stood up. "Please—take my seat for the moment. I'm going to do my best to talk Lei into dancing with me."

"Chief Justice Tanaka, Lindy Lindstrom," Warren said.

They shook hands and made small talk while Lei watched with such a bemused expression on her face that Paul realized something unusual was going on. As Tanaka led her away, Warren remarked, "Interesting, given the fact that he hates to dance. What do you suppose it's all about, John?"

John Pukui, the governor, had no idea, and neither did anyone else at the table. When Tanaka returned, Warren teased him about his sudden affinity for the cha-cha, but he only smiled. He'd wanted to ask after Marshall's health in private, he insisted. Nobody believed him.

Paul was so curious that he excused himself as soon as he possibly could and asked Lei to dance. The band was playing a sultry torch song, but his mind was on business for once, not pleasure. Nobody would bother them here. "So what did Tanaka want?" he asked.

She settled into his arms. "He told you. To find out how Marshall was."

"I don't believe that for a moment." He lifted her chin and smiled his most persuasive smile. "Come on, Lei. Give."

Lei felt his smile clear down to her toes. Her eyes sparkled with amusement. "I love watching you beg, but I'm not supposed to say."

"You will, though."

"That depends. What will it get me?"

Paul wanted to tell her he'd make love to her until she collapsed with pleasure, but that probably wasn't what she had in mind. "The truth about Tracy and Candice," he said.

"A greater bribe than I can resist. Actually, Tanaka asked me to speak with you, but you can't pass anything on. He'll have my head if you do."

"Agreed." He took her back in his arms, holding her a little closer than before. Far from resisting, she snuggled against him.

"What do you know about the Bishop estate?" she asked.

Paul reeled off the facts. "Dates to the late 1800s. The largest private landowner in Hawaii. Set up in accordance with the will of Princess Bernice Pauahi Bishop to benefit children with Hawaiian blood. The income supports the Kamehameha Schools."

"Very good. And the trustees?"

"There are five of them. They earn about a quarter of a million a year each to run the estate. They're appointed by..." Paul stopped for a moment. "By the Supreme Court of Hawaii. Good God. Do they want Marshall?"

"Maybe. There's a vacancy coming up and they could use a savvy developer on the board. Of course, anyone they chose would have to be acceptable to the Hawaiian community."

"And if Marshall builds on that land, he won't be."

"That's true," Lei said, "but Tanaka says his name came up long before the dispute over Waikane arose."

Maybe it had, given all those awards in his office, but the timing was still damned interesting. "So if Marshall satisfies the natives' rights groups, they'll consider him for the appointment. Do you think he'll go for it?"

"I don't know. It's one of the most prestigious positions in Hawaii, but you've seen how he is about money."

Paul certainly had. Marshall thought he'd done enough already. Prestige or not, he'd be reluctant to budge until his financial interests were protected. "I know he's stubborn, but it's one hell of an inducement. Why don't I run it by him on Monday? Once he's had time to think about it, he might decide that a Bishop trusteeship is worth a few additional concessions on his part."

Lei told herself he had to. The world seemed a little brighter now. She closed her eyes and followed Paul's lead, losing herself in the warmth of his embrace.

When the number ended, she looked at her watch and sighed. It was well past midnight. The evening had passed too quickly. "I hate to leave, but I promised my sitter I wouldn't be too late. If you want to stay, though, I could find you a ride home."

"I've met everyone I was supposed to meet. Let's…" He paused and cocked his ear. "You hear that? It's raining again. Give me your keys and I'll drive the car down to the bottom of the driveway."

Lei listened for a second. "It's only a few sprinkles. Anyway, I like walking in the rain."

"You're *pupule*," he said with a grin. The word meant crazy, and people in Hawaii used it all the time.

"And you're going native." She took his hand. "Come on. Let's go."

They thanked the Greenwoods, said goodbye to the people they'd sat with and left. Paul suspected it was raining a little more heavily than Lei had bargained for, but he didn't do the chivalrous thing and insist that she go back. He didn't want her to leave him.

By the time they reached the front of the house, the rain was falling so steadily that he gave her his jacket to hold over her head. The driveway was extremely slick, so he put his arm around her waist to steady her. After a moment, she did the same to him.

He set a measured pace, afraid she would slip if he went too fast. Then the sky opened up and they began to run all out, heads down, clutching each other, trying not to get drenched. They still had a long way to go. The car was near the top of the hill.

Lei was the first one to laugh. She didn't really mind getting wet. The rain was warm, and it was exhilarating to dash up the hill like a child—fast, reckless and free.

"*Pupule*," Paul said. "Just plain *pupule*! What the hell is so funny?" But he was laughing as hard as she was.

She glanced at him. "You," she gasped. "You look like a drowned cat. It's pathetic."

"Yeah?" He grabbed back his jacket. "Now let's see how much you like the rain."

"A little water won't hurt me. We Hawaiians are a tough lot." She stopped abruptly, almost causing him to fall. Then she yanked off her heels, gathered up her dress and took off, leaving him rooted to the ground like a plant. "I'll race you," she called over her shoulder.

Naturally he beat her. He was taller, stronger and had shoes on. Then he made a fatal mistake. He gloated.

Obviously it hadn't occurred to him that she still had the car keys. As he stood there, getting wetter by the moment, she slowed to a stroll to underscore the hollowness of his victory. Then, the crowning insult—she unlocked her door, scooted into the car and made him walk around to the other side to get in. She kept him outside for a full ten seconds longer before she pulled up his lock.

Both of them succumbed to hysterics afterward. They sat there for a good minute, water dripping all over the place, both of them weak with laughter. Paul finally tossed his jacket onto the back seat. "God, I'm wet. I don't suppose there's a towel around."

"An oily rag," Lei said. "Will that do?"

"The idea of drying your face with it has a certain appeal, but, no. I'll use my shirt." He slipped off his suspenders, pulled out his cuff links and went to work on his shirt studs.

Lei studied him, watching him struggle with the studs in the dim light of a nearby lamppost. Despite his disgruntled tone, he was grinning from ear to ear. "Good idea," she said. "Let me help you with those." She grasped the stud just above his cummerbund and began to undo it.

He jerked away, laughing all over again. "Lei—"

"You're ticklish!" She grinned with delight. "A weakness I never imagined existed."

Paul was *very* ticklish. He was also incredibly turned on and trying desperately to behave. Lei looked irresistible soaking wet. Her hair was spilling wildly over her shoulders, and he could see the outlines of her nipples under her wet dress. "Yes," he said. "Don't you dare—"

But he was too late. She attacked mercilessly, reducing him to a state of helpless laughter and shattering arousal within seconds. He didn't know whether to be glad or sorry when she stopped.

He marshaled what was left of his self-control and pulled the last few studs out of his shirt. "You're going to pay for that," he said. It was still a game, but not by much. For a lady who kept saying no, she was being damn provocative.

Lei heard only his threat, not the frustration behind it. "I'm quaking in my—my panty hose. It's *my* car, Paul. Take revenge and you'll walk home."

Scowling, he pulled off his shirt and wiped his face and hair with it. She was giggling at his display of temper when she got her first good look at his body. He was gorgeous—muscular, tanned and whipcord tough. One glance and she was flushed and breathless. Shaken by the strength of her reaction, she turned away. Suddenly none of this was funny.

Out of the corner of her eye, she saw him finish drying himself. "Your turn now," he said.

She held out her hand. After all, she *was* soaked. "Give me the shirt."

"No way." He captured her wrists in a single, large hand. "We'll do things my way for a change."

Before she could say a word, he began to rub her briskly with the shirt, drying her hair the way you'd dry a wet puppy's fur. She didn't know what she'd expected, but it certainly wasn't that. He went to work on her face next. Having little choice, she closed her eyes and endured it.

His revenge, if that's what it was, wasn't enjoyable or erotic, but other things were. The warmth of his body, heating her as he bent over her. The strength of his hand, gently holding her prisoner. The intimacy of being alone with him in the car as rain beat down all around them.

He finished drying her face, then straightened. "Are we having fun yet?"

"You're a sadist," she said, opening her eyes. She tried to glare in mock indignation, but didn't even come close. Her voice was husky, her expression apprehensive.

"Wrong. A sadist would have made you stand outside for five minutes and *then* rubbed you down." He dried her neck and shoulders, rubbing her less vigorously now. His face was blank, unreadable. He didn't look as if he meant to touch her, but he was so close. She shivered. Too close.

She pulled free from his grasp. "If you're finished torturing me . . ."

"Not quite." He dried her chest, moving the shirt in slow, seductive circles. Their eyes met. He wasn't smiling anymore. His breathing was erratic and his gaze was tense and hot. He brushed the shirt back and forth across her nipples until they hardened with arousal, then tossed it aside and cupped her chin.

Lei refused to look at him. She was trembling uncontrollably. "Let's go, Paul."

He didn't move. He knew how excited she was—he could see it, feel it, almost taste it. One move, one word . . . "Is that really what you want?"

"Yes." She raised her hands to push him away, but never got the chance.

"Like hell you do." His mouth covered hers at the same instant as her palms touched his chest. He brought her mouth close to his, then kissed her gently but firmly, nuzzling her lips for several dizzying, seductive seconds.

Her heart pounded violently. She couldn't catch her breath. He kissed her again, slipping his tongue between her lips and teasing her with it, making her want it deep inside her mouth, making her wait an eternity before he granted her wish. Feelings she'd never realized existed exploded out of control. Her hands were still on his chest, but instead of pushing him away, she caressed him feverishly. His kiss became fiercely erotic, a slow, thorough exploration of her mouth that left her weak with longing, her only thought to do as he wished. She was shy with men, but there was nothing hesitant about the way she kissed him back. She gave him her lips and tongue because she simply couldn't help it.

She couldn't help putting her arms around him and clinging to him when he pulled her closer, either. He moved against her, rubbing his chest against her breasts until her flesh ached to be touched and her nipples grew exquisitely sensitive. She moaned deep in her throat when he covered a breast with his hand and took the nipple between his fingers. He massaged it, teased it, pleasured it. She couldn't bear it. She felt as if she were burning up, splintering apart.

Still kissing her, he slipped his fingers under her straps and slid them off her shoulders. She hazily realized she should tell him to stop, but she didn't. She allowed him to pull down the dress until her breasts were exposed. He kneaded her damp, hot flesh with playful, gentle fingers . . . rubbed her nipples with thumbs that provoked and delighted and dominated.

Finally he lightened the kiss and murmured against her lips, "You like that, hmm?"

She shuddered. His thumbs had stilled. She ached to have them caress her again. "Yes. Don't stop. Please . . ."

"Please, what?" His voice was soft, teasing. "Touch you? Kiss you?"

"Anything you want." He began to stroke her again, touching her a little less gently, and she arched frantically against him. "Oh, God... Paul..." He stopped her moans with a kiss that was even more passionate than before, and wildly erotic images filled her mind. She was undressing in front of him, lying down on his bed, beckoning him closer, offering herself eagerly.

Offering herself eagerly. She tensed. It was just like the vision in the glass. *You'll offer yourself, my girl. He won't even have to ask you.* Then the pain would come, and the fear...

She pulled away, gasping for breath, so muddled with arousal she could barely think. It was all coming true. Suddenly hysterical, she shoved him violently and yanked up her dress.

Paul slowly backed away, breathing hard, stunned by the abruptness of Lei's rejection. He didn't understand what had happened. He only knew that every inch of his body ached, that he wanted her desperately and that she looked terrified. He reached for her, but she flinched and cringed away, throwing her arms protectively in front of her face.

She was afraid of him—afraid he was going to hurt her. The idea appalled him. "Lei—sweetheart... I wasn't going to... I would never force you to..." He took a deep breath and tried again. "You're upset. I just wanted to hold you. To comfort you. That's all."

Lei lowered her arms. Her reaction had been pure, panicky instinct. Paul's hand had shot out and she'd thought he was furious with her for stopping him—that he was going to hit her, to beat her up. It was the vision, of course. Her hands had been clenched, her body tense. She'd known what would come next. But Paul had never been anything but gentle with her. It was crazy to think he would hurt her.

Deep in her soul, though, in a place reason couldn't touch, she knew that he would. Hadn't everything else happened the way Liliha had predicted? "I want to go home now," she said. "This never should have happened."

He settled back in his seat. "Why not? Both of us wanted it to."

"You did, not me. I was just—"

"Of course you did. Think about how you acted. The way you teased me, the way we danced... And when you started tickling me before... I know you didn't do it consciously, but you've been asking for this all night."

Lei twisted her hands together in her lap. When he put it like that, she could see he was right. She'd done everything she'd known she shouldn't and justified it by telling herself it was only a game between friends. "I'm sorry," she said, staring at her hands. "I didn't think."

"You were too busy having a good time. There's nothing wrong with that." He lifted her chin. "Come on, sweetheart, look at me." He smiled. "That's better. We like being together. We can't keep our hands off each other. Give me one good reason we shouldn't keep seeing each other."

"We've been through this before, Paul. I want someone I can share my life with. You'll be gone in two months." That wasn't the only reason—Liliha's vision had a lot to do with it, too, but she couldn't say so. He wouldn't have understood.

"It's crazy to get so hung up on the future that you stop living in the present," he responded. "Neither of us knows how we're going to feel in two months. Let's relax and let things take their course."

Now it was Lei's turn to smile. "You should know yourself better than that. There's only one possible course things can take."

"I used to think that. Now I'm not so sure." Paul wanted Lei to keep seeing him, but he also wanted to be fair. "Marriage and a family—I don't think I'm ready for that yet. But I want to be with you, Lei. A lot. And life doesn't provide any guarantees. Next week or next month, I could get hit by a truck or die in a plane—"

"Don't ever say that!" She was suddenly rigid with distress. "My brother and his wife died in a plane crash. Two children were left orphans because of it. It's a real tragedy that can happen to real people. Believe me—I know."

He was stunned. He'd been as far off base about her as it was possible to be. That wasn't like him. "You mean the twins? They're your niece and nephew?"

She nodded and looked away. He didn't press her for the details; he'd noticed how reluctant she was to talk about herself. She'd obviously been through a hell of a lot in her life and he didn't want to hurt her; if anything though, he meant to do the opposite. "I didn't mean to trivialize something serious. I was just trying to make you see that you should focus on now, not later. We can make each other happy. We can have a great time together."

Lei told herself it was pointless to argue. Given Paul's track record, only a fool would have supposed that he'd be able to make a commitment. A two-month affair was all she was going to get, and it was wrong for her and wrong for the children. "No," she said.

He simply smiled. "You're going to change your mind, you know. You won't be able to help it, any more than you could help how you acted tonight. When you're ready, you'll come to me. And I'll be waiting."

Just like in the vision, Lei thought. She felt very cold, very alone and very afraid.

Chapter Eight

Paul had been so busy since his arrival that he'd barely spent any time with the staff, so he held a meeting on Monday to tell them what he'd been up to. They'd no sooner sat down in the conference room than Grace asked, "What's this I hear about Marshall being appointed as a Bishop trustee?"

Like Grace, everyone Paul had met with that day had heard gossip about Marshall being considered for a Bishop trusteeship. That was obviously why Tanaka had approached Lei in public. He'd wanted to start a rumor—to launch a trial balloon. He would either move ahead or drop the idea depending on how the community reacted.

Paul shrugged, doing his best to look puzzled. "Who knows how these rumors get started?"

"Since you were the one who told him about it, I assume you do." She smiled. "I saw him at lunchtime, Lindy. He mentioned that you'd been up at the house this morning."

The damage was obviously done; all he could do was limit it. "And did he tell you that Tanaka wanted the subject kept confidential?"

She looked startled. "Of course, but I assumed you'd tell *us*. Nobody will pass it on."

"I hope not, because Tanaka's in a delicate situation. He'd like to help resolve the dispute, but he doesn't want it to look like he's involving the court in politics. A careless word from any of us and he might withdraw the offer and deny ever making it. Please keep that in mind."

Everyone murmured their agreement. "Unfortunately Marshall wasn't very receptive," he continued. "He says that if the justices want him, they should use their influence to get him some help from the government. Then he'll modify the project so the burial ground won't be disturbed. I hope he'll change his mind, because without some concessions on his part there's probably no chance of a compromise. All I've gotten from the city and state are polite interest and promises that any requests we make will be considered carefully." He took out his appointment book. "Let me run through who I've met with and what we discussed."

His account took the better part of an hour. Ned Beecham and Bob Lum walked in as he was finishing up, helped themselves to coffee and joined the meeting.

Looking somber, Bob explained that the heavy rains of the past few days had left the site so soggy that it was no longer safe to work there, even during periods when the rain let up temporarily. With clear weather predicted for Tuesday and beyond, they had two choices. Either they could wait a few days until the sun dried things out, or they could work on the only uncleared area with good enough drainage to support the heavy equipment they used—the burial ground and *heiau*. The decision was Paul's.

"You mean the decision is Marshall's, and he's already made it." Paul rubbed the back of his neck, working at the tight muscles there. "I spoke to him this morning, Bob. He knows the rains have slowed you down and he's not happy about it. He wants that land cleared, and fast. You'll have to move to the disputed area. You'd better lock the fence even during the daytime from now on."

Bob looked even grimmer. "And if the protesters hop over it, lie down in front of my machinery and refuse to move? Are you going to get me some extra security?"

"There's no point antagonizing people with paid muscle unless we're sure we'll really need it." The protesters might take it as a taunt, or, even worse, a dare. "I'll come out tomorrow and talk to them. Maybe I can convince them to be patient."

He noticed the reproach in Lei's eyes and paused. She'd been extremely quiet, maybe because she was embarrassed about Saturday night. "I can see you're only inches from arguing with me," he said, "but remember, that land will have to be cleared no matter what's eventually done with it. Turning it into a state park would probably take the most work of all—removing the tree stumps, collecting the stones from the *heiau* and rebuilding it, and restoring the entire area to the way it looked a thousand years ago. There's no logical reason for your friends to object to us moving ahead."

"Except that we can't develop the land until we clear it," she said. "They're not stupid. They know that. They'd have to be fools not to try to delay us."

She sounded as if she wanted them to succeed, a position that didn't surprise him. He'd known from the beginning how she felt. "In that case, the less notice we give them, the better. It will take them a while to agree on a strategy." He looked at Bob. "What time have they been showing up?"

"Not too early. Around ten or so."

"I want you to get a solid start out there before they have a chance to stop you. Move your equipment after they leave tonight and start work early tomorrow morning. Use men you can trust and tell them to watch what they say. That goes for all of you. I'll come out there and try to talk to them, but if they won't listen . . . if they try to interfere—''

"You'll hire a squad of storm troopers to throw them onto the highway?" Lei snapped, and then reddened so markedly it was obvious she regretted the outburst.

Paul resisted the urge to smile. "I was going to say I'd request police assistance to help Bob keep order until I could get some security guards to the site." He checked his watch. It was almost five. "Any questions or comments?"

After several seconds of silence, Grace murmured, "I think you all should know . . . I've spent a lot of time with Marshall over the past few days and he's adamant about moving ahead. I've tried to change his mind, but he insists the government will have to give him some help first. Lindy has no choice about what to do."

Paul knew Grace was fond of Marshall, but obviously their relationship had progressed. She'd been widowed last year, so maybe it wasn't surprising. "You've spent a lot of time alone with him lately? That's loyalty above and beyond the call of duty."

She smiled, but didn't reply. "Any other comments?" He waited a moment, but nobody spoke up. "Then that'll do it. Lei, I know you stayed late today to come to this meeting, but I'm going to need another few minutes of your time. Would you come into my office, please?"

Lei nodded and got up. Though Paul had been perfectly civil, he had every reason to be annoyed. She'd said things she had no business saying, slipping into the intimacy of the very relationship she claimed she didn't want. She wondered as she followed him into his office if he'd still be as civil once he got her alone.

He closed the door and leaned casually against the desk. If he was angry, it didn't show. "Sit down if you want to."

She hesitated, then shook her head. "I've been sitting all day. I'd rather stand. About what I said before . . . I'm sorry. I was just—surprised. I thought you'd stall as long as you could before you told Bob to clear that land."

"Only surprised?" He folded his arms across his chest. "I would have said 'disappointed and angry.'"

"All right. I was both those things. But I shouldn't have been so...so..."

"Impertinent? Caustic? Honest?" He grinned at her. "I've been called a lot of things in my time, but nobody's ever accused me of being a fascist before."

"You know I didn't mean it that way, and you don't have to make fun of me. I feel really bad about what I said."

"I wasn't making fun of you. I was just teasing you a little." He paused, then drawled, "You should loosen up, Lei. Stop worrying so much about tact and propriety."

Lei was too upset about Paul's decision to loosen up. "My mother raised me to be polite. Nobody's ever considered it a shortcoming before. If you're not going to yell at me, then accept my apology and let me leave."

"I won't accept it because it wasn't necessary," he said. "You should know by now that you can say whatever you want to. All of you can. After ten years in this business, I have a tough enough hide to survive a little abuse."

"Then why did you ask me to come into your..." She saw the warm look in his eyes and cut herself off. "Oh. So we're back to that again."

"Wrong again, Miss Howe. I asked you to come in here because I wanted to make sure you understood that I only told Bob to clear the disputed area because Marshall will ship me back to San Francisco if I don't. I won't be any use to you there. This way, we can placate him without committing ourselves to anything."

That was true, but only in the short term. "And what happens when the grading is done? Once we start work on the infrastructure—"

"Why worry about that before we have to?"

"And that's what you plan to say tomorrow morning? That you'll keep trying, and that everyone should be patient and trust you?" She shook her head. "I'm sorry, Paul, but as much as they like you, they won't accept that."

"If they won't, they won't, but that's all I *can* say. Look, Lei—it's stupid to stand here arguing about it. Why don't we talk about it over dinner? Maybe we can come up with a strategy I haven't thought of yet."

Lei sighed. All the talk in the world wouldn't change the fact that Marshall had told him to clear the land. As for dinner, she wasn't naive enough to think he'd suggested it because he wanted her advice. "Maybe we can pull rabbits out of hats, too. I realize there's nothing you can do. I'm just worried and frustrated, that's all."

He took a few steps forward. "Then let's have dinner and talk about something else. How bad the weather is or who'll win the Super Bowl or how much fun we had Saturday night."

She automatically backed up. He was too magnetic and handsome—a temptation she didn't need. "I told you then—I don't want to go out with you."

"It's not a date. It's just—dinner. We'll eat and talk." He smiled. "I won't lay a finger on you unless you ask me at least twice."

A few hours in his company and she'd probably do exactly that. Her track record was lousy. "Thanks, but I'll pass. And I'll be a little late tomorrow—the kids have their annual physicals. If that's all you wanted..." She turned to go.

He took her by the arm to stop her. His touch made her skin prickle. "You're not taking the bus home—not in this weather and not when it's so late. I'll drive you."

She glanced out the window. It was pouring again, the wind whipping the rain so furiously that an umbrella would be all but useless. She'd get soaked between here and the bus stop, and again between the bus stop and her house. Wanting to say yes, she politely refused.

"I won't take no for an answer." He released her, but she knew he would stop her again if she tried to walk away. "I'm the one who kept you here. The least I can do is drive you home. I'll stick to business—I promise. Besides, you've got a couple of kids waiting for you to show up.''

He was right, and it would take twice as long to reach them by bus as by car. She allowed herself to do what she'd wanted to all along. ''All right, if you're sure it's not too much trouble.''

He told her it was no trouble at all. They talked about the state legislature on the way to Manoa, both of them acting as impersonally as they possibly could. Even so, sexual tension suffused the air. She lay in bed that night, unable to sleep, remembering how he'd kissed and touched her, and she was hot with frustration one moment and cold with anxiety the next.

According to the doctor, the twins were in perfect health. Lei was relieved they were doing so well. She worried about spending too little time with them and tended to blame herself if they got sick or misbehaved.

She was running later than she'd anticipated, so she took her car to work rather than wait for the bus. Paul's Cutlass was in its usual spot in the garage; obviously he hadn't spent much time in Waikane. She hoped it was a sign that things had gone well.

She arrived at the office to find Amy watering the plants, her back to the door. Helping herself to coffee, Lei began chattering about the twins, repeating what the doctor had said. Then Amy turned around, and Lei was so startled that she stopped in midsentence. Amy looked tense and angry. That wasn't like her at all.

''My God, what's wrong?'' she asked.

Amy pointed at Paul's closed door. ''Him!''

''Paul?'' The two usually got on famously. ''What did he do?''

''Obviously you haven't had the news on this morning.''

Lei shook her head. ''No. Why?''

Before Amy could answer, Paul's door opened and Eileen Fujimoto, the clerk-typist, emerged ashen faced. She hurried back to her desk without a word or even a glance.

Paul walked out a second later. "You're here," he said to Lei. "Good. I want to talk to you."

"Sure." Puzzled, she set down her cup and crossed the room. He was never this brusque.

"Better take a bullet-proof vest with you," Amy muttered, glaring at him.

Paul ignored the comment and strode into his office. Lei followed silently, closing the door before she sat down.

He slid into the chair behind his desk. "There was a mud slide last night at Waikane. A large chunk of the hillside above the *heiau* broke loose and damaged Bob's equipment. It'll take days to get things working again. We're lucky it won't be weeks."

She understood why he was upset now, but not why everyone was mad at him. He wasn't the type to vent his frustration on the staff. "It's a rotten piece of luck, but you can't control the weather. It isn't unusual to have mud slides after rain this heavy."

"Bad luck had nothing to do with it," he answered. "Somebody knew we were going to clear that land. They knew we'd moved our machinery. That slide was induced in order to cause damage and delay us. A little farther and the mud would have buried damn near everything."

"'Induced'? What makes you say *that*?" It was a crazy thing to think, but maybe he had proof.

"The police are out there now, looking for footprints or other evidence of tampering, but I don't need physical evidence to know it wasn't an accident. It's the most stable area of the site—the last place there should have been a mud slide."

"Except that there had to have been slides in the past there or the *heiau* never would have been destroyed and buried the way it was."

"The distant past, maybe. Not for hundreds of years." He took a deep breath, visibly restraining his temper. "First a rope mysteriously snaps and now this.... Don't tell me both were accidents. Somebody wants to cause problems. The only way anyone could have known that we'd moved our machinery was from someone in this office. I want to know who said what to whom before someone else gets hurt out there."

Lei was totally lost. "But you told us to be careful about what we said. I don't see how there could have been a leak—"

"I agree—there was no leak. Someone deliberately passed on confidential information."

She had the picture now, and it was damn offensive. He was accusing people she'd known for years. If he hadn't been concerned first and foremost with safety, she might have walked right out of his office.

Instead she told him in an even voice that he was jumping to wild conclusions. "Even if you're right that the slide was deliberately induced, one of Bob's men could have let something slip. Or somebody could have driven by last night and noticed that the equipment had been moved."

"Bob's four sons helped him—no one else. They wouldn't have made a slip. It was almost dark by the time they started work, and they parked the equipment far enough back from the road that nobody could have seen it. It was pitch-black last night. It rained almost continuously."

"Then it was accidental or fated, because nobody—"

"'Fated'?" he interrupted incredulously. "You can't be serious."

"I'm perfectly serious. Some things—"

"Are not meant to be?" He rolled his eyes. "Give me a break, Lei. There's nothing mystical out there. It's the power of suggestion—nothing but self-hypnosis."

Damned haole cynic, she thought. "The land is sacred," she said aloud. "Every square inch of it. We have no business disturbing it. When you try to do something you shouldn't, things have a way of happening."

"You want to believe in that stuff, fine, but don't ask me to." He shook his head. "'Fated'. Unbelievable."

For a moment she simply stared at him, thinking him a perfect fool—a know-it-all mainlander who knew exactly nothing. Then she said coldly, "There are more things in heaven and earth, Mr. Lindstrom, than are dreamt of in your philosophy."

His eyes lit up with amusement. "The ghost of some ancient *kahuna*, you mean, wandering around like Hamlet's dead father, protecting the land from infidels like me."

"It's possible." Her voice was clipped.

"Ah! You're angry with me for being a skeptic."

"You don't know half as much as you think you do. Even worse, you refuse to learn."

He smiled crookedly. "I can't believe this! You're madder at me for not believing in some ludicrous superstition than you are about my questioning the staff."

"There's nothing ludicrous about it, and we haven't even gotten to what you said to the staff."

"True enough." He lazed back in his chair. "You won't like it very much. Maybe I'm the one who needs the bullet-proof vest."

She smiled sweetly. "Maybe so. We Hawaiians were a ferocious people once. Don't forget, the same natives who welcomed Cook as a god killed him during a dispute only a month later."

"I know. I've read about it." A gleam she was all too familiar with entered his eyes. "Your ancestors were strong and proud, fiery and independent.... You have fascinating genes, Lei." He didn't have to add that he would have liked to become intimately acquainted with them.

"So what did you say to the staff?" she asked, firmly changing the subject.

"Since there's no bullet-proof vest around…" He picked up a letter opener and tested the blade. "A little dull, but it'll do. Just to be on the safe side, you understand."

"Completely. What did you say to them, Paul?"

He sobered. "Problems or not, the land at Waikane is immensely valuable. If Marshall decided to give up and get out, substantial profits could still be made. In my opinion, someone is trying to panic him into doing exactly that."

John Davis, for example, he said. He and Marshall had quarreled bitterly in the past. Davis was interested in the development business and might have decided to go after Waikane. Given how much Amy loved him, there was no telling what she would have done to help him.

Then there was Matsuo Fujimoto, who'd solved his business problems and might want to revive his golf course project. Eileen Fujimoto was his first cousin. Her loyalty to her family might be greater than her loyalty to her boss.

Finally, a rival developer might have bribed someone on the staff to provide him with information that would induce Marshall to sell. Cliff Whitney was an obvious suspect. He was always short of money. Everyone in town knew it.

Lei was almost speechless by the time Paul finished. "Of all the ridiculous, paranoid theories…! Did you actually sit there and accuse Amy, Eileen and Cliff of being involved in this?"

"Not exactly. I told them what had happened and asked a few questions. They understood what I was getting at."

"I'll just bet they did." Given the insult, she was surprised no one had hit him. "I know every one of the people you mentioned, including Mr. Fujimoto, and they're as honorable as anyone you could name. None of them has any tolerance for swindles or betrayals—not for money, family loyalty or even love. You owe them all apologies."

"If so, they'll get them," he responded calmly.

She suddenly realized there was another motive for sabotage—an even stronger one than greed. "And what about me? My friends have more reason than anyone to want the project stopped. Aren't you going to question me? Accuse me of helping them out?''

He stared at her for several seconds. She stared back, not blinking or moving, sure he was judging her, and resenting it bitterly. "No. You wouldn't have said anything except inadvertently, and even then, you would have told me about it by now. You're too ethical and gentle to get mixed up in anything this repugnant."

"That's right. I am." A little of the anger drained out of her. At least he had *some* sense in that thick head of his. "So is everyone else. We wouldn't double-cross Marshall. We happen to care about him."

"Maybe. We'll see what the police have to say."

"And if they don't find anything suspicious?"

"Given how hard it rained, I'd be surprised if they did. The evidence was probably destroyed." He tossed the letter opener back on his desk. "Hawaiians haven't always been peaceful about expressing their opposition to development. I was reading about Nukolii over the weekend."

Nukolii was on the coast of Kauai. It had once been quiet and unspoiled, an area where the locals camped and fished, so there had been strong opposition to development. A resort had eventually been built there, but only after a spate of robberies, arson and vandalism directed at the developers and their backers.

"Nukolii was unusual," Lei said. "Protests in Hawaii are usually peaceful. Nobody in this office—no one in Hawaii Ohana or any other group I've dealt with—would be a party to anything illegal."

He smiled so gently that she knew he thought she was hopelessly naive. "You're too trusting, Lei. Too sweet. Things aren't always the way they seem."

"And you're too skeptical and closed minded." His choice of words was ironically appropriate. "You said it yourself, *haole*. Things aren't always the way they seem."

"So we're back to ghosts and fate again, hmm, Lei *nani*?" The phrase meant beautiful Lei, and it had exactly the effect he'd intended. She remembered Saturday night and blushed. "You and I have some differences to resolve. I'm booked up for the rest of the day, but we could discuss them over dinner. Let's go someplace small and quiet, with soft music, candlelight and waiters who forget you even exist."

"Don't you ever give up?" she asked in exasperation.

"Of course not. How do you think I got where I am?"

"You told me I was going to fall at your feet. That all you had to do was wait."

"But I'm half in love with you," he said softly. "I can't help being impatient. Will you have dinner with me if I make my peace with the staff?"

His voice was so seductive that she felt as if he'd caressed her. She had to remind herself that love meant something different to him than to her. "Make your peace with the staff and I'll let you know."

Laughing, he told her she drove a hard bargain. She started to leave, then changed her mind and turned around. "Actually, I wouldn't even then, but you should make your peace with them, anyway."

"I'll think about it." He paused. "Mostly, though, I'll think about *you*. You keep me awake nights. The outcome may be inevitable, but the waiting is pure hell."

Lei walked briskly out of his office. The waiting—the fear that it was all inevitable—was only nerve-racking. It was the wanting that was pure hell.

Chapter Nine

Bob's equipment was repaired and back at Waikane by Wednesday afternoon. Most of the ground was still spongy from the recent rains, so Paul had no choice but to proceed with Monday's plans. Since the mud slide—and the position of the equipment—had been reported widely, the opposition knew what was coming. They turned out in record numbers . . . and so did the local media.

Paul was speaking quietly with a police lieutenant named Joe Santos as the protesters chanted slogans and marched back and forth. Santos, who seemed intelligent and thorough, had supervised the investigation of the mud slide. Nothing out of the ordinary had been found.

A reporter walked up and asked Paul for a statement. He responded the way he had all day, with platitudes about Marshall's legal right to build here, the demonstrators' legal right to protest and his hope that a compromise would eventually be reached. The reporter tried to trap him into saying something more controversial, but he didn't oblige.

As the reporter walked away disgruntled, Santos remarked, "I don't like the mood here today. It's got a nasty edge to it. That's something new."

Paul nodded. He'd spent the past few days on the phone, trying to calm people down and avert trouble, but it hadn't worked. They didn't distrust him or doubt his good intentions. They'd simply lost faith in his ability to make a difference.

"They have a point they want to make," he said. "If they don't make it strongly, the media won't take them seriously."

"Maybe so, but that's real emotion out there, Mr. Lindstrom. Real passion. They're damn angry. It's not just for the benefit of the TV cameras."

"They've been planning this demonstration since Monday. That's a long time to sit and wait." He glanced at Santos's car, which was parked a few yards away. "You think you'll need to radio for help?"

"Maybe. Like I said, I don't like the way things feel."

A reporter finished interviewing Bernice Kapakala and pointed to a group of demonstrators, telling her cameraman to tape them.

"I'm going to have a word with Mrs. Kapakala. She usually has a good handle on what people are going to do."

As Santos strode away, a teenager noticed the camera on him and shouted insults at Bob's men, oblivious to the fact that they couldn't hear him over the din of their tractors. A young man gestured angrily, then walked to the fence and shook it violently with both hands. A group of women with placards written in both Hawaiian and English chanted a prayer. It would make good television.

Santos returned with Bernice a minute later. Paul had spoken to her twice this week, on Monday after the mud slide and on Tuesday after Hawaii Ohana had gone into court for an injunction to stop the work here. "People are upset," she said. "Very upset. You've got to leave this land alone."

"If I could, I would. You know that, Bernice. I'm sorry it had to come to this."

"So am I." She stared at the protesters for a moment, then sighed. "Today was peaceful. Tomorrow might not be."

"Assuming there is a tomorrow. Maybe Judge Blake will rule in your favor." Blake had promised a decision by Thursday at the latest.

She smiled. "And you wouldn't mind if he did. You're a good guy, Lindy."

"Thanks, but there's only so far we can go. Ross had to make the best case he could."

"A darn good one, from what I hear." She hesitated, then admitted, "The law is on your side. I expect to lose, but some of these people are less realistic. The kids, especially. They're idealistic and hot tempered. They might be tempted to take matters into their own hands if Blake's ruling goes against us, and if they do, that fence might not stop them. It scares me."

Since the police had neither the obligation nor the man-power to station officers here full-time, that left only one alternative. "I was hoping I wouldn't have to use private guards here. Some people see a uniform and take it as a challenge."

"Some," she agreed. "To others, it's a deterrent. Believe me, if I could promise to keep everyone under control, I would. I can't."

Paul knew that. Her own group was peaceful, but others might be less so. "Then I'll have to. I don't want anyone to get hurt." He turned to Santos. "Lieutenant, what's the best private security firm on the island?"

Santos recommended two of them, adding that he'd have a squad car cruise by the site as often as possible. If police help was needed, he promised, it would arrive quickly. Still looking worried, Bernice shook Paul's hand and rejoined the demonstrators.

One by one, the television and newspaper crews departed. The protesters left soon afterward, but Paul knew they'd be back. As Santos had said, this wasn't just for the cameras.

He got stuck in traffic on the way downtown and didn't arrive till four. Amy gave him a cool look as he walked in, still angry with him even though he'd taken Lei's advice and apologized.

"Ross just phoned, she said. "Blake's ruling came in. He's on his way to the courthouse. Your other messages are in your office."

"Thanks." Amy wasn't the only one who was mad at him—the whole damn staff was. He walked to her desk and leaned casually against it. "It's pretty hard to work in a place where everyone would like to string you up by your thumbs. What do I have to do to be forgiven?"

"Not much," she answered. "Just trust us. Until you do, your apologies won't mean a thing."

The odd thing was that he did. "You want the truth? My instincts tell me two things—that it wasn't an accident and that none of you had anything to do with it. It doesn't make sense, but that's how I feel. In the meantime, I'm responsible for keeping the project on schedule and ensuring everyone's safety. I need answers, but I'm not getting them. Try to be patient with me until I do. Please, Amy."

"You would try the patience of a saint," she grumbled.

He could see, however, that she was a lot less angry. He grinned at her, then went into Cliff's office and asked about the security firms Santos had mentioned. Cliff replied that Marshall had used both in the past and considered them equally good. Paul called the one that came first in the alphabet, Aloha Security, and hired four guards to patrol the site starting the following morning.

He was about to hang up, when he realized there was a possibility he hadn't investigated yet—that somebody had gotten information by bugging the place. He asked if Aloha conducted electronic sweeps, was told that they did, and arranged for someone to come out the next morning.

He was still returning phone calls when Ross stepped into the office. Judge Blake, Ross said, had ruled in their favor. They could move ahead. It was the first time in Paul's life that he'd won when he'd wanted to lose.

Aloha's surveillance expert arrived at eight o'clock sharp with a caseful of sophisticated equipment. An hour later, Ned Beecham called from Waikane to report that the security men seemed experienced and proficient and that the site was tense but under control. Paul told him to keep in touch, then left for some meetings at the capitol. By the time he returned, the surveillance expert was gone and there was a sealed envelope on his desk. The letter inside stated that no recording or listening devices had been found.

Again, it wasn't the outcome Paul would have preferred. A bug traceable to some obscure enemy would have explained everything. He would have been able to stop watching and worrying.

Ned called again at noon with a report just like the first one, but there was something in his tone that Paul didn't like. Anxiety, maybe, or fear. Deeply concerned, he canceled his next few meetings, grabbed some lunch and drove out to Waikane to evaluate the situation for himself.

He arrived to find the four guards on the *mauka* side of the fence, spread out at even intervals in front of the demonstrators. There were almost twice as many protesters as on Wednesday, some carrying signs mentioning groups that hadn't come here before.

As he got out of his car, a couple of burly kids wearing T-shirts reading Students to Save Waikane pointed at him and began to shout, yelling that he should go back to the mainland and stick to bribing judges in California. Paul didn't lack for physical courage; he couldn't have survived his childhood if he had. He went over to talk to them, hoping to convince them that he sympathized with their position and was trying to help.

Unfortunately they were in no mood to listen. He was a *haole*, a member of .the same despised establishment as Judge Blake and Marshall Canning. Within minutes he was surrounded by an angry, threatening mob. This was the ugliness Nick Nakamura had predicted, the hostility Lieutenant Santos had spoken of. He was wondering which kid would throw the first punch when Mr. Leinau, the old *kahuna* from Hawaii Ohana, came over and calmed everyone down.

Sweating from the tension and heat, he walked over to a guard and identified himself. "I want to have a word with Bob Lum. Are the four of you going to be able to handle this situation, or will you need additional help?"

"Only about a dozen of them want to cause trouble." The guard unlocked a gate and pulled it open so Paul could pass through. "As long as they're on the other side of the fence, we'll be able to keep things under control."

"If you change your mind, let me know," Paul said.

The guard nodded and relocked the gate. Paul walked over to Bob and Ned, who were standing together near the work site. "How are things going? Are you on schedule?"

"Ahead of schedule," Bob said. "We should be finished by tomorrow afternoon assuming nobody smashes up my equipment in the meantime."

"I'll arrange around-the-clock security." Paul noticed a TV van pull up. "Here we go again. It's show time." Two more television crews arrived within the next few minutes to tape footage of what had become a nightly story, and the protest grew louder and more rancorous.

Then, so unexpectedly that the three of them flinched, there was a brief, violent explosion. One of the students had shot the lock off a gate a hundred yards up the coast and dashed through. Half a dozen of his friends followed. He ran toward the tractors, waving his gun high in the air. Paul told Bob to call the police—there was a cellular phone at the site—and took off toward the students. The four guards did the same.

They couldn't catch the kid with the gun; he fired wildly and darted around them, then hurled the gun away. A guard chased after him, while everyone else moved to head off his friends. Paul tackled one of them to the ground and tried to pin him. They rolled around in the dirt, fighting furiously. The kid had the build and strength of a gorilla, but Paul somehow managed to keep him away from the workers and tractors. The tussle ended only when some men from Hawaii Ohana ran up, pulled them apart and led the kid away.

Panting, Paul stood up and spit the dirt out of his mouth. He wiped his face with the sleeve of his jacket, barely looking at the mixture of sweat, dirt and blood that came off. The kid had kicked and punched at every spot he could reach, which was most everywhere on Paul's body.

The site was eerily quiet now. Then, as the wail of a siren pierced the silence, Paul noticed a cluster of men gathered in front of one of the tractors, staring somberly at the ground. He broke into an anxious trot, then winced and slowed down.

There was a crumpled body in front of the tractor—the kid who'd shot at the fence. His eyes were glazed with pain and his leg was bent at a hideous angle. Bob was standing with his arm around the driver, who looked badly shaken.

"He threw himself in front of Kenny's tractor," Bob said. "Kenny never even saw him coming. He was busy with the stump... These engines are so loud ... And the kid was so damn quick—nobody could grab him in time. *Goddammit, these people are crazy!*"

Passionately committed, Paul thought, or young and rash, but not crazy. If the kid had been crazy, he probably would have killed someone.

The siren died and a car door slammed. Two policemen ran toward them. A second squad car arrived a minute later, and then an ambulance. The kid was moaning and cursing by then, his color good and his breathing strong.

Marshall probably would have pressed trespassing and assault charges, but Paul decided not to—not unless they made trouble again. The site was extremely tense, but at least it was peaceful. He didn't want to arouse resentments that would make a bad situation even worse.

He trudged to his car, ignoring the photographers who snapped his picture and the reporters who shouted questions. He locked the door because they would have opened it and kept bothering him otherwise, then looked in the mirror. His face was abraded and filthy; his suit was a lost cause. He was emotionally spent and he ached all over.

He got back to Emerald Plaza at a quarter of four. He would have liked to go straight to the apartment to clean up, but he was fifteen minutes late for a meeting with Mack Mackenzie about the shopping center project. It wasn't his responsibility, of course, but Mack needed some help and Paul was the best one to provide it.

He knew something was wrong the moment he opened the door. The whole staff was gathered in the reception room, the women on the love seats and the men on chairs from the conference room. Grace's eyes were puffy and red; Lei was sitting next to her, comforting her. Paul had a feeling her tears were for Marshall.

Everyone looked up when he entered the room. Cliff gave a low whistle. "Jesus. What happened to *you*?"

"To me? Oh. Right." He'd forgotten how he looked. "We had some trouble out at Waikane. What's wrong? Marshall...?"

"Had another heart attack. Grace was up at the house when it happened. He's in intensive care." Cliff paused. "What kind of trouble?"

Paul gave them a quick run-down, adding that he planned to double the security force at the site. "About Marshall... How bad a heart attack? Has anyone called Everett yet?"

"I did," Grace said hoarsely. "I thought—I wanted to tell him whatever I could, but it wasn't much. It looks bad, though. Those damn cigars..." She began to cry softly. "He—he has the flu. Everett, I mean. He's at home. He said—he said he would keep in touch. The doctor..." Sobbing, she turned into Lei's embrace.

"The doctor told Grace he would call around five—that they were going to do a heart catheterization and would know more by then," Lei said. She stroked Grace's back. "He'll be okay, Gracie. He's too stubborn not to recover."

In fact, Lei was cold with apprehension, afraid that Marshall would die, or, even worse, that he would turn into a mere shell of a man. *"Forget Marshall Canning,"* Liliha had said. *"He won't matter."* And now he didn't.

And Paul... When she thought about the boy with the gun and how he could have shot Paul instead of throwing it in the dirt, she felt so queasy she could hardly breathe. "You look awful," she said. "Those scrapes—you need to clean out the dirt. Get some antiseptic on them. There's some hydrogen peroxide in the medicine chest upstairs."

"They won't get infected." He smiled weakly. "It's sacred soil, remember? No germs." He looked at Mack. "Can you wait here while I shower and change?"

"Sure, but we can talk some other time. You should see a doctor, or at least lie down—"

"I'm okay. I'll be back in twenty minutes." He left, walking a lot more slowly than he usually did.

The phone rang, but everyone ignored it. Amy had switched on the answering machine after Grace arrived with the news about Marshall, leaving the volume just high enough to hear callers' voices. It was another reporter—the fourth in the past half hour—so they didn't pick it up. Now they knew the reason for all those calls.

The conversation continued, jumping from Marshall to the trouble at Waikane to Paul's insistence that the two incidents there hadn't been accidents. Everyone had pretty much forgiven him, in part because they liked him and in part because they respected the job he was doing. Still, they thought he was either paranoid or *pupule*. Too much pressure, they all said. It had affected his common sense.

The abrasions on his face looked less grisly when he returned, but there were also bruises Lei hadn't noticed before. He poured a cup of coffee and pulled over a chair, then asked Mack about the problems at the shopping center.

The most important concerned the wiring. Paul offered to take a look at it and talk to the subcontractor. Leasing and promotion weren't going as well as expected, either. With Marshall ill and Ned assigned to Waikane, both areas were currently in limbo. The vacuum could prove costly if it weren't filled soon.

"I could try to help out," Lei said. "I've always been interested in that part of the business, but I never had a chance..." She grimaced. Marshall had never *given* her the chance, but she didn't want to say so when he was fighting for his life in a hospital. "Anyway, I was thinking that Amy is good with the media, so maybe she could take over press relations while I work on leasing and promotion."

Paul turned to Amy. "Is that okay with you?"

"Yes. I'd like that." She paused. "Thanks, Lindy. I appreciate the opportunity."

"You might not thank me a few days from now. It's going to be a tough job."

He looked exhausted, Lei realized, emotionally worn down.

"The reporters were all over me when I left Waikane," he went on, "so you'll probably get requests for a statement. For now, just—"

"We've already gotten calls. The messages are on the machine. I turned it on because no one felt like... It probably wasn't very professional of us, but..."

"I don't blame you. If anyone else phones, tell them we regret that a protester was injured and that I'll have a more detailed statement in the morning. I want to talk to Ross before I say anything more. Lei—if you're going to help with the shopping center, you should probably come out there with me tomorrow morning. Can you get here by eight?''

''Yes.'' She preferred to see the children off herself, but Mrs. Keala was always happy to help out in emergencies.

''Good.''

He finished his coffee and got up—very gingerly, she noticed. She wanted to help him, to pull his arm around her shoulders and support him as he walked, but of course she didn't.

''I'll be down in Ross's office,'' he continued. ''I'll be back in time to hear what the doctor says about Marshall.''

Amy switched off the answering machine, and everyone returned to work, even Grace. She had some tapes to transcribe for Paul and hoped it would take her mind off Marshall. Lei pulled out the files on the shopping center and began to review them. The phone rang often—more reporters, probably—but Amy handled the calls.

The doctor phoned exactly at five. Grace took the call on the speaker phone in Marshall's office so everyone could listen in. When he told her that things didn't look good, her eyes filled with tears and she asked Paul to do the talking.

The second attack had been far more serious than the first. There was enough blockage to make bypass surgery an option, but Marshall had refused to consider it. He was convinced he would die on the operating table. He was still in the ICU, conscious but disoriented and in pain. All they could do was wait.

Chapter Ten

Amy was finishing up a phone call when Lei arrived at work the next morning. "That was Grace," she said. "She's at the hospital. Marshall isn't any better, but he isn't any worse, either." She pointed to the newspapers on her desk. "Have you seen those yet?"

Lei nodded. The trouble at Waikane had been front-page news, with pictures of both the injured protester and Paul featured prominently. She shuddered each time she thought about how badly he'd been hurt.

"Reporters kept calling Lindy all evening," Amy went on. "He finally agreed to hold a news conference at noon today at Waikane. He plans to drive out there after he finishes at the shopping center."

Paul emerged from his office a moment later. Lei smiled at him, trying to hide her distress. "Good morning. You seem a little less stiff this morning. Did you wear that aloha shirt because it matches your bruises so well?"

"Sure. Anything for the TV cameras." He rubbed his right temple. "I have a headache that won't quit. Would you mind driving?"

"Of course not." She reached for the attaché case he was carrying. "Let me take that for you."

He surrendered it without a peep. It was heavy, but not so heavy that carrying it would have been a burden unless he was in considerable discomfort. She could hardly keep from touching him as they walked to the elevator—gently stroking his cheek or giving his arm a reassuring pat.

Since she had no right to do either, she tried to coax a smile out of him. "Next time you decide to fight, maybe you shouldn't choose a UH football player."

"The kid was a football player?" He looked startled.

"A lineman. Didn't you read the papers this morning?"

"I didn't have time. Between studying the blueprints for the shopping center and drafting a news release..." They stepped into the elevator. "A lineman. Hell, no wonder I'm covered with bruises."

Without stopping to think she lifted up his aloha shirt and looked at his stomach. There were several large, ugly bruises on it. Her eyes softened with compassion. "Oh, Paul! You should be in bed, not chasing around—"

"In bed, huh?" He smiled tiredly. "Nice thought. Are you going to keep staring at those or do something constructive like kiss them and make them better?"

She dropped the shirt and took a step backward, embarrassed by how badly she wanted to. "Being thrashed senseless obviously hasn't affected your libido."

"Not when I'm alone with you, it hasn't. I'd have to be dead first." He fingered the sleeve of her muumuu. As usual, her pulse rate soared and her face grew flushed. "You were wearing this the first day we met. I thought you were so damn beautiful—so sweet and gentle, like someone from another time and place...."

As he reached for her, the elevator stopped and the doors slid open. She moved to the opposite side of the car. Several people got in.

She told herself she would have turned her head if he'd tried to kiss her, but if he'd pressed her against the wall, if he'd lifted her chin and taken her mouth... She shivered. She would have let him. Even though it would have been insane. Even though they had no future together. Even with Liliha's prophecy hanging over her head.

They rode downstairs and got into his car. She knew she had to say something about what had happened. She couldn't let it happen again. "I don't want you to touch me or even say anything personal." Her hands were clenched around the steering wheel. "It makes me—uncomfortable. I can't work under these conditions."

Paul leaned back in his seat and closed his eyes. Lei was kidding herself—it was obvious from the way she looked at him and spoke to him—but he couldn't force her to admit what she insisted on denying. In any event, he felt like hell. His chief goal was just to make it through the next few days.

"I'm sorry," he said. "I just want you to know—it wasn't really about sex, Lei. I didn't get much sleep last night. I had too much on my mind, and the pain..." He grimaced, disgusted with himself for whining. "Anyway, we were alone together, and you were so soft and sympathetic... I haven't been able to do a damn thing in Hawaii, and sometimes I feel..." He shook his head. He was at it again. "Never mind. It would have been nice to hold you. That's all."

Lei hadn't realized he had so many doubts, or such deep feelings. She ached to do what she'd told him not to—put her arms around him and comfort him. In other words, she was a total hypocrite. "You're too hard on yourself. You've done as well as anyone possibly could, but you're disappointed in yourself because you haven't worked miracles. Please, just keep trying."

He smiled at her. "I will. I'm just tired, I guess. Would you mind if I tried to sleep?"

"Of course not." She started the engine and backed out of the parking space. He was asleep within minutes.

The shopping center was in a rapidly growing area of central Oahu about twenty miles from the office. Paul and Mack inspected the wiring while Lei walked around with a construction worker, noting which space was still available and jotting down the names of possible tenants. She finished before they did, so she strolled around the neighborhood for a while to kill some time.

Paul was negotiating with the electrical subcontractor when she got back. He hadn't spotted any defects, but a lot of the wiring was covered up already and would have to be exposed and reinspected in order to locate the source of the problem. The two men haggled for a while about how to divide the costs in numerous different situations, reached an agreement they both could live with, and shook hands.

Later, in the car, Paul remarked that Marshall would still be arguing. "That's why Mack was stymied. The deal we made is fair, but he didn't want to take the heat for conceding more than Marshall would have. The contract provides for a fair amount of bargaining room in this situation."

"But your agreement is within its limits."

"Sure, except that I had no authority to negotiate. Still, somebody had to settle this if you want to open in three months. I'll check it out with Ross this afternoon. Let him dot the i's and cross the t's." He stifled a yawn. "Any chance you could drive me to Waikane?"

"I was planning on it. Go back to sleep, Paul. I'll wake you when we get there."

"Thanks." He settled back in his seat and closed his eyes.

He slept for about an hour, waking a few miles short of the work site. They were running a little early, so they stopped at a roadside stand for a snack. Lei had to restrain herself from helping him in and out of the car.

She'd seen film of Thursday's protest on the news, but it didn't prepare her for what she found at Waikane. There were more protesters than ever, and they were louder and angrier than she'd dreamed possible. Reporters and cameramen were everywhere. Eight security men were strung out along the fence, watching the crowd warily, while behind them, Bob and his men ate lunch. As she pulled off the road, a patrol car arrived and two police officers got out. The place looked like a war zone.

She'd barely come to a stop before reporters spotted the Cutlass and swarmed over. Paul sighed wearily, got out of the car and made his way to the fence. She would have stood beside him if he'd let her, but he ordered her to wait a few yards away. She'd never felt so torn in her life. She hated hostility and violence but agreed passionately with what the protesters stood for.

The two cops and four of the security men stationed themselves near Paul. Reporters formed a semicircle around him and the protesters crowded in behind. The usual questions were followed by the usual answers. Most people listened politely, but the courteous majority was no match for the hostile, disruptive minority.

They hooted him down when he tried to defend Marshall's legal right to proceed. His comments about the desirability of a compromise were greeted by scathing sarcasm. He tried to talk about the meetings he'd attended, but every name he mentioned was drowned out by either cheers or jeers depending on the crowd's opinion of the person in question.

When he expressed regret that a student had been hurt, someone shouted that it was a shame he hadn't been hurt just as badly. Similar sentiments were bellowed regarding Marshall when a reporter asked about his current condition.

Finally, hoarse from shouting over the noise, Paul announced that he would make one final statement and then leave. "Marshall Canning has vested rights to this property and he intends to exercise them. I can't—"

A roar of disapproval rose up, cutting him off. Lei felt the crowd's antagonism and trembled. It wasn't just a minority now—it was all of them. If it hadn't been for the cops and security men, she would have been terrified for his safety.

"He's given me an order to proceed with the work here. I can't disobey it, but—" There was a second, even stronger wave of animosity. "I want to help. I'll keep looking for a solution. That's all I can do."

"The only solution is for you to get the hell off our land," someone screamed. It was one of the few responses that wasn't too obscene to be aired on the nightly news.

Between the cops and the security men, they made it to the car unharmed. Lei didn't argue when Paul said he would drive; she was shaking too badly to get behind the wheel. "That was awful," she said. "The fury... The hatred and suspicion... You're not even responsible for what's happened, but some of them wanted to tear you apart."

He started the car and pulled onto the highway. "I'm the only target they've got. Besides, their bark is worse than their bite."

"You think so? Look at yourself in the mirror, for God's sake!" She knew she was getting hysterical, but couldn't help it. "And all of it over removing a bunch of tree stumps! When rough grading begins... They'll never let it go forward, Paul. Never. And even though I disagree with their tactics, they're right. That land—"

"Is sacred. I know your position, and *you* know that I sympathize with it. But Marshall has a legal right to proceed—he's got a judge's ruling that says so."

"Legal isn't the same as moral. Please, call a halt out there before someone gets hurt."

He shook his head. "It's not my land, Lei. I can't disregard a direct order. As far as safety is concerned..." His expression hardened. "If I need to, I'll station more guards out there. If there's trouble again, I'll press charges and get a restraining order to keep the people responsible away from the site. I have a job to do and I'm not going to let a bunch of foulmouthed punks intimidate me into running away from it."

She took a deep breath, forcing her emotions under control. He was turning a dispute based on principle into a macho showdown. "But they're right."

"That's your opinion. Not Marshall's."

"But Marshall's in the ICU. He can't—"

"That doesn't change the fact that he gave me an order. There's not a damn thing more I can do."

"But if you only understood—"

"Drop it, Lei. I'm not going to change my mind."

She bit her lip and stared out the window. He was tired, in pain and utterly fed up. It had been stupid to press him. "I'm sorry. You've been through enough today without having to listen to my nagging."

"Meaning, I assume, that you'll nag me some other time," he said with a sigh. "I don't suppose I can stop you, but I'm telling you right now—it won't work."

She didn't answer. Her deepest beliefs—her very soul— told her to keep pleading with him, but he sounded so intransigent. She didn't know *what* to do.

They stopped for lunch on the way back to the office, but she was too afraid of antagonizing him to try to talk to him. Amy greeted him with a stack of messages and some grim news: Marshall had taken a turn for the worse, responding to his nurses with moans and incoherent complaints—or not at all.

Paul went into his office to return his messages, while Lei shut herself up with the shopping center files. She'd barely pulled herself together and started working when the phone calls began. Her friends wanted her to speak to Paul about the larger issues involved, to convince him that morality and justice were more important than cold legalities.

She couldn't have lived with herself if she hadn't agreed to try, but she didn't expect to succeed. He was too tired and frustrated to listen. Her best bet, she decided, was to approach him after work so they could speak in private. For the third time that week, she called Mrs. Keala to say she'd be late.

Paul, meanwhile, was down in Ross's office talking about the shopping center project. As he outlined the agreement he'd reached with the electrical subcontractor, it struck him that he was now working for a man who was incapable of rational thought or speech. He described Marshall's condition, then asked Ross if anyone else could sign the agreement he'd negotiated or make binding decisions on the company's behalf.

Ross replied that he himself could—he had power of attorney for Marshall and often signed papers when Marshall was out of town. And years ago, he recalled, Marshall had been so terrified of impending hernia surgery that he'd signed a document directing Everett to make all important decisions if he should die or be mentally disabled. He hadn't trusted anyone else to look after his wife's future. Ross checked his files to see if the document was still in force. It was.

Paul didn't need a lawyer to explain the implications of that. Maybe it was the break he'd needed. He went upstairs to the apartment, gulped down a couple of aspirin and changed into a bathrobe. Then he settled down on the bed and called Everett in California. They'd last spoken on Monday, before Everett had gotten the flu.

He delivered the bad news about Marshall as gently as he could, then brought Everett up to date on Waikane. At best, he said, the protests would cost a bundle in security and delays; at worst, they would stop work completely. Public opinion was turning against the project, the governor was being pressured to take action and there was talk of a referendum. If it passed, the ensuing court fight could take years. Politicians with an eye on the next election could always find ways to rescind zoning decisions or require additional permits they had no intention of granting. Again, a court fight would be costly and time-consuming.

"According to Ross," he continued, "you have the authority to make decisions if Marshall is incapacitated. I feel like a vampire approaching you when he's so sick, but—"

"Don't worry about it. The biggest favor we could do him would be to arrange a compromise behind his back. What do you want me to do?"

"Graham Smith's design is a large part of the problem. It doesn't generate the kind of enthusiasm that loosens up official purse strings. Let me commission a new design for the site. If it's good enough—if the community and the politicians like it enough—maybe I can squeeze out concessions that will satisfy even Marshall. In the meantime, we can move ahead with clearing and grading."

"Sounds reasonable. I'll send you a letter of authorization tomorrow morning." Everett paused. "You going to hire that Hawaiian architect with the big ego?"

He meant David Kapakala. "Yes, assuming I like his work. I definitely want to use someone local. The protesters don't have much use for mainlanders."

"Including you, obviously. I'm sorry you're having such a rough time out there. I'll fly in as soon as I can, but between business and the flu, it may be another week or two."

They talked shop for a while, then hung up. Paul didn't feel like dressing and going downstairs afterward, so he phoned Amy to say he'd pick up his messages later. Then he fixed himself a sandwich and a cup of coffee and carried them into the bedroom to eat in front of the TV.

As usual, Waikane was the top story, with the station running tape from his news conference, followed by reactions from local leaders. He dozed off in the middle of some editorialist's comments about how people on both sides of the issue had a right to be heard.

That was how Lei found him—fast asleep, with a half-eaten meal on the night table and the television set on. He was wearing a knee-length robe that was open at the throat and chest, revealing bruises she hadn't realized existed. Her heart melted. He was probably exhausted and in pain.

She wanted to turn around and leave, but she was desperate to get their conversation over with. Telling herself she wouldn't bother him if he were sleeping soundly, she murmured, "Paul? Are you awake?"

He opened his eyes halfway. "Lei." He smiled drowsily. "Hi, there. What are you doing here?"

If he hadn't been half-asleep, he would have known. She hoped it was a lucky break—that with his guard down, he'd be willing to listen. Right now, not tomorrow night. "I stayed around to talk to you, but you never came back to the office. So I came up here, but you didn't answer the door. I figured you were out, so I let myself in to wait."

"Talk to me, huh?" He pulled himself up and straightened his robe. "Would it be too much to hope that the subject is something other than Waikane?"

She heard the dry humor in his voice and realized there was no help for it. He wasn't going to listen unless she made it worth his while. She would have to stick to her original plan.

Her heart began to race. One by one, the predictions in Liliha's glass had come true. A blue-eyed, blond-haired man had appeared. She'd been almost irresistibly drawn to him. Marshall had become irrelevant to the future of Waikane. The rest of the prophecy would undoubtedly follow. She would become Paul Lindstrom's lover—and suffer for it. It was her destiny. But if she had to offer herself, she might as well get something in return.

She took a deep breath and plunged ahead. "I know you're sick of being nagged, but there are things you don't understand—things you've never tried to feel. If you really listened, though, I think you would. I know this is the wrong time to talk—you've had a terrible day—but I was hoping we could discuss it over dinner tomorrow night."

Paul clicked off the TV with the remote and sipped his coffee. He wasn't completely alert yet, but he had the feeling he'd just been bribed. And if he had, there was no way on earth that he was going to admit it was totally unnecessary.

"Dinner?" he repeated. "You're asking me out?"

She blushed so hotly that he *knew* he'd just been bribed.

"Yes. You keep suggesting it, and I thought..." She looked at the floor. "You said your mind was made up— that you weren't going to change it—but I don't believe that. You wouldn't be where you are if you were really that closed-minded. I'll have dinner with you if promise to listen—really listen—to everything I have to say."

He'd never had a woman go to such lengths to give herself an excuse to do what she'd wanted to do in the first place. "You talk, I listen and we both eat," he said, somehow keeping a straight face. "That's it. That's the total package."

Lei didn't answer right away. He might have been her destiny, but *he* didn't know that. Inevitable or not, there was only so much she could bring herself to offer.

"Yes," she said.

"No dancing? No fondling you in the car?"

She looked up. He was grinning at her. "No to both. I mean it, Paul."

"You're tough, Lei *nani*, but the truth is, I'm probably in no shape for either one. I'll pick you up at seven."

"I thought we could meet—"

"No. I'll pick you up and I'll take you home. That's *my* total package. Take it or leave it."

He wasn't smiling anymore. He looked just as determined as she was. "All right, then. Seven o'clock." She paused. "You promise you'll really listen?"

"To every single word," he said.

By eight the following night, Paul was telling himself he'd missed his true calling. He should have been an actor. For the past thirty minutes, he'd listened attentively while Lei gave a lecture worthy of a professor on the native Hawaiian religion and the passionate, mystical bond between the people and the land. Every now and then, he'd asked a brilliantly incisive question. He'd even managed to look increasingly convinced.

Now she was finally finished, and the greatest challenge of all lay ahead. "I understand the situation much better than I did before," he said solemnly. "Of course, I have to admit that I've given the matter a lot of thought since last night. When I met with Ross yesterday, he mentioned a document that authorizes Everett to make decisions if Marshall is incapacitated. And I was thinking... Maybe I should talk to Everett."

He could see the hope in her eyes shining so brightly that only a skunk wouldn't have been ashamed. He felt a twinge of guilt, but it was a very small twinge. It wasn't his fault they had to go through this elaborate charade before she would allow herself to go out with him. Even her appearance was a form of self-defense; she'd French-braided her hair and put on a long-sleeved, high-necked dress.

"Would you be willing to ask him to leave the sacred lands alone?" she asked. "To turn them into a park?"

He pretended to think it over. "I can't go that far, but maybe..." He frowned, as if pondering the matter further. She was hanging on every word, looking optimistic but nervous. He *was* a skunk. There was no doubt about it.

"Maybe what?" she finally prompted.

"Maybe he would let me commission a new design for the site. I could speak to David Kapakala about it." David hadn't been home when he'd called that morning, so he'd left a message on his machine. "Having actual plans would make it easier to put a reasonable deal together—if the plans are good enough, that is."

"They will be, Paul. I know they will. He's a wonderful architect!" She was flat-out thrilled, looking at him as if he were some sort of savior. "Thank you. I knew you'd understand if only you listened." She brushed away a tear.

"Oh, God. I'm going to bawl. I should probably go to the ladies—"

"No, you shouldn't." He smiled his most reassuring smile. "You can cry right here if you need to. I don't mind. You've barely touched your dinner. Do you want me to have it reheated?"

"Yes. I was too nervous to eat before." She sniffed and smiled. "I didn't think it would be this easy. I expected to have to nag you and argue with you all night. That would have been awful. I hate fighting with people."

He caught the attention of their waiter, asked for some coffee and sent back her meal. Then he said softly, "I don't enjoy fighting, either. I'd rather learn about you. There's a special passion in your voice when you talk about Hawaii. I assume it comes from your background. Tell me about it."

Lei had felt many different emotions that night—nervousness and determination, then hope and joy—but not discomfort. Not the deep sexual anxiety that Paul had evoked in her from the moment they'd met. He'd been too distantly polite for that, too businesslike. Until now.

He was looking at her as if he ached to touch her—ached to and meant to, both physically and emotionally. It was unnerving. Her feelings for him were unnerving. Gratitude, admiration, desire... Talking about herself was hard enough, but the deeper she let him see into her heart, the more it would hurt when he left.

All her defenses slammed into place. "There's nothing much to tell. My mother is pure Hawaiian and my father was an anthropologist who specialized in Polynesian cultures. Naturally I have a special feeling for the islands."

"In other words, you don't like talking about yourself." He looked more amused than offended. "Okay. I'll go first."

Learning about him might be just as dangerous—she might be drawn to him even more strongly—but she was too curious to object. He was sophisticated and well educated, but he'd denied being upper crust. Where had he come from? How had he gotten the way he was?

"If you want to," she said.

"To be honest, usually I don't. You're an exception." He paused while the waiter poured their coffee. "My parents were from a small town in Nevada. My father got my mother pregnant while they were seniors in high school, and they ran off to Las Vegas and got married. They had dreams of making it big there. They were dirt poor—rejected by their parents, too young for good jobs in a casino and un-qualified for anything but minimum-wage work. I was a difficult baby—a month premature, sickly and constantly crying. My father stuck it out till I was two, then left. I don't remember him, but I've seen his picture. I look a lot like him."

Lei couldn't hide her astonishment. Nothing about the man in front of her tallied with that kind of background. "Your father just walked out? He never even came to visit?"

"No, but he didn't live that long. His body was fished out of a lake when I was five. I found out about it when I was in my teens. A kid in school taunted me about my father working for the Mafia and I asked my mother if it was true. She honestly didn't know, but obviously he'd been mixed up in something dangerous."

"So he was—murdered? He didn't just drown?"

"Either murdered or killed in a fight. My mother had a job as a dealer by then. She worked days while I was in school. She was blond and pretty, so she must have done okay, but she wanted things even good tips can't buy. When I was seven or eight, I asked her why she left late at night and stayed out till dawn sometimes, and she told me she had to work. It wasn't exactly a lie, I suppose. Everyone in the neighborhood knew what she was. Some of the other kids used to throw it in my face. I got beaten up a lot trying to defend her, but eventually I got big enough and tough enough to hold my own. I knew they were right, though.

The house, the car, the flashy clothing and stereo equipment . . . She couldn't have afforded those things on what a dealer made.''

He sipped his coffee, looking as cool and emotionless as a robot. Lei was relieved when the waiter brought her meal. She couldn't think of a thing to say. She was too stunned.

"You're shocked," he said.

"Yes. You sound so hard when you talk about her." She suddenly realized why. "It still hurts, doesn't it?"

"She wasn't all bad. When she paid attention to me, we had great times together. She was more like a sister than a mother. We played games, laughed and horsed around, pulled practical jokes . . ."

He hadn't responded to her question, so obviously the answer was yes. "Most of the time I was on my own," he continued, "so it wasn't surprising that I wound up totally undisciplined. The saving grace of my life was the man who lived next door. He was a retired carpenter. There was nothing he couldn't build or fix. He was always doing favors for people, and he used to let me tag along. I hated school, but I loved working with my hands. He taught me as much as I was willing to learn and gave me affection and approval for whatever I managed to accomplish. I might have gotten into drinking and drugs or died on the streets of Los Angeles if it hadn't been for him.''

"Los Angeles?" she repeated. "How did you wind up there?"

"My mother remarried when I was sixteen. Her husband knew about her past and wanted to start off fresh, so we moved to Bakersfield, California. I didn't get along with him, so I ran away a year later. I thought I was all grown up and ready to be on my own.''

The story he told was as incredible as what had preceded it. One of his mother's regular "clients" had been arrested while she was in his hotel room and charged with embezzling his company's funds. Originally a reluctant witness against him, she'd wound up cooperating fully and marrying the detective in charge of the case. He was a huge, tough man with firm ideas about how to handle a defiant teen-ager, but Paul was too used to doing as he pleased not to resist. After a year of verbal and physical warfare, he'd left.

His mother hadn't tried to stop him; she'd always sided with her husband during their fights and was relieved to have him out of the house. Although he admitted he'd been a source of constant tension, Lei sensed it was yet another way in which she'd hurt him.

He seemed reluctant to talk about what had followed, saying only that he'd scratched out a living doing odd jobs for a while, then met Everett Canning's daughter, Melissa, who'd hired him to take care of her house and grounds. Eventually she'd introduced him to her father, whom he'd worked for ever since.

They lingered over their coffee, talking about the hap-pier parts of his childhood. The retired carpenter was in his nineties now and still going strong. Paul visited him once or twice a year. He reminisced about his first few months in Los Angeles, and how people had been amazed that a kid his age could do everything from repair a water-damaged ceiling to build a serviceable bookcase. Lei was fascinated by these tales and enthralled with the man who told them. He'd pulled himself up from nothing. There was a lot to admire in that.

It wasn't until they left the restaurant that she realized that the very thing she'd feared had happened. She was crazy about Paul Lindstrom—crazy about a man who'd been scarred by a traumatic childhood, found it difficult to trust and wanted no part of commitments or obligations. It was no wonder Liliha had seen a lover in her glass, not a husband.

She wasn't very talkative after that—she was too upset. They lapsed into silence during the ride home. Then he drove straight past her house instead of stopping, and her distress turned to anxiety.

He parked in a dim cul-de-sac half a block away.

"Why did you stop here?" she asked.

"I wanted to talk for a few minutes."

He took off his seat belt and pushed up the center arm-rest.

To Lei, those weren't preparations to talk. She stiffened. "Paul . . . You promised—"

"I'm aware of that." Before she could unfasten her seat belt, he covered the release button with his hand. "Don't look so terrified. I'm not going to touch you. Tell me something. Did you have a good time tonight?"

As he'd promised, he wasn't touching her, but he was so close he might as well have been. They stared into each other's eyes. She could feel the warmth of his breath, the heat of his body, the strength of his *mana*. She trembled—with nerves or desire, she wasn't sure which. "What difference—"

"Just answer the question."

He knew she had. "Yes."

"And last Saturday night? Did you have a good time?"

"Yes."

"Why did you suggest having dinner with me tonight?"

"I didn't think you'd be willing to listen unless I..." Her face grew hot with embarrassment. "Unless I made it worth your while."

"So you bribed me." He slowly smiled.

She caught her breath at the intensity of her response. It was fluid and hot and totally beyond her control, like the havoc Pele unleashed from Kilauea. It was awful to want someone so badly and know you couldn't have him.

"Don't worry about it," he said. "I enjoyed it. Of course, I wish you didn't feel you had to give yourself excuses to go out with me."

"I don't. I didn't want to." She lowered her eyes, unable to hold his gaze when she knew it wasn't true. "I do and I don't. You know that. We've been through this before. Do we have to have the same conversation—"

"Not if you stop telling yourself that things won't work out and act as though they will. Believe me, you'll have a lot more fun that way. When are we going to see each other again?"

She shook her head. "We're not. I can't think about fun. I have two children—"

"Whose mother is going to shrivel up inside if she runs away from every guy who takes an interest in her."

It was pointless to talk. It was the same argument all over again. "I want to leave now. Should I walk, or do you want to drive me?"

Paul wasn't normally one to push, but Lei was making him crazy. She was so aroused she was damn near smoking. How could she say she wanted to leave? "I'll drive you," he said, moving closer. "In a minute."

A moment later, Lei felt his lips against her neck. She closed her eyes and swallowed hard. Not just against her neck, but everywhere, as if he were kissing her nipples and belly and thighs, too. He nuzzled the hollow below her ear, nipped the lobe, and kissed his way along her jawbone to her chin. She couldn't seem to move, only to feel, her fingers clenching convulsively even as she sagged weakly against the seat. When his lips moved to her throat, she tipped back her head, helplessly inviting more. He freely gave it, nuzzling her throat and neck and face until all she could think about was having his tongue deep inside her mouth.

Finally, when her heart was racing wildly and her breathing was quick and harsh, he drew back a bit. "Lei?"

She opened her eyes. His lips were poised above hers. She parted them and waited, all but begging him.

"I'd like to kiss you," he said, "but I won't if you don't want me to."

He knew she did, damn him. He was reveling in the victory. "I don't."

"Okay." He smiled for a moment. "But someday soon, I'm going to undress you very slowly, and kiss and caress every inch of your body until you're so damn hot you can't think straight, and ask you if you want me to make love to you. And you'll say yes.''

He slid back to his seat, started the car and drove to her house. She didn't say a word, just bolted outside and hurried to the door. He didn't follow. He didn't have to. Eventually she would come to him, and he seemed to know it.

Chapter Eleven

The old *kahuna* from Hawaii Ohana had once said that David Kapakala could look on a piece of land and see wonderful visions. On Sunday, David took Paul through several houses he'd designed, showing him some of those visions. Then they continued up to Waikane, where he painted such a vivid picture with words and gestures of what he wanted to build there that Paul was astonished and then dazzled.

David admitted the site had obsessed him from the moment he'd first walked there—that he'd spent countless hours dreaming and making sketches when he should have been working on existing contracts. Fortunately, he said, his clients valued him enough to tolerate delays. When Paul offered him the commission, he accepted with a wry smile. Paul might be an ignorant *haole*, he teased, but at least he had the good sense to recognize genius when he saw it.

Paul phoned Graham Smith later the same day. Though disappointed to lose the project, Smith promised his full cooperation. The following morning, Paul announced that David would be their new architect.

Public reaction was immediate and positive. The involvement of a native Hawaiian with strong ties to the community reassured even the most militant protesters. They continued to show up at Waikane each day, marching and chanting as Bob and his men pulled out tree stumps at the north end of the site, but they didn't cause any trouble. They'd decided to wait for David's design, then give Paul a chance to fashion a compromise around it.

He should have had an easy week after that, but people seemed determined to keep him busy. On Tuesday, Mack asked whether he thought some substandard work at the shopping center could be salvaged. It could, but the job was so painstaking that Paul felt he should supervise it himself. On Wednesday, he got a call from Harry Topping, who asked him to fly to the Big Island in a few weeks for a meeting about the condo project. With Marshall still in the ICU, Paul knew Everett was counting on him to hold things together. That night, he tackled his third set of files.

He would rather have been with Lei, of course, but he'd pushed her as hard as he dared. Unless she came to him, she would only castigate herself for getting carried away and grow warier than ever. He spent a lot of time in the health club that week, exercising away his tension and frustration.

Lei was busy, too. She'd begun contacting store owners about leasing space in the shopping center and discussing her ideas for advertising and promotion. On Wednesday, she held the first of a series of meetings with community groups about Waikane, describing David's initial ideas to a large, enthusiastic crowd. Her job was challenging and enjoyable.

Her private life was something else again. At the end of each day, Paul called her into his office for a report. The impersonal manner he adopted in public disappeared and a gentle warmth took its place. He listened attentively, encouraging, advising and praising her in a way Marshall never had. It was wonderful.

But then, just before she left, the boss disappeared and the lover took his place. Sometimes he lazed back in his chair and smiled tenderly, as if he were remembering intimate pleasures they'd shared. She thought of the prophecy then, and told herself it was only a matter of time. Other times he gazed at her with such tense, hot hunger in his eyes that she had to look away. Erotic, graphic memories flooded her mind, leaving her shaken and aroused. He could probably have seduced her, but she knew he wouldn't. He was waiting for her to offer herself. It was her destiny.

Grace had a big smile on her face when she walked into the office Friday morning. Marshall had rallied dramatically during the night. If his condition stabilized, he would be transferred to a private room on Saturday.

More good news arrived that afternoon, when David came by with some computer renderings of his design, an artist's conception of the completed project and preliminary cost estimates. The plans were both stunning and original, with sweeping curves that soared across the landscape and architectural detailing that echoed the unique Hawaiian heritage of the burial ground and *heiau*. Paul told David that no developer worth the name could look at the design and not ache to build it. He certainly did.

Everett flew to Hawaii two days later. He spent the afternoon with Marshall, then joined Paul and David for a working dinner in the apartment. Like Paul, he loved the design. His only reservations concerned the price, but they gradually disappeared as David described how he could cut costs without sacrificing too much in the way of looks.

Marshall had improved so much by Monday that Everett managed to talk the doctors into letting him hold a brief business meeting in Marshall's room. Paul arrived at the hospital to find Everett waiting for him in the lobby.

"I told Marsh what you'd been up to," Everett remarked. "He wasn't pleased that we'd gone behind his back to commission a new design, but he calmed down amazingly fast. It seems Grace has been singing your praises. She softened him up."

They went upstairs. Marshall looked gaunt and pale, but there was no sign of the mental confusion that had plagued him the previous week. Although he grumbled about Paul and Everett's spending money without his permission, Paul sensed it was mostly for show.

Then, looking at the renderings Paul was holding, Marshall grumbled, "I might as well see what I've paid for. Always wondered if Kapakala is even half the architect he thinks he is."

After fifteen minutes of careful study, he muttered, "Okay, he is. Brilliant, in fact. But this will cost even more than Smith's design. I can't afford it."

"There's a greater number of apartments, sir," Paul pointed out. "The unit cost is only—"

"Apartments that people won't be able to afford without a subsidy. If I can't rent or sell them, I'll lose even more."

"I'm working on—"

"Then there's the financing. I'm committed up to my ears. I've borrowed as much as I can afford to."

Paul explained that David would work with them to reduce costs. With plans this good, he added, the government was bound to allocate additional funds for the project. The allocation would serve as collateral, enabling the bank to increase the size of its loan.

Marshall was too astute not to see this for what it was—a fragile house of cards that would collapse with the failure of any single element. "You've been talking to people for three weeks and you've gotten nowhere. I knew you wouldn't." He looked at the artist's conception and sighed. "It's a damn shame, but even this design won't change that. I've worked with the people here all my life and I know how they operate. It would take you a good year to put together the kind of deal you're talking about, and I can't afford that. Do what you were hired to do, Lindy. Move ahead with the original project."

"But there's tremendous opposition," Paul said. "One way or another, we'll be stopped."

Marshall shook his head. "For every politician who worries about natives' rights, there's another whose first concern is affordable housing. The two sides will stalemate each other."

"The governor is Hawaiian. He's being pressured to order a halt to the project, and he's leaning toward doing it." Actually, Pukui was only considering it, but Paul was willing to shade the truth if it would buy him more time.

Again Marshall looked at the plans. Again he sighed heavily.

"Spectacular, isn't it?" Everett said. "Don't tell me you wouldn't like to build it, Marsh. it would be the crowning achievement of a wonderful career. Let Lindy keep trying. Bob can move ahead with grading in the meantime."

Marshall slumped against the pillows. For all his mental sharpness, he was extremely debilitated. "All right. I know you've been working hard for me, Lindy. Grace and Everett have seen to that. The least I can do is let you take a shot at it." His eyes hardened. "Still, the bottom line comes first. If the government doesn't come up with funding by the time grading is done, you're going to use Smith's design. That's an order. Disregard it and I'll sue you for every extra dime you cost me."

Paul was about to object, when Everett touched his shoulder and said, "Fair enough, Marsh. We'll let you get some rest now." He led Paul out of the room into the empty lounge next door.

"He's talking about a few weeks," Paul said. "That's not enough time."

"He was letting off steam. He's much too grateful for all your help to pay you back with a lawsuit." They sat down on the couch. "Besides, I know my brother. We got to him today. He loves that design—sees it as something special and lasting he can build. He'll come around in time."

"He's a sick man," Paul replied. "Two weeks ago he wouldn't budge. Two weeks from now it could be the same thing. As much as I want to keep trying, I can't afford a lawsuit."

"If he sues, I'll pay your legal expenses—not that there's any real chance of it. Given the documents he's signed, Ross would be the first to tell him he can't win." Everett smiled reassuringly. "Don't worry about it, Lindy. Just hang in there and do the kind of job I know you're capable of doing."

It was a nice vote of confidence, but Paul *was* worried. Getting bogged down in a lawsuit, even one Everett paid to defend, would take a great deal of his time and might damage his reputation. He agreed to stay out of old-fashioned loyalty. After all Everett had done for him, he probably would have surfed through shark-infested seas for the man.

The next morning, Everett returned to California and rough grading began at Waikane. For the rest of the week, Paul sat in meetings trying to put a workable deal together. Day after day, he got the same old answers. Kapakala's ideas were wonderful and people wanted to help, but... But a project this complicated required further study. But their funds were committed for this fiscal year. But they'd never made such extensive concessions before.

Finally, on Friday, two key legislators agreed to sponsor a bill to buy the burial ground for a state park. The price was too low and they refused to buy the *heiau*, but it was better than nothing.

Thinking some positive news, however meager, might win him more time, Paul drove to the hospital to see Marshall. The receptionist stopped him with a sympathetic apology. Mr. Canning had developed pneumonia during the night.

The doctor had left orders that only his brother and Mrs. Pepperman were to be permitted to visit.

Paul returned to his car and sat motionless behind the wheel. Nothing was going right. He'd hoped Marshall would become more supportive of David's project as his health improved, but instead he'd gotten sicker. With work on the infrastructure about to begin, he was running out of time. He'd seldom felt so frustrated or drained.

Then there was Lei. The same woman who looked at him with stars in her eyes when he helped her with her job stiffened and withdrew whenever he got personal. On Wednesday, she'd refused another dinner invitation. It was hopeless. He wasn't going to ask again.

Grimacing, he started the car. There was no point dwelling on what couldn't be changed.

Amy and Lei were talking by the coffee machine when he arrived at the office. As always, he put the best possible face on things, accentuating the good news about the burial ground and minimizing the bad news about Marshall. As the boss, it was his job to keep everyone's spirits up.

Afterward he went into Grace's office, took her in his arms and told her what had happened. "It couldn't be too serious or he'd be in the ICU," he pointed out. He could feel her trembling. "You can visit him if you want to. You're on the list at the reception desk."

"If you don't mind, I'll go up there now," she said.

"You're in no shape to drive. I'll ask Eileen to take you." He released her and smiled. "It'll be okay, Grace. I know he's going to make it through this."

He left the room and fetched Eileen. As the two women left, he turned to Amy and Lei, who were watching with deep concern. "Eileen's taking Grace to the hospital. I'm sure she'll feel better once she's seen Marshall for herself. Don't worry—he'll be better in a few days."

Amy and Lei looked at each other as Paul disappeared into his office. "Something's wrong," Lei said. "He keeps saying things are fine, but he's almost as shaky as the day that football player got hold of him.'' She paused. "Maybe someone should talk to him.''

Amy sat down at her desk. "Don't look at *me*! The only one he ever confides in around here is you.''

Amy was right. Although there was tension between her and Paul, there was also empathy and trust. She knocked on his door. "Paul, it's Lei. Can I come in?''

She interpreted his grunt as a yes and went inside.

He looked up from the report on his desk. "What can I do for you?''

"I have a feeling that things aren't going as well as you keep saying. Am I right?''

He stared at her for a moment, then closed the report. His shoulders suddenly drooped, his whole body registering discouragement. "Yeah. You're right.''

She closed the door and sat down. "Tell me about it.''

He talked for twenty straight minutes. Lei's heart went out to him. He'd done everything he could, only to come away with too little money and too small a park. "It's a start,'' she said. "It's also more than anyone else could have gotten so quickly. Give it time, Paul.''

"Time, huh? I could pull this off if I had a year, or even eight or nine months, but I don't. A week ago, I really thought . . .'' He shook his head. "Never mind. My ego got in the way of my common sense. Anyway, it's not your problem.''

He expected more of himself than any man she'd ever met. "Talking about your problems isn't the same as whining or complaining. You should do it more often.''

He smiled. "Who has the time? Monday is another week. I'll keep trying.''

"That's another thing. You work too hard.'' When he wasn't reading or studying files, he was at meetings or helping the staff. "Promise me you'll relax this weekend. Play golf or go to the beach.''

"I can't. I have a stack of reading to get through.''

She pursed her lips in exasperation. "You can't go on this way. You're still recovering from that beating you took. You need a break."

"Don't worry about me. You've got your own problems to deal with. You're doing a terrific job, too."

"If I am, your help and encouragement have a lot to do with it." She hadn't given much in return, she thought guiltily. When it came to receiving rejection and abuse, he was always out in front. "I'm not leaving until you promise me two things—that you'll come to me when things go wrong and let me cheer you up, and that you'll take some time off this weekend."

"Okay. I promise." He opened the report again. "Go home to your kids, Lei. I'll see you on Monday."

She doubted he'd do either one, but she'd learned not to argue with his dismissals. She said good-night and left.

It was only later, on the bus, that she was struck by how peculiar the dismissal had been. She'd demanded that he let her cheer him up; once he would have suggested that she do it over dinner. She'd insisted that he take some time off; once he would have asked her to join him. For some reason, he'd stopped pursuing her.

The realization left her puzzled and disoriented. He wasn't supposed to lose interest. It was their destiny to be lovers.

Maybe the prophecy was wrong, then. Or maybe she'd reversed it by the sheer force of her will. She should have been relieved, but instead she felt restless and confused.

On Monday morning, Marshall's pneumonia took a turn for the worse and he was returned to the ICU. By evening, he was semicomatose. Paul hated to call Everett with that sort of news, but he had no choice.

The following afternoon, Bob Lum stopped by the office to report that the grading at Waikane would be finished in another day or two. The sacred lands would be the last area they worked on. He needed a decision on what to do next.

Paul called everyone into the conference room. "Last Monday, Marshall ordered me to move ahead with the original project unless the government came through with funding for David's design," he began. "Unfortunately a modest amount of money for a park isn't the kind of funding he meant. We'll have to start laying out Smith's infrastructure." That was what their permits were for.

He looked at Lei, waiting for her to argue, but she didn't say a word. "David and I spoke on Saturday and came up with some tentative plans. He's duplicating as much of the original infrastructure as he can. I'll have him meet us at the site at noon tomorrow to show us what he's come up with, Bob. If you can start with what's identical, it'll keep our options open and buy us more time."

"So you can keep talking to the politicians?" Bob smiled and shook his head. "You're a professional optimist, Lindy. They don't do anything unless a bomb is about to go off under their butts."

Paul wasn't optimistic at all; he was simply taking the only course open to him. "There hasn't been any pressure on them yet. Maybe they'll come up with some money if we move ahead with the original project."

"Will we really do that?" Lei asked quietly.

"I'm afraid so." Again he waited for her to object, but there was only silence. "I wish I had a choice, but Marshall was perfectly lucid when he gave me that order. Lucid enough to threaten me with a lawsuit if I disregard it and cost him extra money."

She looked appalled. "You can't be serious!"

He was more tired than he'd realized, he thought, or he wouldn't have mentioned it. Playing for sympathy wasn't his style. "Don't worry about it. Everett said he was only letting off steam. I know your friends will be angry and upset, but I don't have much maneuvering room."

"Of course you don't!" She shifted restlessly. "You're not taking the heat by yourself. I'm coming to the site with you tomorrow."

It was his job to take the heat, but he enjoyed her company too much to object. "You can come if you keep away from the protesters. If things get ugly, I want you somewhere safe."

She agreed and the meeting continued, touching on the shopping center and condo projects as well as the specifics of his discussions with government officials. The staff demanded honesty, so he provided it. He shouldn't have. They didn't so much walk out of the conference room as forlornly straggle out.

Lei slept poorly that night and found it hard to concentrate the next morning. That was nothing unusual. All she did lately was worry about Waikane—and Paul.

It had been two and a half weeks since they'd had dinner together, but it seemed like months. She winced when she recalled how she'd lectured him that night, caring more about a piece of land than a human being. The land was important, but not more important than a man's health. He drove himself too hard. He took failure too personally. He was under enormous pressure from Marshall and felt responsible for everyone in the office. Although she knew she couldn't change him, she longed to ease the burden.

Paul being Paul, they'd no sooner gotten into the car than he asked her how things were going. "Everything's fine," she replied. "Let's not talk shop." She forced a smile onto her face. "You've lived in so many different places—Los Angeles, San Francisco, Seattle.... Tell me about them. I've never been out of Hawaii."

"Trying to get my mind off my troubles?"

"You're too perceptive, but I *am* interested. Which was your favorite place to live?"

"San Francisco."

He started talking about it, visibly unwinding as he drove Diamond Head. Some funny stories about Everett followed; she matched them with stories about Marshall.

He was relaxed and smiling by the time they reached the work site. Dozens of protesters were milling around on one side of the fence, while clearing and surveying took place on the other. Ned was up the coast with the workmen, while David was standing with Bob at the edge of the burial ground. Lei sobered. She wasn't fooled by the outward calm. When the first foot of trench was cut into sacred soil, this place would explode.

They got out of the car and walked across the burial ground. Lei thought she was prepared for what she would feel, but the land was like a living, pulsing being. It caught her and trapped her, moved her emotions and wrenched her soul. She stopped and fought for breath, stunned by the power of it.

Paul took her arm. "Are you okay?"

"Yes. The land..." She swayed, feeling hot and dizzy. Paul settled her head against his shoulder and murmured words of comfort. Her eyes filled with tears. "I know you can't feel it, but it's so strong. And the pain of the dead... Please. Don't let them disturb—" She bit her lip. "I'm sorry. I know you've done all you can."

"Maybe not." He stroked her hair. "I promise you, Lei... this will be the last place we dig, even if it costs more to do it that way."

"Thank you." She allowed herself the solace of his embrace for a few moments longer, then straightened.

He put his arm around her and continued over to Bob and David. She couldn't focus on the conversation that followed. It was too technical and she was too distraught. She desperately wanted to think he could work a miracle, but he was only a man—and a very tired, discouraged one at that.

After twenty minutes or so, the sound of chanting caught her attention. The protesters were marching and singing; a TV crew had arrived to film them. She glanced around the site to see if something specific had set them off. A phalanx of bulldozers was approaching the *heiau*. The work up the coast was finished.

She felt physically ill. Only the *kanaka*, she thought, would really understand. "I can't bear it, David. It's obscene—a violation. They're going to crush our ancestors."

"They're safe for the time being. They're deep beneath us." He touched her gently on the cheek. "Sometimes it takes obscenity to make people listen. The protesters know that. Maybe it has to happen this way."

She swallowed and nodded, praying he was right. Paul took her arm. "We can't stay here. Let's go."

They walked over to the fence. The bulldozers rolled onto the *heiau*. The protesters continued to march and chant, but as David had said, it was more sound than genuine fury.

Lei went rigid as the machines began to strain and belch, scraping the sacred land smooth.

"I shouldn't have let you come," Paul said. "This is upsetting you too much. David, could you take Lei—"

"No. I want to stay." She put her hands over her ears. "It's just the noise—it's so loud. It makes me..." She stopped short. Paul had jerked around to stare at something behind them. So had Bob and David. Bewildered, she dropped her hands and looked over her shoulder.

The noise was deafening, unbearable. A small plane was approaching on their left, flying much too low and vibrating violently. Paul pushed her to the ground and covered her with his body. Time slowed down. Ever so gradually, the plane flew over the fence. The workers bolted to safety. The plane crashed to earth on the *heiau*, landing nose down about five yards from one of the bulldozers.

Everyone raced across the burial ground. The pilot freed himself and staggered away. Miraculously, he was only slightly hurt. He was an experienced pilot, he said, but he hadn't been able to control his plane. He had no idea what had gone wrong.

He was startled to learn where he'd crashed. He wasn't a *kamaaina*—he only wintered here—but he'd followed the events at Waikane closely. When Lei murmured something about fate, it was all Paul could do to hold his tongue. In his opinion, it wasn't destiny, but the latest in a string of suspicious accidents. He wanted to hear what Santos and the FAA had to say about it.

A squad car arrived a few minutes later. A local resident had realized the plane was in trouble and called the police even before Bob Lum had. The officers asked a few questions, then took the pilot to the hospital.

Bob told his men to resume work *makai* of the plane, but to a man, they refused to set foot on sacred land. The more superstitious among them insisted the area was under the protection of some powerful deity. Hadn't the plane crashed mere minutes after they'd violated sacred ground? Wasn't it the third such incident? Only fools, they said, would continue to work here.

Others, more rational in Paul's opinion, thought someone was out to cause trouble. They weren't willing to risk their lives by exposing themselves to further danger. The entire crew simply left, and there wasn't a thing anyone could do about it.

Chapter Twelve

Dramatic footage of the plane crash at Waikane led off the evening news. Interviews with workers and protesters followed, and then a brief clip of Paul declining comment. Finally, there was a profile of the pilot, who turned out to be a midwestern millionaire who owned a string of luxury hotels, including one on Maui.

Paul snapped off the TV. For the second time that day, he called Joe Santos. Didn't Santos find it suspicious, he demanded angrily, that a hotel owner just happened to crash on a troubled construction site, fanning workers' superstitions—and miraculously escaping serious injury?

Santos replied that the pilot had cooperated fully when they'd spoken that afternoon. There was no indication that he'd ever evinced an interest in building a hotel on Oahu. Still, if the FAA investigation failed to turn up evidence of mechanical failure, he would pursue the possibility that the crash had been deliberate.

Paul wearily hung up. Odd things kept happening at Waikane, but nobody could prove they weren't accidents. He'd been hitting his head against a wall for over a month now, and he was running out of patience.

Less than an hour later, someone called to make an offer on the property. There was a second offer the same evening and three more the following morning. Between Marshall's illness and the publicity about their problems, people had begun to wonder if the land might be available at a bargain price. Paul told them that the burial ground wasn't for sale—it would go to the state for a park—but all five callers remained interested.

He did some long, hard thinking after that. Maybe it was time to cut Marshall's losses and get out. Work at Waikane was at a standstill because Bob couldn't persuade his men to return there. The politicians weren't going to come up with any more money—not in the foreseeable future. And Marshall remained desperately ill.

Even if he recovered completely, it would be months before he could take charge of his business again. Paul's life and work were in California. He couldn't stay in Hawaii indefinitely. If Waikane were sold, he'd be able to turn over the reins to the best person available and go home.

By early afternoon he'd decided to contact Everett and ask for authorization to negotiate a sale. He called a staff meeting for three o'clock, then phoned Santos to find out if the FAA's investigators had finished examining the plane.

They had, finding a defect that would have made the aircraft extremely difficult to control. Paul's mood was more dour than ever when he hung up. Each incident had a plausible explanation, but when you put them all together...

His feelings were only too clear as he explained his decision to the staff that afternoon. From his clipped tone to his rigid back, he radiated irritation and frustration.

There was a stunned silence when he finished. "If there were anyone here to replace you, Marshall wouldn't have asked for Everett's help in the first place," Cliff finally said. "If Everett can spare you for a little longer—"

Paul cut him off. "I was sent here to deal with Waikane. Once the land is sold, my job will be finished."

"What about the other two projects?" Grace asked. "We need your help. At least stay until the shopping center opens."

"Until April?" He shook his head. "I'm sorry, Grace, but the answer is no. Mack is handling things just fine. And if nobody here has the expertise to oversee the project on the Big Island, we'll find someone suitable and sell him Marshall's interest."

"But then there would be nothing left for Marshall to come back to. It would break his heart."

Paul didn't blame her for fighting for the man she loved; he just didn't want to take part in the battle. "He'll be able to relax and enjoy life. It'll be the best thing in the world for him."

"You don't know Marshall," Lei said. "He'd be bored stiff without his work." She looked at him imploringly. "Besides, that's not the real issue. You loved David's design. You really wanted to build it. Bob's men will return if they don't have to step on sacred land, so why can't they work elsewhere while you go ahead with your original strategy?"

"Because I have no reason to think I can succeed in the short time I'd have. I have an obligation to protect Marshall's financial interests, and the best way to do that is by selling. We've got five potential buyers who could change their minds by next week. If we sell right now, I can play them off against one another and get a decent price."

"But they'll build a hotel or a golf course or condominiums there. We need affordable housing for average people." She leaned closer to him. "They'll desecrate the *heiau*, Paul. Please...don't let that happen."

Her pleas would have softened him once, but now they only irritated him. She knew how she affected him. She was using it to get what she wanted. Maybe it was personal and unfair, but he couldn't stop himself from striking back. "Appeal to the city council, not to me. I'm sure you can talk them into denying approval."

"I thought you understood," she said hoarsely. "I thought you really cared. Obviously I was wrong."

His temper flared. "I got you money for a park, didn't I? Do you have any idea how hard that was? I could have rammed Smith's project down your throat, but I busted my ass trying to arrange a compromise. I've been patronized, threatened, insulted and beaten since I got here, but I still kept trying. Don't tell me I didn't care."

Amy touched his shoulder. "Please, Lindy—try to calm down. Lei didn't mean it. She's just upset."

He studied Lei for a moment. She was pale and trembling, obviously because of what might happen to her precious *heiau*. He found himself wishing she'd cared for him even half as much. "There's no point going on with this." He jerked to his feet. "I tried my best and I failed. I'm sorry about that. And Lei—I'm sorry I yelled at you. I'm sorry I couldn't do more. Okay?"

He waited for a response, but she avoided his eyes. "Fine. Don't answer me. You've driven me half-crazy by now, so why not finish the job?" Utterly fed up, he stalked to the door, mumbling, "I'm sorry I ever came to this damn island, too."

Lei didn't say a word. She couldn't. She felt naked inside, scraped raw. She heard the hall door slam shut and flinched. Paul had stormed out.

Without looking at anyone, she hurried into her office and closed the door. Tears filled her eyes as she stumbled to her desk. A minute later Amy walked in, pulled over a chair and held out her arms. Lei turned into her embrace and sobbed against her shoulder.

"Are those tears over a man or a piece of land?" Amy asked.

"I don't know. Oh, God, why did I say those things? I know they're not true. I hate it when he's mad at me." She straightened, rubbing impatiently at her eyes. "He hates me. It's my fault he's leaving."

"Because you drive him crazy, I suppose." Amy smiled a little. "What did he mean by that? Crazy with aggravation because you nag him, or crazy with frustration because you won't sleep with him?"

Lei reddened. "Both, I guess. I'd rather not talk about it."

"Umm. Nothing new there." Amy paused, then added gently, "It would do you good, though. If you change your mind, I'm a pretty good listener."

Although Lei nodded, she wasn't going to change her mind. Not only were her feelings too private, she wouldn't have known where to begin. She only knew that she couldn't bear the thought of Paul leaving—of never again working with him, talking to him or laughing with him. Given the pain he would have brought her, that was reason enough to be glad he was going. And given the pain she felt right now, it was reason enough to beg him to stay.

Paul changed into shorts and a T-shirt, then rode down to the health club and tortured himself for a solid hour on a variety of diabolical machines. He was sweaty and tired afterward, but he was also calmer and rather sheepish.

He'd really lost it downstairs—let emotion govern his actions instead of logic. Some of it was impatience with the protesters and politicians, but most of it was frustration over Lei. Her rejection had hit him hard, filling him with an unfamiliar mixture of dejection and anger. In a way, though, he'd only gotten what he deserved. He'd been too damn confident he'd get what he wanted. He'd even been arrogant enough to assume that her sweetness and compassion had been for him personally rather than for someone who was in a position to help her people.

Only a quitter or a coward would have run away to forget her, and he was neither of those things. He returned to the apartment and took a cool shower, dressing in a comfortable pair of gym shorts. The he phoned Everett.

They spent the first few minutes discussing Marshall, who was improving physically but remained torpid and mentally confused. Then Paul simply talked—about the plane crash and its aftermath, about his myriad frustrations, about his uncharacteristic bursts of temper and self-doubt. "I don't trust myself to be objective anymore. Maybe selling is the only realistic option, but I don't want to give up on David's design if there's any hope of getting it funded. I don't know what the hell to do anymore."

"Tell me something," Everett said. "What have you done to relax lately?"

"I work out at the health club—"

"To keep in shape and preserve your sanity, but not to relax. Have you played any golf? Gone out to dinner? Taken in a movie?"

Paul frowned. "I haven't had time. I've been playing catch-up since—"

"Then make time. You're burned out, Lindy. You're so emotionally involved in this situation that you're no damn good to anyone. Put Waikane out of your mind for a few days. If Topping still wants you to go to the Big Island on Wednesday, then go—and stay for a while to play golf."

Paul opened his mouth to argue, then remembered that Everett was seldom wrong about anything. Maybe he *was* burned out. "And Waikane? What do I tell Bob?"

"That we're going to let things cool off for a week or two. Maybe the politicians will wake up and do something once they realize they could lose the housing project entirely if they don't. A week from Sunday, when you're relaxed and fresh, we'll decide how to proceed."

"But Bob and his men will still have to be paid," Paul pointed out.

"My brother can afford it, believe me." Everett paused, then added firmly, "Remember—no work till Monday. That's an order, Lindy."

Smiling to himself, Paul said he'd look forward to following it. He felt as if an elephant had been lifted off his back. His fatigue forgotten, he went into the living room and pulled a guidebook off the shelf.

He was checking on whether any of the local golf courses were lighted, when the doorbell rang. If his sense of duty hadn't been so strong, he would have ignored it. Instead he looked through the peephole and saw Lei outside, staring at her toes while she twisted her hands together nervously. He sighed, wondering if she'd come here to apologize to him or nag him.

He opened the door. She glanced up, then quickly looked down. Her face went from pale to flushed. The fact that he was practically naked seemed to unnerve her.

He stepped aside. "Come on in. About this afternoon— I'm sorry I lost—"

"No, *I'm* sorry. I shouldn't have questioned your integrity." She walked inside and he closed the door. "I'm too emotional. I get upset and I say things I don't mean. I'm so ashamed of myself..."

He smiled. "Don't take it so seriously. I spoke—"

"Anyway, that's not the reason I came to see you. Not the main reason. I wanted to talk to you about—about you and me. I was wondering if...if..." She turned bright red and started to tremble.

Paul had no idea what she was so wound up about, but the news about Waikane would probably calm her down. "Take it easy, Lei. I have some good—"

"What I'm trying to say is, I know I'm part of the reason you're leaving, and I thought that maybe if the two of us... That is, if you and I were—together, maybe you'd stay and keep trying. Maybe you'd want to, that is." She looked at him anxiously and croaked, "Would you?"

He wasn't sure what she was offering, but obviously she wouldn't have been here if she'd known he wasn't leaving. Waikane could wait. He wanted to find out what was going on.

"I'm not sure. Why don't we talk it over? Go on into the den. I'll bring you something to drink. What do you want? Lemonade? Iced tea? A soda?"

Lei was so mortified she wanted to slide through the nearest crack. She'd offered herself as baldly as she could, and he was barely even interested. "I shouldn't have come. I'm sorry I bothered you." She turned to leave.

He grabbed her arm. "Wait a minute. How can I say yes or no when I don't even know what you're suggesting?"

How could it have been clearer? Was she supposed to explain it in clinical language? "I told you... I'm willing to be... I mean, I *want* to be with you."

"Fine. I'd like that." He sounded as if he were humoring someone *pupule*. "I'm going to make some lemonade. Do you want some?"

"Okay. I'll wait for you in the den." She pulled away and fled down the hall.

She resisted the urge to cower in a corner of the couch. After all, nobody had dragged her up here. She'd come because she'd wanted to—because she wanted Paul, even if it were only for a few weeks or months.

She knew now that the prophecy was right. She was in love with him, trapped by the force of her feelings, willing to give him whatever he asked. Destiny worked in strange ways. It had presented her with a choice—offer herself or watch him leave. It was really no choice at all.

Still, the future frightened her. Liliha had spoken of anguish and fear. Paul had spoken of living for the moment. The memories made her shudder. If there hadn't been faint rays of hope, she never would have come. *"Don't fight him,"* Liliha had said. *"Do what he wants."* And Paul... *"I used to think that. Now I'm not so sure."* When she thought of the future, those were the words she tried to remember.

Paul walked into the den with two glasses of lemonade, set them on the table and sat down next to her. He was half-naked, and his virility was almost overwhelming. Almost, because she could see the faded bruises on his body. His male strength aroused her passion, but his human frailty touched her heart.

"It's tough just to sit here," he said. "I can hardly keep my hands off you. But before I touch you, I want to make sure we understand each other." He picked up a glass and cupped it. "You said you wanted to be with me. That can mean anything from going out to dinner once in a while to living together."

"Somewhere in between," she mumbled. To her relief, he desired her as much as ever. Gym shorts didn't hide much, and his hands were so unsteady that the lemonade was sloshing around in the glass he was holding.

He took a sip, then set the glass down. "It would help if you were a little more specific." He smiled weakly. "I mean, I wouldn't want to interpret that as meaning an intimate love affair if all you had in mind—"

"You can interpret it that way if you want to." She wanted to make him happy, not frustrate him. Besides, once she got used to it, it would probably be wonderful.

She waited for him to take her in his arms, but he simply sat there. Finally he said, "Before—in the hall—you started to say 'willing,' and then you changed it to 'want.' But if it's really only 'willing'..."

He grimaced. "Look, you don't have to sleep with me to keep me in Hawaii. I'm staying for the time being. I spoke to Everett a little while ago. He said I was burned out—that I needed some time off. We're going to talk again a week from Sunday. We'll decide then whether to sell the property or keep looking for funding. But you have to understand—when it comes to business, my first obligation is to

Marshall. Even if I'm sleeping with you, I can't let that influence my recommendation.''

So her actions were irrelevant. He was staying in any event. He could make love to her now, then break her heart next Sunday. Somehow, none of that mattered.

"You can't?'' She ran a teasing finger down his arm. "Not even if I'm incredible in bed?''

"Not even then.'' He pushed away her hand and took a deep breath. "Lei—I want to make love to you so much I can hardly think straight. Please—don't start something you don't plan to finish.''

Things were happening a little too fast, but she didn't see the point of waiting. "Okay.'' He didn't move. Puzzled, she asked, "Do you want me to take my clothes off, or wait for you in the bedroom?''

"No.'' He slid the rubber band off the end of her braid, then separated the strands. His touch was tender, soothing. "I wasn't sure what okay meant.''

He ran his fingers lightly down her arms. A wave of desire rippled through her. "It meant yes,'' she said.

"Umm. I figured that out.''

He grasped her shoulders and turned her so that her back was to his chest. Then he combed out her hair with long, sensuous strokes of his fingers.

"So beautiful,'' he murmured.

He buried his face in it and she shivered, wanting his lips on her neck.

"I love the smell. And the color... where does it come from?''

He nuzzled his way to her bare skin. Her heart raced faster and faster as his mouth teased and caressed her.

"An *ehu*...'' She swallowed and tried again. "It's, uh, a red-haired Hawaiian. It's from my mother's side.''

"Really? Remind me to thank her.'' Still kissing her neck, he threaded his fingers through her hair and massaged her scalp.

Her body went slack. Relaxation mingled with desire. If she'd been a cat, she would have purred.

"That's heaven." She closed her eyes and let her head loll forward. "You'll put me to sleep."

"We can't have that." He settled her against the back of the couch and bent over her. He trailed kisses against her throat, arousing her all over again. Finally he murmured, "Look at me, sweetheart."

She opened her eyes halfway. His gaze was fiery, consuming. It excited her still more, but it also frightened her a little. Passion that hot could rage out of control.

Still staring at her, he began unbuttoning her blouse. Slowly. Provocatively. His hands kept brushing her breasts, and she knew it wasn't by accident. Her flesh swelled, and her nipples began to throb. She remembered the first time he'd touched them—how aroused she'd been, how eager and submissive. She ached to feel that way again, but he was taking his time, making her wait.

She raised her arms to caress him. His skin was hot and a little damp. She felt a surge of possessiveness, but also a sense of belonging, of surrender. "Such power and strength," she whispered, running her fingers over his arms and chest. "Such a dominating *mana*. It was foolish to resist you. I never had a chance."

Paul knew the term *mana*. Her admiring words and adoring touch made him feel ten feet tall. Even now, he could hardly believe what had happened—that she'd come here, that she wanted him purely for himself, that she was giving herself with such sweetness and abandon.

She caressed his belly, and he stiffened. "Don't touch me that way," he groaned. "Don't say things like that. They make me crazy." He'd lose control, go too fast. He hadn't been with a woman in a long time. He'd never wanted one the way he wanted Lei.

She dropped her hands. She understood his reasons well enough. His breathing was ragged, almost labored. His hands were clumsy with anticipation as he pulled her blouse free from her skirt. "I love the feel of your skin," she said. "Later, can I—"

"Yes. When I tell you to." He slipped off her blouse and bra, cupped her breasts and rubbed his thumbs gently back and forth across her nipples. Then he took them between his thumbs and forefingers and tenderly massaged them.

Her eyelids drooped down. The pleasure was exquisite.

His touch grew more demanding. She arched against his hands and moaned his name, offering whatever he cared to take. His fingers stilled, and then she felt his tongue on one of her nipples, lightly tasting her, making her want more. Unable to bear it, she thrust her hands into his hair and held him close. His lips and teeth were pure magic, nipping and suckling her until a throbbing, intimate ache invaded her body.

He pleasured her other breast, then raised his head. "Lei. Open your eyes."

Trembling, she did so. "You keep saying that. Why?"

"They tell me what you're thinking." He stroked her lips with a playful finger, then slipped it between her teeth. "Like now. They're helpless and sort of glazed. You're dying to have me kiss you. Do you have any idea what that does to me?"

She sucked his finger deeper into her mouth. He shuddered and pulled it away, then cupped her face and took her mouth in a deep, hot kiss. His tongue tasted and probed with an urgency that she met and matched. He stroked her hair, then pulled her close and teased her breasts with his naked chest until she was clinging helplessly.

The kiss went on and on. Lei thought it was ecstasy, perfection. She didn't object when he unbuttoned her skirt and pulled down the zipper, or when he caressed her belly. Slowly his hand inched lower. She was shocked by how badly she wanted him to touch her. Wild with anticipation, she moaned and dug her nails into his back.

Then, with confusing abruptness, he pulled away. "Not here. In the bedroom." He cupped her breasts. "God, Lei— I can't stop touching you."

He nuzzled her nipples, then slid his hands to her waist and tugged at her skirt. She tensed a little. He was going so fast, and there was still the prophecy hanging over her....

She'd promised, though, so she let him undress her and lift her into his arms. As he carried her out of the room, she put her arms around his neck and buried her face against his chest. She didn't say a word as he strode down the hall, just clutched him and waited. But she was shaking with anxiety as he settled her on the bed, and as he turned away to pull off his shorts, she bolted up and grabbed the spread to cover herself.

He turned back and approached the bed. She saw his aroused nakedness and hastily looked away. She couldn't. She just couldn't. "We have to stop. I don't want to right now."

He sat down next to her and she cringed. Her hands clenched. She'd aroused him and then stopped him and he was furious. When he was angry, he struck back. He'd told her so. Liliha's vision... It was time now.

She was terrified. "Paul, please. Don't make me..."

She almost jumped out of her skin when he touched her shoulder.

"Don't look at me that way," he said. "If you don't want to, we won't."

She shook her head wildly. "You're lying. You're angry. You're going to hurt me."

Paul didn't know whether to be confused or offended. This had happened twice now. What in the hell was she afraid of? "I'd never hurt you," he said, feeling his way carefully. "I'd never force you to do anything you don't want to. Why do you think I would?"

"Your—your past.... There was so much violence..."

That was nonsense. She'd been afraid of him before he'd even mentioned his past. Still, if the facts would reassure her, he was willing to provide them.

He slid off the bed and started toward the closet. It was the wrong time to be naked. "I had my share of fights as a kid, but all of them were with boys my own age or older. I've never hurt a girl in my life, unless you count Sue Ann Hodge. She was fifteen and I was eight."

After pulling on his robe, he took a large cotton throw out of the dresser and returned to the bed. Lei still seemed apprehensive, but she let him drape the blanket around her. They sat side by side on the bed, propped up against the headboard, not touching.

"She was standing next to a puddle," he continued, "and I ran past her and splashed water on her dress. She called me a dumb little son of a whore. I wasn't sure what that meant, but I knew she'd insulted my mother. I launched myself at her, trying to knock her over, and she picked me up like a pesky little mutt and dropped me into the puddle." He winced at the memory. "God, she was a brute."

"Was she?" Lei smiled tremulously. "Then you've never hurt a woman? You've never even been tempted?"

"I was tempted once. I didn't, though." He sighed. She'd tensed up again. "Lei...sweetheart...I wish you'd tell me what this is all about." He suddenly felt icy inside. He made his voice as gentle as he could. "Was there a man in your past who—"

"No. It's nothing like that." Lei knew there was no point explaining. If something wasn't tangible or rational, he thought it couldn't be real. "The woman you wanted to hurt... Who was she? What did she do to make you angry?" Maybe Liliha had misinterpreted the vision. Maybe the story would provide a different, less frightening explanation.

"I don't want to shock you, but if you really want to know...." He ran his hand through his hair, looking uneasy. "The woman was Melissa Canning—Melissa Montgomery at the time. She was still on her first husband. I'd been in

L.A. for a few months, and I was working in a fancy grocery store near her kids' school, building some shelves. She
shopped there all the time, and she used to stop and talk to
me—a minute or two at first, then five or ten. She was tall
and blond, and she always wore clothing that showed off her
body. I thought she was the most beautiful woman I'd ever
seen. One day she asked if I wanted a job looking after her
place in Bel Air—doing repairs, maintenance and yard
work. There was a small guest house on the property where
I could live. I was staying in a seedy rooming house in a
rough area of town, so it sounded like paradise.''

Lei had a feeling she knew where this was going. ''I suppose you looked older than seventeen. A perfect body,
movie-star handsome....''

He was startled. ''You're not as innocent as I thought. *I*
was, though, especially since she treated me like a kid
brother at first. Then, two months later, her husband moved
out and filed for divorce, and she started coming around to
talk to me late at night—to tell me her troubles. I had my
share of fantasies about her, but it never occurred to me to
do anything about them.'' He smiled crookedly. ''Until I
turned eighteen, that is. She gave me one hell of a birthday
present that night.''

Lei felt a stab of jealousy. ''Obviously you remember it
fondly,'' she said tartly.

His smile widened. ''Very fondly. At the time, I figured
it was a one-time bonanza. It wasn't.''

She couldn't contain herself. ''That's disgusting. A thirty-
year-old woman with two young children carrying on that
way—''

''She was twenty-eight and we were very discreet. She
even saw other guys. I assumed they were camouflage.'' He
laughed and shook his head. ''God, I was naive. I fell so
hard that when she suggested signing up for junior college,
I figured she wanted me to be more educated before she
would tell people about me. I studied hard. I learned to talk
right and dress right. Eventually I transferred to L.A. State

and got a B.A. So five years later, there I was, the proud new graduate, drinking champagne with her in the guest house, thinking I'd finally turned myself into something worthy of her. I pulled out a ring—the diamond was a third the size of one of her earrings, but it was the best I could afford—and asked her to marry me."

"And she turned you down."

"She didn't just turn me down. She giggled, patted my cheek and told me not to be ridiculous. We were both a little drunk. She was getting married, all right, to a plastic surgeon named Harvey Rice. She told me I would have to move out—that she couldn't see me anymore." He sighed. "Hell, Lei, I was young, angry and very hurt. I raised my arm to slap her face—and then dropped it and walked away."

If he hadn't hit Melissa Canning, Lei thought, he would never hit anyone. The vision couldn't possibly have meant what Liliha thought. "What an awful woman," she said, feeling a wave of empathy for the vulnerable, wounded young man he'd once been. Between his mother and Melissa, it was no wonder he was wary. "I can't believe she's Everett's daughter. What were you to her? A cute little plaything to amuse herself with?"

He shrugged. "Someone to feed her ego, or Galatea to her Pygmalion. I know she was fond of me, and the sex was terrific. Once I got over her, I was grateful for all she'd done. We're good friends now. A few years ago, she told me she'd been a fool not to marry me. That was just after she'd divorced her third husband."

"And were you tempted to ask her again?"

"Are you kidding?" He broke into a grin. "According to her ex-husbands, she was a wife straight from hell—insecure, extravagant and demanding. Definitely better mistress material."

"I feel sorry for her children," Lei said, screwing up her face in distaste.

"Oddly enough, she's a good mother." Paul ran his finger down Lei's cheek. "Not as good as you, of course. Not as beautiful or exciting, either. I'd never hurt you, sweetheart. Do you understand that now?"

She nodded. "Yes. It was all a mistake." Obviously he expected to pick up where they'd left off, but she just couldn't. If only they'd had more time.... "I should go now. It's late. The kids are waiting for me."

Although he looked disappointed, he didn't argue. "Can I see you tomorrow night?"

"I already made plans to go to Niihau this weekend." The lie came out before she could stop it. She blushed and looked away. She wanted this man. It was crazy to say no for weeks, finally say yes and mean it, and then say no again.

"I'm going to the Big Island on Wednesday for a meeting." His tone was a little cooler, as if he expected another rejection. "I'll be there through Sunday. Can you find someone to stay with the kids and come along?"

Lei didn't want to lose him. She didn't want to waste what little time they had left. "Yes," she said.

Chapter Thirteen

Paul usually played golf with intense concentration on the next shot, the next pin, but on Friday it was all he could do to keep his eye on the ball. Early that morning, he'd stopped by the office to tell everyone he was staying. They'd been so damn grateful, so confident he could work things out! How did he live up to expectations like that? What if he failed? He'd wanted to go straight back to work, but Everett had been so sure he needed a break....

And Lei. How could he concentrate on golf after holding her in his arms, tasting and touching her, hearing her moan with pleasure and feeling her nails dig into his back with excitement? Wednesday couldn't come soon enough. He was so charged with anticipation that he was already worried about botching things completely.

Somehow he managed to play passably well, carrying on a coherent conversation with his companions. In time, he began to relax and enjoy his surroundings. The course sat on gently rolling terrain. Some of the holes hugged the shoreline, reminding him of Pebble Beach, but the sea was more tranquil here; the surf lapped rhythmically at a sandy beach rather than crashing over rocks onto a jagged coast. Birds of paradise, poinsettias and bougainvilleas bloomed brightly against a field of verdant green, and the lush Koolau Mountains rose serenely in the distance.

He decided that another few days of golf would do him good, but the public courses were booked solid on weekends. Fortunately, he'd met a lot of people who belonged to private clubs and who'd invited him to play. When he got home, he sat down with the phone and started making calls. An hour and a half later, he was set.

He spent the evening walking around Waikiki, looking in shops and open-air stalls. It reminded him of the parts of San Francisco he generally avoided—lots of energy and noise, but too many tourists and too much schlock. Having satisfied his curiosity, he stopped into a market for some groceries and then returned to the apartment.

He felt pleasantly tired when he got into bed, but also a little lonely. If Lei hadn't been on Niihau, he would have called her to talk. Instead he lay there thinking about her. It was hours before he fell asleep.

Although his game the next morning was early—at seven—the weather was so hot and sticky that he was soaked with sweat by the time he finished. He seldom went to the beach, but he suddenly felt like taking a long, cool swim and relaxing in the brisk salt air with a good book.

He showered and changed, then stopped into a bookstore at the Ala Moana Center and bought a thriller. Lei's favorite beach was right across the street, in Ala Moana Park. She'd once mentioned that it was fairly quiet, and that was exactly what he needed.

Still, it was very crowded. He found an empty patch of sand for his things, then went into the water. It wasn't cool, but warm and soothing. He swam out past the throng near the shore and floated on his back, bobbing up and down on the waves until he lost all sense of time. He didn't feel like reading after that, so he took a walk in the surf, letting the waves splash against his legs.

He'd always been something of a people watcher, learning interesting things about new cities that way. Here, though, it wasn't the foibles of the adults that drew him, but the charm of the children. They came from such an appealing mixture of backgrounds and took such joy in the simplest pleasures that it was impossible not to be enchanted by them.

When he spotted a pair of towheads building a large sand castle a few yards inland, he was tempted to walk over and ask if he could help. He watched them for a while, and then, playing a game with himself, tried to pick out their parents. Would they be tourists? Foreigners?

That's when he saw her. She was wearing a baseball cap and sunglasses, sitting with her arms wrapped around her knees. Long wavy hair, blazing in the sun.... Tall and slender, with sensational legs.... She even had a gold chain around her neck, but he couldn't tell if there was a tiny hand on the end of it because it was tucked beneath her cover-up in front.

He went closer. It *was* Lei. Either she'd changed her mind about going to Niihau and hadn't told him about it, or she'd never planned to go there in the first place. He was annoyed at first, but it didn't last. He was too conscious of how difficult she'd found it to come to him on Thursday night. Besides, he was happy to see her.

He looked around for her kids, but not a single pair on the beach seemed as if they belonged with her. She was facing the ocean, so maybe they were in the water.

He walked up to her, stopping by the edge of her blanket. "Hi. It's a small world. Mind if I join you?"

She started and whirled around. "Paul! Yes. I mean no. Please—sit down." Looking back toward the water, she continued in a rush, "I shouldn't have lied. I'm sorry. I needed more time and it just—slipped out. And then it was easier to keep quiet than tell you the truth." Nervous, she tightened her arms around her knees as he sat down beside her. "Are you very angry?"

"I'm not angry at all." He could see she felt guilty, but didn't know whether that was good or bad. He was too confused and unsure of himself. "Do you still want to come with me on Wednesday?" He grimaced, thinking it was the wrong question. "Did you even want to come in the first place? Or did you say yes just so you could leave without getting into an argument?"

The tension seemed to seep right out of her. "Oh, Paul! Don't ever think that. Of course I want to come. I've already made arrangements for the kids. Mrs. Keala's daughter and son-in-law are going to stay with them."

"Then I can't wait till Wednesday." He didn't know what else to say, so he stuck to the kids. "I was trying to spot the twins, but nobody looked quite right. Where are they?"

She pointed to the two towheads. "There they are. They're pure *haole*."

"Really? I was watching them before. They're beautiful." He looked at her quizzically. "Were they adopted?"

She shook her head. "No. Tom was from my father's first marriage. His mother was French—a Parisian, and very bohemian. Dad met her when he was in the army and married her after the war. They lived in New York at first—he'd gotten a teaching job there—but he was from an old missionary family and he'd always wanted to return to Hawaii. He finally got a position at UH, but Marie was miserable here. She thought it was provincial and boring. When Tom was ten, she went to France for a visit and never came back. She met some artist and moved in with him. They led a pretty wild life from what I've heard—sex, liquor, drugs. Dad divorced her and married my mother three years later. Marie died of an overdose that same year."

"God. Your poor brother.... My mother had her faults, but at least she didn't abandon me." He paused for a moment. "Do you realize that's the first time you've said more than a few sentences about anything personal?"

"Yes." She waved at the twins, who'd spotted Paul and were staring. "It doesn't come easily to me."

Paul had hoped she would tell him about her mother, but the kids ran up, interrupting the conversation. Lei's little daughter planted herself right in front of him.

"I know who *you* are," she said.

"Do you?" He frowned, pretending to be confused. "Could you tell me, then? I've forgotten."

She giggled. "You're Mr. Lindstrom. I've seen you on TV. You work for the other Mr. Canning in California and you're helping out there until our Mr. Canning gets better. Mommy's going to the Big Island with you on Wednesday."

He'd never expected to find himself discussing the subject with Lei's daughter. Disconcerted, he said, "You're right. Why don't you call me 'Paul'?"

"Okay. I'm Jessie. That's Jason." She poked her brother's shoulder a little too hard and he poked her back in silent retaliation. "Mommy, can you take us for a swim?"

"I'm sorry, honey, but I'm still kind of tired. You can go wading if you want to, though."

"Does your stomach still hurt?" Jason asked.

"A little. I'll be fine by tonight."

Given the symptoms, Paul figured it was probably her period, but he still wanted to scold her for taking the kids to the beach instead of staying at home and resting. "I'll take them swimming," he said. "Lie down. Take a nap."

"Thanks, but they're a pair of fish. I have to watch them every minute. Everett wants you to relax, and you can't do that if—"

"Don't argue. Just rest. I promise I'll take good care of them." He stood up. "I need to get my stuff. Why don't you guys keep me company?"

They weren't the least bit shy, agreeing immediately and questioning him about Disneyland as they pranced along by his side. Trying to tire them out, he gave them his things and told them to run back to Lei. The moment he caught up with them, they took off toward the water.

He satisfied himself that they swam as well as Lei had said, then took them out beyond the crowd and played with them, lifting them high in the air and tossing them a few yards away, over and over again. Every now and then he glanced at Lei, who watched intently for a while and then lay down on her stomach and buried her face in her arms.

He ran out of steam long before the twins did. "How about something to eat?" he suggested. "We could walk to the shopping center, get some ice cream, look in the stores...."

They thought that was a wonderful idea. Lei was fast asleep when they reached her, so they quietly dried themselves and pulled on their clothes. Paul figured they were afraid of waking her and being told they couldn't go.

He left her a note, led them to his car to pick up his wallet and continued into the shopping center, where they ordered enormous sundaes. Jessie chattered about school while Jason squirmed and tapped his feet. They didn't finish their ice cream; either their eyes were bigger than their stomachs or they couldn't sit still for that long.

Paul had realized by then that they didn't *walk* anywhere; they trotted, darted or dashed. He had visions of losing sight of them amid the store racks and never finding them again. Maybe it was divine justice, because according to his mother, he'd been the same way as a kid.

Finally, to his relief, they stopped to admire some clothing and he was able to let down his guard. "That's the best sweatshirt I've ever seen," Jessie said. "Jill has it in yellow, but the red one's better. Isn't it cool, Jason?"

"For a girl, maybe." He pointed to a black one nearby. "I like that one. You think we can get Mom to buy them?"

She glanced at Paul and giggled. "Yeah."

Paul bent down a little. "Yeah what? What's so funny?"

She hesitated. "You'll tell my mother."

"Me?" He shook his head. "No way. Not a word."

"Well..." She looked at the sweatshirt again. "We can get her to buy them 'cause she's going away for five whole days. That's the longest she's ever been gone for. She feels bad about it."

"So she'll buy you presents to make up for it. You've got it all figured out, haven't you?" he teased.

"She always brings us presents. Not as expensive as the sweatshirts, though." Jessie studied him for a minute. It was a little unnerving. "She likes you. Do you like her?"

If she meant what he thought she did, there was no way he wanted to answer. "Sure I do. Your mom makes my job a lot easier. She's a smart lady."

"Not like that," Jason said impatiently. "She *likes* you. You know. She even went out on a date with you."

"She said it was work," Jessie added, "but she kept changing her clothes and fussing with her hair so we knew it was a date. So...do you like her, too?"

He was trapped. Kids saw every damn thing that happened, and, unlike adults, didn't hesitate to say so. "Yes. I do. Do you mind?"

"Maybe. She's never had a boyfriend before." She looked at her brother. "Rachel's mother has a boyfriend. She's always going away with him. They never take Rachel."

"Mom wouldn't do that," Jason said. "Anyway, he doesn't even live here."

Meaning, Paul supposed, that he'd be back in California soon and out of their hair. "Your mom loves you more than anything in the world," he said. "She told me so. I could never take her away from you, and neither could anyone else." He motioned for them to follow him into the store. "Let's go inside. Your mom wouldn't be going to the Big Island if I didn't need her help, so the least I can do is buy you those sweatshirts." A fib if ever there was one, but there was such a thing as being too honest.

Jessie raced ahead, but Jason hung back. "She won't let us keep them. It's not like you're a relative or anything."

"Sure she will." He winked at the boy. "Trust me. I'm good at talking people into things."

They spent the next twenty minutes looking at clothing and knickknacks. Paul got a kick out of the way they darted around, commenting on everything as if they were a pair of fashion critics. He would have bought them more than just the sweatshirts if they'd asked him to, but they didn't. Lei had obviously trained them well.

They thanked him politely as he led them out of the store. "You're welcome," he replied. "Where to next? The cookie store, maybe? We could buy some to take home."

"Maybe," Jessie said.

He was surprised and touched when she slipped her hand into his.

"Could I ask you something?" she went on.

"Sure. What?"

"Are you buying us stuff to get us to like you?"

He grinned at her. "Nah. You like me already."

She giggled and rolled her eyes. "Are you, Paul?"

"Sort of, but it's more because I like *you*." He put his hand on Jason's shoulder. "When you like people, it's only natural to buy them presents."

The boy gazed up at him. "Do you buy Mom presents?"

"I bought her dinner, but I don't think that counts." He stopped in front of a jewelry store and pointed to a pair of silver earrings in the window. "What about those cat earrings? Do you think she'd like them?"

Jessie nodded. "She likes cats. We have two of them. But her absolute favorite thing in the whole shopping center is this nene in a store downstairs."

"A nene?" Paul said. "What's that?"

"It's the state bird," Jason answered. "We learned about it in school. It's a kind of duck—"

"A goose, stupid. They're almost extinct, and—"

"Endangered, dummy."

Jessie stuck out her tongue at him. "I said 'almost.' The one downstairs was carved by a famous artist."

"Out of koa wood," Jason added.

Sibling rivalry rears its ugly head, Paul thought in amusement. "Why don't you show it to me?"

They led him into a small gift shop crammed with fragile items and pointed to a wooden bird in a glass cage. He was afraid they might break something, but they seemed to understand that they had to be careful.

The owner unlocked the case, took out the goose and set it on the counter. It was about ten inches long and exquisite. "It's by an artist named Jimmy Akala. He lives on the Big Island. Isn't it magnificent?"

Paul nodded. Such lifelike features had been carved into the wood that the bird looked as if it could take flight. He ran a finger down its feathered back. It was cool to the touch and amazingly smooth, a joy to feel.

It was also seven hundred dollars. That wasn't a trivial sum of money to him, but he could afford it. He'd spent very little recently. Besides, this rare and graceful Hawaiian bird and his gentle Hawaiian lover somehow belonged together.

He handed the owner a credit card. "Would you gift-wrap it, please?"

Jessie's eyes widened. "You're really going to buy it?"

"Sure, since it's your mother's absolute favorite thing in the whole shopping center. My only problem will be getting her to accept it."

Jason grinned at him. "I thought you were good at talking people into things."

"Maybe not *that* good. Come on—let's get some cookies. We'll be back in a few minutes," he added to the owner.

They bought a dozen cookies and ate three of them, then picked up the nene and returned to the beach. Lei was awake by then, and so visibly relieved to see them that he couldn't help smiling. "Did you think I'd kidnapped them?"

"No, but you were gone for such a long time...."

"We were shopping, Mommy." Jessie pulled out the two sweatshirts. "Look at what Paul bought us. Aren't they great?"

Lei checked the price tags and frowned. "They're very nice, but he shouldn't have. Go work on your castle for a while. It's still there."

"But Mom . . ."

"Go on, Jessie."

Jason poked his sister in the ribs with his elbow and said in a stage whisper, "Wait till she sees the nene." Then the two of them giggled and ran to the shore.

"The nene." Lei looked at the bag from the gift shop. "That wouldn't be Jimmy Akala's nene, would it?"

He sat down beside her. "Let's not fight about it. Here. Have a cookie." He held out the box.

"No, thanks. Cookies, too, huh?"

"And ice cream sundaes they didn't finish. They're good kids, but they were running me ragged. I figured I could slow them down if I fattened them up and weighed them down with clothing. It didn't work." He put his arm around her shoulders. "They grilled me, Lei. Made me admit we like each other. It was terrifying."

Lei's emotions were in turmoil. Paul was wonderful, maybe too wonderful. He hadn't been angry that she'd lied, only concerned that she didn't feel well. He'd taken the kids so she could rest, played with them like a devoted father and spoiled them with gifts. He even seemed to like them.

She'd prayed for that. She was thrilled about it. But what would she do if things didn't work out? If they got attached to him and he left?

He was rubbing the back of her neck now, distracting and arousing her. "Don't do that," she murmured. "They'll see."

"I told you—they already know." He started playing with a strand of her hair, winding it around his finger. "God, I want to make love to you. I was up half the night thinking about it."

She blushed. "I can't. It's the wrong time of the month."

"Wednesday, then." He dropped his hand and moved a few inches away. "Let them keep the sweatshirts, Lei. It's not that big a gift."

"Maybe you're right, but the nene—"

"Is a beautiful work of art. I want you to have it."

Obviously he had plenty of money. She wondered if he was in the habit of spending it on his girlfriends. "Did you buy expensive things for Karen, too?"

"Never anything spontaneous. Never anything I saw and bought just because it was so perfect for her, the way the nene is for you." He removed her sunglasses and lifted her chin. "Keep it, sweetheart. Please. It's rare and graceful and beautiful, just like you. You belong together."

Lei was utterly bewitched. No one had ever spoken to her like that before. No one had ever bought her such a wonderful gift. Finally she nodded. "All right, but only because it has a special meaning for you. Thank you."

He kissed her on the nose and stood up. "Good. Rest a little more. I'm off to work on a castle."

She smiled at him, radiant with happiness, and lay down on her stomach to watch.

Paul strolled to the shore. He was happy, relaxed and pleased with how things were going. He and Lei were closer than ever and he even liked her kids, especially after the awestruck looks they gave him when he told them they could keep the sweatshirts. They thought he was some kind of magician.

The three of them worked on the castle for a while, then went for a swim. Afterward he took everyone to dinner and a movie. It was obviously too long a day, because the twins fidgeted, then whined, then squabbled.

He wasn't used to that, and it grated on his nerves. The kids could be a lot of fun, but they never let you relax. Fatherhood would be damn tough, especially on top of a demanding job. He was happy to play golf the next day in the company of three sedate adults who talked about politics and the stock market.

Chapter Fourteen

Paul was so preoccupied with business on Monday and Tuesday that Lei barely saw him. Although he kissed her goodbye each day with a tender passion that was both heady and reassuring, she was visibly nervous as they flew to the Big Island on Wednesday. She was about to take a huge and irrevocable step. She couldn't give her body without giving her heart and soul as well. Besides, awful things might begin to happen—things Liliha had called inevitable, things she couldn't control.

Their hotel was north of the airport on the Kohala coast. Marshall owned a small interest in the place and conducted his local business out of an opulent two-bedroom suite there. As usual, there was a complimentary basket of fruit and wine in the lounge. Paul told the bellman to put the luggage in separate bedrooms, but Lei still felt awkward and self-conscious.

She walked to the window and opened the drapes. The golf course was below her, an oasis of irrigated lushness in the harsh Kohala desert. The ocean was beyond, surging over the black volcanic rock so typical of this young island.

Some people called South Kohala a wasteland, but Lei thought it had a sparse, wild beauty all its own. She barely saw that beauty now; she was too nervous. She didn't understand how she could want something and fear it at the same time.

Paul tipped the bellman and let him out of the suite. "What a spectacular course! I can't wait to play it," he said as he strolled to her side. "I don't want to keep Topping waiting, though. We should probably get going."

She reminded him that their appointment wasn't for three hours yet. "It'll only take an hour or so to have lunch and drive to Waimea. We could make love now if you want to."

"Actually, I'd rather drive around a bit first," he said.

She looked at him in bewilderment. "You want to go sight-seeing?"

"Not sight-seeing. I'd like to get a feel for the area before I see the condo site. Then, when we get back, I thought I'd go to the driving range for a few hours. If I turn in early tonight, I can get on the course at dawn and play eighteen holes before our meetings."

Lei stared at him. There wasn't even the hint of a smile on his face. He was actually serious. "And what am I supposed to do while you're playing golf?"

He looked abashed. "I assumed you'd want to read or sunbathe, but if you'd rather tag along—"

"You've chased me for over a month and you finally get me alone and you want me to follow you around while you hit a little white ball?" She couldn't believe it. "No, thanks."

"Actually, no." A slow smile spread over his face. "I want to rip off your clothes and drag you to bed, but you'd probably faint from nerves before I even kissed you."

Confusion gave way to embarrassed pleasure. "You shouldn't tease me, Paul. I can't help it if I'm nervous. It would serve you right if I left."

"I was trying to be sensitive. Show a little class." He put his arms around her. "We have five whole days, Lei *nani*. There's no reason to rush. Between work and the kids, you never get a break. I want you to relax this afternoon. The sign downstairs said the Alii Room has a band. We could have dinner there and dance a bit. If you want to make love tonight, we'll make love, and if you don't, we won't. Okay?"

Lei snuggled closer. She wasn't nervous anymore, just happy. "Okay. You're sweet, do you know that?"

"Sweet?" He held her at arm's length, looking so woeful that she smiled. "How boring."

"Sexy and exciting, too. Are you sure you want to—"

"Yes. An hour or two isn't long enough. I don't want to rush." He took her hand and led her out of the suite.

They had lunch at an outdoor coffee shop near one of the swimming pools. It was one of four restaurants at the resort, which also had enough athletic facilities to stage a mini-Olympics, a full schedule of activities and classes and a variety of posh shops. Lei had joined Marshall's staff during the hotel's construction, so she was able to tell Paul about some of the problems they'd faced.

Later, as they drove north up the coast through progressively greener terrain, she filled him in on Marshall's previous projects here, an office building in Hilo and some condos in Keauhou. As much as Paul appreciated the briefing, he wished she would talk about something more personal for once.

They rounded the northern tip of the island and turned south, driving parallel to the coast through the Kohala Mountains. Far below him, Paul could see the grassland and volcanic desert they'd passed through on the way up. The highlands, by contrast, contained a series of verdant cattle ranches broken up by brushland. It began to rain, storming violently where it was lush but barely sprinkling where it was dry. He'd heard of microclimates, but this was the first time he'd seen such dramatic examples of them.

The mountains were so unexpectedly cool and lovely after the coast that he hated to see them disturbed. "This is sacrilege from a developer—I can hardly believe I'm saying it—but it's a shame to ruin all this with condos," he remarked.

Lei's face lit up with pleasure. "It's a perfect thing to say! You have the soul of a Hawaiian. If the project were really going to do that, I could never work on it, but fortunately it's down near Waimea. The area is more suburban than agricultural."

She added that most Big Islanders favored growth for the wealth and jobs it would bring. They drove the final few miles to the site, parking next to the trailer that served as the project's office. Harry Topping was waiting inside.

He told them that Thursday's meeting had been put off for a day to accommodate the county's planning director, then took them on a tour. The complex would be luxurious but unexceptional, a typical compound for the wealthy. Paul left with a stack of material to review for Friday's meeting.

They drove back through Waimea, once the company town for the three-hundred-thousand-acre Parker Cattle Ranch but now the sprawling little hub of this area. Their hotel was about ten miles to the west. When they got back, Lei went down for a swim, while Paul headed for the driving range.

He went shopping afterward, taking so long that she was dressed and waiting when he returned. He found her sitting in the lounge, wearing a strapless sundress with a fitted bodice and softly draped skirt, her hair tumbling sensually down her back. She smiled at him, and suddenly he desired her in every way there was—not just physically, but mentally and spiritually, as well. He wanted intimacy, not just passion.

"I'm sorry I'm late." He handed her a shopping bag. "This is for you. I wanted it to be exactly right."

Lei reddened a little. The gift was from a shop that specialized in intimate apparel, all of it feminine and seductive. "Is it for later?"

"If you want it to be. I'm going to get cleaned up. I won't be long." He strode into his bedroom.

She took out a gift-wrapped box. A white silk nightgown and matching peignoir were inside. The present was much too expensive to accept, but if she refused it, Paul would be hurt. He'd obviously put a lot of effort into selecting it. She caressed the delicate lace trim. She'd never owned anything this beautiful.

She was still arguing with herself when he walked back into the lounge. "This is very beautiful," she said, "but it must have cost you a fortune. I really shouldn't—"

"I can't wait to see you in it."

"But Paul—"

"It's more for me than for you. A totally selfish present. Besides, I enjoy buying you things."

That was the crux of it. He enjoyed spoiling her and she enjoyed being spoiled. It wasn't right. "That's very generous of you, but—"

"Generous?" He rolled his eyes. "Hell, Lei, before I was 'sweet' and now I'm 'generous.' If you're going to keep insulting me, I'll stop giving you things."

She couldn't help smiling. "You *should* stop. We can return this on our way to the restaurant."

"Okay, but don't say you didn't ask for this." He helped her up from the couch. "Keep it and I won't buy you anything else. Refuse it and I'll bury you with gifts. You'll get sick of returning them. I'm warning you—I can be ruthless."

She stopped fighting him. The truth was that she adored the gown and peignoir and wanted to wear them for him. "Then I have no choice," she said. "Thank you. I love it."

They went down to dinner, sitting at a quiet table for two overlooking the ocean. They made small talk about their favorite books and movies as they ate, but Lei was so besotted that Paul could have recited the dictionary and she would have thought he was brilliant. She was thrilled just to be with him.

The band arrived, playing a Hawaiian standard and then a ballad. He led her to a dark corner of the dance floor and pulled her close. She sighed and closed her eyes. He was so warm, so strong.

Toward the end of the song, he slid his hand downward and pressed her intimately against him. Her mouth went dry with excitement. He'd never done that before. He moved slowly and provocatively, coaxing her to do the same. Her arms tightened around his neck, and her body grew hot and eager. If the feel of him fully clothed could do this to her...

"Paul..." she whispered. "Let's go upstairs."

"I'd rather dance awhile longer." He nuzzled her hair. "And talk. I know so little about you."

The song ended and they separated. His face was flushed and his eyes were hot and intense. "You don't look like you want to talk," she said shyly.

"But I do. I want to make love to someone I really know, not to an enigma. I was hoping you'd tell me about yourself, but you don't seem to trust me."

"Of course I trust you." How could she explain it when she didn't understand it herself? "I'm just a very private person. I'm not sure why. My childhood, I guess."

He walked her back to the table and helped her into her chair. "So tell me about it," he said as he sat down. "Your parents—how did they meet?"

She hesitated. "Does it really mean that much to you?"

"Yes." He took her hand. "Think about how you felt when I told you about my childhood...about Karen and Melissa. Think about what it meant to you."

She'd understood him better. She'd felt closer to him. God help her, but she'd fallen in love with him—and wanted him to do the same with her.

The barriers dropped a little. "I'd have to start with my grandparents. My mother's parents."

He smiled in approval. "The *kahuna* and her husband."

"Yes—Liliha and Kapahe. She was from Kauai. He'd gone there to work. Niihau men used to do that when

drought struck the island and times got hard. They met and
fell in love. People thought he was brave to marry her.
Everyone knew about her family—about their powers.''

"She probably cast a spell on him." He kissed her palm,
then released her hand. "It runs in the family."

If it had, she would have made Paul fall in love with her.
Blushing, she continued with her story. "They returned to
Niihau and had two children, my uncle and my mother. Liliha was a great believer in education. She wanted her children to have options. Niihau only had a few grades of school
at the time, so she sent my uncle to her family on Kauai for
junior high. He came back to Niihau to work as a *paniolo*—a cowboy—but my mother was more ambitious. She
wanted to be a teacher. She went to junior high and high
school on Kauai, then to UH."

"Where your father was one of her professors. I'll bet she
fell in love with him."

Her eyes widened in surprise. "How did you know?"

"Just a lucky guess."

Or maybe *he* had powers. "She never showed it, though,
because he was married. She returned to Niihau and devoted herself to the children there. Over the next dozen
years, he wrote four important books about the islands and
grew more and more famous and admired. He'd always
been fascinated by Niihau, and he was able to get permission to go there one summer to do research. He hired my
mother as his assistant."

"And the poor guy never had a chance. She cast a spell
on him."

"I'm sure she tried to," Lei said with a smile. "She fell in
love with him all over again, and with Tom, too. He was
thirteen and he desperately needed a mother. Mom married
Dad that fall and moved to Manoa. I was born a year later."

Ella's ties to her homeland had been strong, Lei added, so
she had taken Lei there for the summer each year. "Nowadays people think of Niihau as a unique part of our heritage that should be left in peace, but in those days it was

considered backward and deprived. People wanted to bring it into the twentieth century. The other kids were always asking me questions, always making fun of it. I tried to defend our way of life, but they wouldn't listen. I wasn't more than seven or eight when I decided it was none of their business and stopped talking about it."

"Then you felt closer to Niihau than Oahu?"

She looked at the table, remembering the pain and confusion of those times. "I guess so. Dad died of a heart attack when I was ten and Mom moved to Niihau permanently. Eventually she got her old job back. It wasn't easy being *hapa haole* when almost all the other kids were pure Hawaiian. I got teased about my looks, my perfect English and the funny way I spoke Hawaiian. Finally I threatened to have Liliha pray them to death if they didn't stop, and they were so frightened they hardly spoke to me after that. When Mom asked if I wanted to go to high school at Kamehameha, I jumped at the chance. For one thing, Tom was a chemistry professor at UH by then and I knew I'd see a lot of him. He was my big brother and I idolized him. And almost everyone there was like me—part Hawaiian. For the first time in my life, I felt I belonged somewhere."

"So you were happy there."

"Very happy. And I was happy at UH, too. I lived with Tom and his wife, Cindy. She'd just had the twins, but money was tight so she'd gone back to work. I took care of the kids more than she or Tom did. They called me 'Mama' before they called her that." She looked at the table, overcome by emotion. "They're so like Tom! I miss him so much."

Paul signed the check and got up. He put a comforting arm around Lei's waist as they walked out of the restaurant, and after a few seconds, she rested her head on his shoulder. "They still call you 'Mommy,'" he said gently. "That surprised me. How old were they when . . . ?"

"Three. I was 'Auntie Lei' by then, but after a while they switched to 'Mommy.' I was thrilled. In my mind, I *was* their mother. I'd even started adoption proceedings."

"You were only twenty and you took full responsibility for them?" He hugged her close. "You're a marvel. They're lucky to have you."

"They'd known me all their lives. We loved each other." She hesitated, then told him something she'd never told another soul. "They were as much mine as Tom and Cindy's, Paul. I would have fought anyone who'd tried to get them. But I was lucky. No one did."

"Cindy's family...?"

"She was from Boston. Tom met her in college. Her parents agreed I was the best one to take over. The kids' only other relatives are Marie's family in France and some cousins of Dad's on Maui they hardly know."

They went upstairs to the lounge and sat down on the couch. Lei waited for Paul to say or do something, but he seemed to be lost in thought. Finally she asked, "Was there anything else you wanted to know?"

"No. It's just that you're so..." He paused and started again. "What I'm trying to say is, I've finally put things together. You've had the kids since you were a girl. They told me you'd never had a boyfriend. Whatever you need those pills for, it's not birth control. I can't do it, Lei. It would be like violating the Madonna."

Given the way he'd pursued her, his sudden reservations were as unexpected as they were irrational. She was suddenly tired of all the evasions, tired of fighting both him and herself, tired of resisting fate. She'd told him everything else. She might as well tell him about the prophecy. Whether he believed it or not wasn't her problem.

"My grandmother can see the future," she said softly. "She told me I'd offer myself to a blue-eyed, blond-haired man. I thought she was wrong. I'd never been attracted to a *haole*. But then you came. I tried to resist you, but I couldn't." She paled. "I tried because you're going to hurt me badly—physically, I mean. I know you won't want to, but for some reason you will. Liliha saw it in her—it's like a crystal ball. And she saw fear and anguish, too. I'm tired of waiting and being afraid, Paul. If that's my destiny, I just want to get it over with.''

For a moment, Paul was too dumbfounded to speak. Fortune-telling and crystal balls...? How could someone as intelligent as Lei believe in things like that?

He stared at her. So she wanted to get it over with, did she? That was swell. He was nothing but the fulfillment of some lunatic prophecy. "And that's why you came with me? Because it was fated and you had no choice?''

She shrank from him as if he'd seared her soul. "I came because I wanted to," she said in a small voice. "I'm in love with you. What choice did I have but to want to?''

He felt like a total heel now. She loved him and he'd upset her, made her cringe. The least he could do was keep an open mind. "Look, Lei—I'm not saying there's no such thing as prescience. Maybe there is and maybe your grandmother has it. Maybe she even saw us together. But the rest of it is just plain nuts. I'd never hurt you. I'd cut off my right arm before I—" He stopped abruptly. Maybe he *would* hurt her. The room began to spin. He felt queasy with confusion and shock. "You're, uh, a virgin. It might hurt no matter how careful I am. But only a little—not badly. And that stuff about fear and anguish..." He shook his head. "She makes it sound like I'm going to torture you, make you afraid of me. And that's impossible. There's no way I'd do that.''

"But you'll leave me. And it's going to hurt so damn much when you do." Her eyes welled up and she turned away. "If that isn't fear and anguish...''

He cursed softly and pulled her into his arms. "You think I don't want to love you and be your husband? You think I don't want to love your kids and be their father?'' He lifted her chin. "I do, Lei, but only if I can give you everything you need. I want to be sure, because otherwise I'll hurt you even more. And I'd hate myself if I did that.''

Lei put her arms around him and buried her face against his neck. He didn't want to leave her. He was simply afraid of giving too little, of falling short and hurting her.

She prayed that it wouldn't happen—that if he truly tried to love them, he'd succeed; that the fear and anguish would have some other cause; that whatever it was, whenever it struck, they would conquer it together.

She nuzzled his neck, murmuring between kisses, ''You'll give me what I need. You already do. Make love to me, Paul.''

''I can't. I told you . . . it would be like—''

She brushed her lips across his mouth to silence him, and he sucked in his breath. ''Don't do that,'' he groaned. ''You're not being logical about this.''

''Logic is an overrated commodity. I prefer emotion.'' She kissed him more insistently, gently nipping his lips. ''And magic.'' And again, teasing him with her tongue. ''And pleasure. Nobody's ever made me feel the way you do.''

''God, Lei . . .''

It was as if a dam had burst. He took her mouth with such need and passion that she knew he wasn't going to stop. Then he pulled away, led her into his bedroom and silently undressed her. She got into bed and slid beneath the covers as he stripped off his clothes. It seemed impossible that his nakedness had once frightened her. Now it only excited her.

He slipped in beside her and took her in his arms. ''Lei . . . I want you to know—I haven't been with anyone since Karen left in August. I had a complete physical in December. You don't have to worry that—''

''I wasn't worried.'' He never would have risked her health. She stroked his cheek and smiled. ''Stop stalling and make love to me, *haole*.''

He caressed and kissed her with a tender ardor that brought a fierce joy to her heart. Then, as his lovemaking became more intimate and intense, she stopped telling herself how sweet he was and thought only of the next arousing touch, the next hungry kiss. Finally he slid on top of her and rubbed himself gently against her, and there was nothing but the warm, exciting feel of him driving her higher and higher. Desperate for release, she wrapped her legs around him and strained closer.

After a few moments, he grasped her hips to still them. "Easy, sweetheart. Let's take this slowly."

She reddened. "Yes. All right. I'm sorry."

"Don't be. You're incredible. Passionate, sweet, exciting...."

He began to ease himself inside her, going a fraction deeper with each gentle stroke. It was so erotic and pleasurable that the first stab of pain caught her off guard, and she flinched in shock.

He immediately withdrew. "Try to relax, sweetheart. It'll be okay."

She nodded. "Don't worry—I'll be fine."

He entered her again, working his way inside her with the same tender restraint as before, then applying a shade more pressure. The pain was even worse this time; she recoiled even more violently. She took a deep breath and fought down the tension in her body. "I'm all right. Keep going."

"But Lei..."

"Please, Paul. Just keep going."

"Yeah. All right." There was another stab of pain as he pressed himself against her, but she didn't move an inch. She simply gritted her teeth and endured it.

He pulled away, looking ashen. "I've never done this before, but I don't think it's supposed to be this hard. Maybe you should see a doctor."

"No. I don't want a doctor to touch me that way." It had been bad enough going for the pills. "I love you. I want *you* to do it. Don't be afraid of hurting me. You don't have to be so gentle." She saw how reluctant he was and forced herself to smile. "Believe me, this is nothing compared to the cramps I used to get every month. You can make it up to me later."

He nodded grimly and parted her thighs. It was just like the vision after that. She lay there, as stoic as a board, wanting to run after the first powerful thrust but trusting him enough to stay. Two more deep, hard thrusts and it was over. He withdrew at once, turned onto his side and cuddled her against his chest.

She didn't realize there were tears in her eyes until he brushed them away and asked if she was all right. He looked thoroughly shaken.

"Yes. It doesn't hurt anymore." He was still aroused; she could feel him against her thigh. "You didn't have to stop. Come back inside me."

"You can't possibly want me to—not after that. You must think sex is the pits."

"Of course I don't. It was wonderful at first. Anyway, I want to make you happy." He didn't look impressed with that particular argument, so she added softly, "Just touch me and kiss me. You know how it affects me."

When he didn't answer, she reached under the covers and took him in her hand. He tensed, but he didn't pull away. As she stroked and teased him, his fingers found her breast and his lips found her mouth. He went slowly at first, but there was no real need. The lightest caress, the briefest taste, and she wanted him all over again.

It wasn't as sweet and tender this time; they were both too aroused. She was so eager for him by the time he entered her that the slight soreness she felt barely registered. She got hotter and hotter with each skillful, erotic thrust, and then he caressed her with his fingers, and wave after wave of pleasure coursed through her body.

His own release came moments later. She was panting and dazed by then, able only to hold him tightly and ride out the storm.

Afterward, while they were still fused and breathing raggedly, she broke into giggles. It was a crazy reaction, but she couldn't help it. "Wow! That was just like in the movies. If Liliha had seen *that* in her glass, I wouldn't have cared a whit about the pain part."

"No?" He smiled and smoothed her hair. "And the rest of it? Are you still worried about fear and anguish?"

Her greatest fear—that she wasn't truly important to him—had proved groundless. As long as there was hope, nothing else mattered. "Liliha's other visions came true and that will, too. I can't change it. I can only accept it and hope for the best."

"Talk about self-fulfilling prophecies! You believed we were going to be lovers so you came to me last Thursday. You were frightened of being hurt so you tensed up, and that made it hurt even more. The next time something bad happens, you'll probably say to yourself, 'Aha! *That* was the fear and anguish my grandmother saw.' She can't lose."

Lei screwed up her face. "*Haole* skeptic! You have an answer for everything, don't you?" She tried to wriggle away, but he grinned and kept her pinned beneath him. "Bossy, too," she said, not really minding. "Okay, Mr. Know-it-all-from-the-mainland, if there's no such thing as destiny or the supernatural, why have there been three accidents at Waikane? You tried to find people to blame, but you couldn't, and do you know why you couldn't? Because—"

"I know. It was fate. Some things are not meant to be. When the moon is full and the wolfsbane is blooming—"

"Oh, shut up." Laughing, she pushed against his chest. He grinned and rolled onto his back. "The fact is, things keep happening out there. Somebody could get hurt."

"I'm surprised you don't think fate will prevent us from building there," he said.

"Fate is strong, but so is the human will. I don't know which will win." She wiggled back to him and draped herself over his chest. She was suddenly very serious. "Paul? Can I tell you something?"

"Sure." He toyed with the amulet around her neck. "What is this? Some kind of good luck charm?"

"Yes. My mother gave it to me. Don't you dare make fun of it." She paused. "About Waikane...I want you to know that I have faith in you. If you decide to keep trying—"

"If?" He laughed softly and shook his head. "Remember what I said about my first obligation being to Marshall and not letting our relationship affect my recommendation?"

"Of course. I'd never ask you to—"

"You can forget it. I can't make love to you and not move heaven and earth to try to make you happy. I've been a total idiot. I don't know why it took me so long to figure out how much I love you, unless it's because I've never felt this way before."

Lei had never expected to hear that—not so soon and not with such quiet certainty. She threw her arms around his neck and hugged him fiercely. "Oh, Paul! I love you so much."

He moved his hand to her bottom, caressing rather than massaging. "In that case, am I forgiven for being a bossy skeptic?"

"I haven't given up yet. I know I can turn you into a believer if only..." He stroked the inside of her thigh, and she shuddered. "Is that what you're going to do every time I argue with you? Make love to me?"

"You're sure it's okay? There wasn't any pain?"

"No." There had been, just a little, but there was no way she could stop herself from having him again. Her passion for him was too overwhelming.

Chapter Fifteen

Liliha had been right about Lei having a strong will. She wanted Paul to understand that there was more to human existence than the physical, perceptible world, and when she wanted something, she went after it.

She lay beside him in bed the next morning and brooded about it. Maybe she *was* worried about the future, just a little. She wanted his comfort and support, but his words would be empty platitudes unless he could accept the validity of Liliha's visions. Besides, his arguments about Waikane would carry more passion and conviction once he'd recognized that transcendent forces were at work. People in Hawaii took fate seriously. A believer might be able to sway them.

Convincing him wouldn't be easy, though. His mind was only inches from closed. She'd have to carefully lead him, not hit him over the head and drag him.

He woke and reached for her, and she snuggled into his arms. "Let's go to the volcano today," she said. "It's fascinating country. They show a film of Kilauea erupting that's just spectacular.''

He ran his hand down her back and fondled her bottom. ''Who needs Kilauea?'' He nuzzled her neck and throat. ''We'll make our own eruption.''

''But Paul...''

He caressed her breasts. ''But what?''

She couldn't think straight when he touched her that way. ''Never mind. It doesn't matter.''

He pulled away, repeating the question so firmly that she didn't dare not answer. ''It hurt a little the last time we made love. I know I should have said something, but I was too excited to stop. Just be careful, okay?''

''I'll be careful in a couple of days. Let's eat and go sightseeing.'' He reached for the phone. ''I'll have breakfast sent up. What do you want?''

She made a face at him as he punched in the number. ''How come you have so much willpower? I don't.''

''Room service just answered. Are orange juice and Danish okay?''

''I guess so, although how you can think about food at a time like this...'' She reluctantly sat up.

Smiling, he ordered and hung up. ''Actually, I don't,'' he said. ''Have much willpower, that is. Do me a favor and get dressed, because if I walk out of the shower and find you naked in my bed...''

Mollified, she pecked him on the cheek and told him she'd meet him in the lounge. They left immediately after breakfast, driving south through the Kohala desert past Kailua, then climbing into the cool, green hills of the Kona district, where coffee and macadamia nuts were grown. The area had been a favorite of Hawaiian royalty and was dotted with ancient temples and petroglyphs and charming old towns where the earliest *haole* settlers had lived. Paul would have liked to stop and explore, but Lei told him there wasn't time. The volcano was two more hours away and would take the whole afternoon to see.

As a result, he was puzzled when she turned off the road south of Kealakekua Bay, where Cook had been killed, and drove *makai* to a national historic park on the stark, wind-whipped coast. *Pu'uhonua o Honaunau*—the place of refuge of Honaunau—dated to the early fifteenth century, she said. The home of a long line of ruling chiefs, it had also been a sanctuary for violators of the *kapu* system, the ancient religious laws. The penalty for that had been death, but if an offender could escape to a refuge like *Honaunau*, powerful priests would purify him so he could live out his life in safety. During wartime, women, children and the elderly had also found protection in such sanctuaries, as had defeated warriors.

Huge, fierce figures guarded the land, wooden replicas of the ancient gods. An L-shaped lava-stone wall, three hundred feet long and ten feet high, ran inland from the shore and divided the sanctuary from the palm-shaded area where royalty had once lived. Great chiefs had probably chosen this spot because it was sacred, but Paul also found it very beautiful—the black lava rock, the graceful green palms, the whitecaps foaming in an azure sea. He walked among the thatched houses on the reconstructed palace grounds and spoke with people in native costume demonstrating ancient crafts, thinking that if it hadn't been for the other tourists, he might have believed he'd gone back in time.

"It makes me feel guilty that white men ever came here," he said, wondering if Lei had stopped here so he would understand her people's history better. "We brought disease and devastation. We destroyed your way of life."

"Expansion and conquest. It's the history of the world, even of early Hawaii. The first people to reach these islands were much gentler than the warlike tribes who followed and conquered them. The arrival of the Europeans was just the next inevitable step." She took his hand. "Come. Let's visit the *pu'uhonua*."

They crossed in front of the great stone wall. A reconstructed *heiau*, one of three here, was on the other side. "The bones of twenty-three chiefs were once buried here," she said. "Their *mana* was very powerful. It protected this place. Even though their bones were removed and hidden in 1929, I still feel something when I walk here."

"Because the land is sacred?"

"Yes, and because the chiefs who lived here loved this spot so much. I think that something of them remained behind—that they still watch over it."

She was looking at him so expectantly that he realized more than history was at stake. "You want me to feel what you feel, but I can't. Maybe I have the wrong blood in my veins."

"Blood has nothing to do with it. It's a question of opening your heart and spirit." She paused. "We'll walk a little more. It takes time to absorb the aura of a place."

As they followed the trail past the other two *heiaus*, she said softly, "Look around you. Imagine that you're a *kapu* breaker in the time of Kamehameha. How do you feel?"

"Awestruck, I suppose. Frightened of the priests. And relieved to be alive."

Lei told herself that he'd answered too quickly, from his mind rather than his heart. "But Paul Lindstrom of twentieth-century California sees only piles of rock and feels nothing, hmm?"

"It's beautiful and fascinating," he replied. "I'm sorry, but that's the best I can do."

She told herself to be patient. The forces of so-called reason had had over thirty years to infect him. It would take time to effect a cure.

They walked back to the car and continued south through the coffee country to an area ravaged by lava flows from Mauna Loa, which was about twenty miles *mauka*. In the sections reached by rain, ferns, lichen and then trees had sprung up on the harsh, charred land, but the drier areas remained black and barren. Like the Kohala Mountains, South Kona was a patchwork of microclimates.

After rounding the southern tip of the island, they drove northeast through rolling countryside planted with sugarcane, grasses and fruit trees. Paul found the area peaceful and very lovely, especially after the sea came into view, crashing turbulently against the black lava rock at the shore. If he'd lived and worked on this beautiful island, he would have fought for careful, thoughtful development—for affordable housing and for projects that provided good jobs without raping the land. One Oahu was enough.

Then, with jarring abruptness, they came to a place so gray and wasted that even the grass and scrub looked sickly—Volcanoes National Park. Lava flows crisscrossed the land, some smooth and ropy, others chunky and jagged, and the smell of sulfer filled the air. Kilauea Caldera came into view about fifteen minutes later.

They ate lunch in the Volcano House, a small inn near the rim of the crater, and then stopped into the Art Center across the street. Paul bought gifts carved from milo wood for his friends in San Francisco and a small seascape that reminded him of the coast near their hotel.

They reached the visitor center just as the film was beginning. Molten lava, bright orange and spewing flame, spurted hundreds of feet into the air in curtainlike rows of pulsating fountains; cascaded over towering cliffs in great, wide torrents; flowed to the sea with amazing speed, a fiery river that destroyed everything in its wake. Paul could see why Hawaiians were superstitious. Nature, usually so gentle in these islands, could turn on them at a moment's notice.

There hadn't been any major eruptions lately, but the entire area was seething with geologic activity. They circled the two-mile-wide caldera on Crater Rim Road, leaving the car to look at sulfurous gases hissing out of cracks and vents, to gaze across smoking firepits, to stare *mauka* at Mauna Loa, tranquil and snow-capped in the distance. Halemaumau Crater, where the volcano goddess Pele was said to live, was on the far side of the caldera, at the halfway point of the road.

After parking the car, they started along the trail to the crater's rim. A short distance ahead of them, two young men dressed in ragged jeans knelt by a smoking fissure and scavenged around on the ground. When one of them picked up a couple of lava rocks, Lei bolted forward and marched up to them. Paul stopped about a yard behind her. He didn't want to intrude unless she needed him.

"This is Pele's domain," she said in a pleasant but firm voice. "Those rocks belong to her. Please put them back."

The man holding the rocks looked her up and down appreciatively. "Listen, babe, Pele has more rocks than she knows what to do with. She won't miss a few."

Lei smiled coolly. "You never know. She's jealous of what's hers. She's been known to make people pay for stealing from her."

He stuck the rocks in his pocket and stood up. "She'll have to go all the way to Texas to do it, then. Cause quite a stir, I'll wager. Maybe I'll sell tickets."

"This is a national park. It's against federal law to remove anything—even rocks," she pointed out.

His friend laughed and got to his feet. "Come on, Jeff. Let's get out of here before she sets the rangers on us."

Paul told himself they were total jerks. Even more to the point, they'd upset the woman he loved. He stepped forward, then said in a cool, foreboding tone, "I'd obey the lady if I were you. She comes from a long line of *kahunas*—powerful native priests." His voice grew softer and more sinister. "She can see the future. Cure the sick. Kill people with her mind. And she's very protective of her islands."

Jeff laughed nervously. "Yeah, sure." He glanced at his friend, who was looking at Lei uneasily. She stared back, fierce and implacable. "Hell, if it means that much to her..." He tossed the rocks onto the ground and the two of them walked away.

Paul and Lei smiled at each other as they continued toward the crater. "That was well done," she said. "My grandmother says *kahunas* shouldn't use their powers to hurt people, but those two make it tempting." She sighed and shook her head. "They have no respect. They'll probably go someplace else and pick up other rocks."

"Maybe not. They were afraid of you. You looked damn menacing." They stopped by a metal barricade a few yards in front of the rim of the crater. Flowers, fruit and trinkets had been left on the ground between the fence and the rim. "What you said about Pele controlling this land and protecting what's hers... You didn't really believe that, did you? You just think people have no business taking anything."

Instead of answering, she climbed over the barricade and took some fruit out of her purse. After leaving it with the other offerings, she rejoined Paul and said gravely, "I hope she wasn't listening. She can be spiteful at times."

He gaped at her. "You've got to be kidding. I mean, a goddess who spews fire when she gets cranky—who has to be bribed and placated... No rational person could believe stuff like that."

"A friend once told me that he'd picked up a beautiful red-haired woman between Kona and Hilo. She fell asleep in the back seat. He never stopped the car, but when he finally arrived in Hilo, the seat was empty. There are many such stories. I was raised on them. I consider myself perfectly rational, but I don't disbelieve them." She gazed out over the crater. "There's something eerie and otherworldly about this place. Don't you think so?"

Paul loved Lei and wanted to understand her, but he wasn't going to pretend he felt something he didn't. "It's a volcano, Lei. It probably looks like every other volcano on the planet. It erupts because this area is geologically active, not because some goddess is in a snit."

"Her anger might have nothing to do with it. Some say she can sense impending disaster and appears to warn us." She turned to face him. "Every year dozens of people send back rocks that they've stolen from Pele's domain, saying they've had nothing but bad luck ever since. You can call it a coincidence, but I doubt many Hawaiians would agree with you. There's talk of developing geothermal energy here, but some oppose it as a desecration of Pele's sacred grounds. Nobody laughs at them or calls them *pupule*."

"So everyone pays lip service to a charming old legend. That doesn't mean they really believe in it."

"But they do." She smiled serenely. "Standing here, I feel things that can't be seen or heard. I rejoice in that. The world would be a very dull place if everything were logical and easily explained."

"You think I disagree?" He grinned and added in his best Rod Serling voice, "You're traveling through another dimension, a dimension not only of sight and sound—"

"But of mind. Absolutely." She laughed and took his arm. "So you're a *Twilight Zone* fan. There's hope for you yet."

"I hate to disappoint you, but I've never taken a single episode seriously. I've never confused fiction with real life."

They started back to the car. "You wouldn't like the show if it didn't touch something deep inside you. Open your mind to it and let it grow."

Paul didn't reply. Lei's notions were too fanciful not to challenge, but he didn't really want to change her. Her Hawaiian view of life was as captivating as her exotic Polynesian beauty.

They spent the rest of the day in the park, driving to the coast and then circling up to Hilo. By the time they'd had dinner and continued on their way, it was very late and Lei was half-asleep. The last stretch of road, from coast to coast through Waimea, was so dark and deserted that Paul half expected to spot a flame-haired goddess on the way. Almost, but not quite.

Lei awoke the next morning to find a bouquet of red anthuriums on the night table with a note from Paul tucked into the blooms saying he'd see her later. She yawned and stretched. She vaguely remembered him asking her if she'd mind if he played golf this morning. She didn't, of course. She wanted him to enjoy himself.

They'd been curled up in bed at the time, Paul snuggled up behind her, holding her as she drifted off to sleep. She wished he could do that every night for the rest of their lives. She'd felt so loved and secure....

She spent the morning window-shopping and swimming. It was pleasant but a little lonely, especially when she spotted some children who reminded her of the twins in the coffee shop. She'd called them each evening, but she hadn't missed them badly until now. She wished they could come for the weekend.

It was out of the question, though. She couldn't share a bed with her lover when her children were around, and besides, they would get on Paul's nerves. She knew that from Saturday night. Even *she* got tired and impatient at times, but she loved them, and that made all the difference. She could only hope that someday he would, too.

He was sitting in the lounge when she returned, eating a sandwich as he skimmed material for the meeting that afternoon. They left for Waimea an hour later. All in all, things went very well. Unlike Waikane, there was no opposition to the project. Paul and the planning director made a number of suggestions that the architect promised to incorporate, and everyone agreed to keep in touch.

As they walked back to the car, Lei said, "There's a place I'd like to visit—a very special *heiau*. We passed the turnoff on Wednesday, but there wasn't enough time to go there. It's very old—fifteen hundred years—and very sacred. King Kamehameha I was born a short distance up the road. His birth rites were observed there."

If he suspected she had an ulterior motive, he didn't say so, although he smiled tolerantly when she asked him to stop at a florist so she could buy a couple of leis—a traditional offering, she explained. Until the 1960's, the *heiau* had been *kapu* to everyone but priests. It was still relatively inaccessible, located at the northern tip of the island on a rutted dirt path off a narrow, unmarked road. Lei thought that was as it should be. Casual tourists and curiosity seekers didn't belong at such a sacred place.

There was only a single car in the dirt parking lot. As they walked up a gentle hill to the *heiau* itself, they passed a family of five going the other way, all of them dressed in aloha attire. Paul stopped for a moment to look around. The land here was spare and hard, the sea endless and fierce. Perhaps it had taken a place this harsh to produce a king great enough to unify the islands.

The *heiau* was very large, a high, rectangular platform made of layer upon layer of black volcanic rock. They followed a dirt path through a break in the rocks into the *heiau*'s center, then stood all alone, surrounded by the past. The sole reminders of the twentieth century were the offerings people had left.

Neither of them spoke for a while. Then Lei handed Paul one of the leis and set the other on the stones. In a soft, sweet voice, she chanted something in Hawaiian—a prayer for her islands and her people, she said.

"This is the most affecting place I know," she added. "The *kahuna nui* of this *heiau* has made it her mission to bring Hawaii's children here to learn about their past. They feel joy and pride here. Some see warriors—their *kupuna*, their ancestors. The heiau touches their spirits. That's a rare and important thing in this cold, material world."

"Yes. It is." Paul set his lei next to hers. "And you? Have you ever seen warriors?"

"No, but I've felt their presence." She paused. "Sometimes people experience the past here. The distant past. Before they were born."

He was beyond surprise by now. Even reincarnation didn't faze him. "You mean a past life, I take it."

"Either that or a tribal memory. I had a vision the first time I came here. I was only sixteen. I like to think I have the same spirit as the girl I saw."

"Who were you? What happened?"

She hesitated, then blushed and shook her head. "Maybe some other time. What do you think of this place?"

He told himself it must have been one hell of a vision. He couldn't wait to hear about it. "It's forbidding, but there's also a sense of peace. I like it."

"So you feel more here than you did at Waikane or Honaunau?"

He smiled gently. "Of course I do, but there's nothing mystical about that. I've read about Kamehameha. I admire him tremendously. It's so isolated and timeless here that I can almost picture him standing beside us."

"But don't you feel something spiritual, too? Don't you sense the aura of sanctity here?"

"Not really." She looked so dejected that he added quickly, "The scale here is immense. It makes me feel small and insignificant. It's only natural to wonder why I'm here and ask myself what I want to accomplish during my life."

"And do you have an answer?"

"Once I would have settled for leaving the world a better place." He looked at her tenderly. "Lately I've gotten more selfish."

Glowing with pleasure, she teased, "Have you really? And what more could you possibly want?"

"Happiness. Real, honest-to-God happiness—with you." He took her hand. "Would it be profane to suggest going back to the hotel?"

She smiled. "I don't think so. How can love be profane?"

They stopped at Kamehameha's birthplace, then drove home. Lei told herself she'd made real progress that day. There was more inside Paul then he knew. She simply had to show him the way.

She pulled him into her arms the moment they were alone in the suite. "You know what I think, *haole*? If you want happiness, you'll have to be liberated first."

He cupped her bottom and pressed her erotically close. She fought the urge to forget about educating him and caress him back. "Liberated, huh? From what?"

"Logic. Reason. You deny—" He cut her off with a kiss. She allowed him a brief, exciting taste, then pulled away and finished unsteadily, "You deny the spiritual side of your nature, but that doesn't mean it doesn't exist. It's just that—"

"Later, sweetheart. I'd rather concentrate on the physical side of my nature right now."

"But if you won't listen—"

"I'll listen later." He pulled her blouse out of her skirt, unhooked her bra and took a nipple between his fingers. Her body remembered the pleasures of Wednesday night and responded swiftly and ardently.

It was hard to concentrate, but she was very determined. "I don't want to make love yet. I want to talk."

"Whatever the lady wants..." He smiled rakishly. "There are two conditions, though. We have to talk naked together in bed, and you have to tell me about the vision you had at the *heiau*."

Since he could have seduced her in thirty seconds flat, it was probably the best deal she could hope for. "Okay, but no touching. And you really have to listen."

"Sounds logical and reasonable," he said. She shook her head, silently pronouncing him hopeless.

They undressed and got into bed. Seeing him naked and aroused, she was a lot less set on talking, but she wouldn't have admitted it for the world. That was obviously what he'd counted on.

"In my vision, I paddled out to an English ship in my canoe," she began. "It was hundreds of years ago. My breasts were bare and I had leis on my head and around my neck. I was curious about the sailors—about whether they were men like our own men or spirits of some kind. I decided to choose one and make love to him. I picked the tallest and strongest. He had—'' She stopped, jolted by the memory. "He had yellow hair and blue eyes. I'd forgotten that.''

Paul groaned softly. "You talk about naked breasts and making love and I'm not supposed to touch you?''

She forced back a smile. "Do you want to hear the rest of it or don't you?''

"There's more? I may have a nervous breakdown, but, yes. Go on.''

"He resisted me. His captain had forbidden any contact. I took his hand and pulled him below. Then I undressed him and—explored him. Very thoroughly. I ran my hand—''

"You can skip the details," he said gruffly. "I get the picture.''

"Oh. Well, the thing is, I was only sixteen—in real life, that is—and very naive. But the vision was very accurate. About men, I mean. About their physical—''

"Right. I understand. What happened next?''

He sounded so frazzled that she couldn't resist milking the story for all it was worth. "We were naked together. I was fascinated by him. The hair on his body, his fair skin, the size and shape of his—''

"Dammit, Lei...''

"Of his hands," she finished innocently. "They were large and slender. He was very passionate and virile. He kissed and touched me until I was desperate for him. I'd never had such a lover. And then the captain walked in and chased me out, so I never did satisfy my curiosity.'' She smiled coyly. "Maybe I've been searching for him ever since.''

Paul rolled onto his side and pulled her against him. "You've found him, sweetheart. And you can satisfy your curiosity as many times as you want.''

She pushed against his chest. "Why should I want a man who breaks his promises?''

"All that passion and virility, probably." He nuzzled her lips. "Anyway, I'm not breaking it, just delaying it."

He had the spirit of a conqueror, she thought, and such men enjoyed the battle as much as the victory. She turned her head. "Don't you dare try to seduce me. You said we could talk about—"

"Later." He threaded his hand into her hair and brought her mouth to his lips.

She glared at him. "Try to kiss me and I'll bite you."

"Umm. Sounds exciting." He nibbled her lower lip and she nipped him back. He probed with his tongue, and she pressed her lips together firmly. Finally, with a lazy smile, he pushed her onto her back and took one of her nipples in his mouth. She tried to twist away, but he pinned her with his body. Ignoring her struggles, he stroked her belly, then moved his hand downward. She closed her thighs, but he wedged them open with a hard, determined leg and caressed her with playful, intimate flicks of his fingers.

She was too aroused to keep resisting by then. He suckled her until she was caressing him feverishly and touched her everywhere but where she ached to be touched. By the time his mouth moved lower, she was beyond shyness, beyond rational thought. She moaned and writhed against him, wanted him inside her but unable to get a word out.

Somehow he knew. He knelt between her legs, lifted her hips and entered her. She stared at him for a moment, then shuddered and closed her eyes. His strokes were slow, deep and tantalizing. When she was tense and panting, he settled himself on top of her and brought them both to a fiery release that seemed to go on forever.

"Now *that*," he said afterward, "is what I call magic."

Lei hugged him tightly. It *had* been magic—literally. Surely she could make him see that. "Before, when I was fighting you—why didn't you stop?" she asked.

He was taken aback. "You weren't fighting me. You were only pretending to fight me. It was a game."

"Yes, but how did you know?"

"Your eyes, your voice—you wanted to provoke me. And the way you described the vision—you knew you were turning me on. You *wanted* me to do what I did."

Naturally he had a logical explanation. "What about later, then? You always do exactly what I want, as if you can read my mind. How?"

"It's easy. You're so expressive. You don't hold anything back when we make love."

"I couldn't even if I wanted to. Not from you." She took his face in her hands. "Don't you see, darling? It isn't only your physical senses that tell you what I feel. We touch each other with our minds and spirits."

He kissed her nose and rolled onto his side. "Maybe you're right. It's so perfect with you I can't believe it. I feel incredibly close to you when we make love, like we're inside each other's skins, linked together somehow. It's not logical, just wonderful." He drew her against him. "I hope you're as happy as I am. I hope you're glad you came."

She wondered how long it would last, but it was the wrong time to ask. He'd finally begun to understand, and that was enough for now. "Of course I am," she said.

He smiled. "Even though you couldn't convince me that Pele wanders the local roads? Even though I couldn't feel the spirits at the place of refuge or sense anything sacred about Kamehameha's *heiau*?"

She tickled his chest in retaliation, and grinning, he captured her wrists and pulled them above her head. Undaunted, she said, "You're a defeated man, *haole*. Now that I've put a dent in that rational armor of yours, it's only a matter of time before I convert you."

"If you say so."

Still holding her wrists, he ran his other hand down her body, touching her wherever he pleased. She loved him in his playfully arrogant mood.

"Until I see the light, I suppose I'll have to appease you however I can," he drawled.

"You can't possibly be conceited enough to think sex would work," she retorted, "so you must plan to break your word and bribe me with another gift. That seascape, for example."

"So you knew it was for you." He continued caressing her, rubbing her nipples until they were taut and tingling. "Don't argue with me about accepting it. I bought it to remind you of our stay here."

He was totally impossible. How could she make him see that she didn't want him to spend his hard-earned money on things she didn't need? "Why should I argue? It's different now. We're lovers. In fact, I was in the art gallery this morning and I saw the most wonderful tiki..." Somehow she kept a straight face. "I know it would bring me good luck, but it was a little out of my price range. Will you buy it for me?"

Smiling indulgently, he released her wrists and pulled her on top of him. "Of course. I'm all for good luck."

She kissed him soundly. "Thank you. You're so good to me. Wait till you see it! It's by Jimmy Akala. It's carved from koa wood and worth every dime of the five thousand dollars he's asking."

She waited for him to howl in protest or burst out laughing, but he simply lay there. Finally he said, "We'll buy it after dinner. The gallery will still be open, right?"

He was downright pale, either appalled by her extravagance or worried about the cost. "For heaven's sake, Paul, I wasn't serious. I thought if I asked for something expensive enough, I would cure you of this crazy habit you have of spoiling me—"

"You're just saying that. You'd love to have it." He fingered her amulet. "I know how you feel about good-luck charms. I'm going to buy it for you."

He couldn't afford it; that was obvious now. "And how are you going to pay for it? I can tell you don't have the money."

He didn't deny it. "Don't worry about it."

"Men!" She rolled her eyes in exasperation. "Listen to me, will you? The things you've given me are beautiful, and I love them, but I don't want anything else. It would make me feel like a mistress, not a partner. In case you haven't noticed, I'm very independent."

"I noticed." He paused. "You're sure?"

"I'm sure." She smiled at the relief on his face. "Besides, I wouldn't want to bankrupt you. I love you."

"The tiki wouldn't have bankrupted me. Things are just a little tight right now." He settled her head on his chest and played with a lock of her hair. "Everett invited me to invest in one of his projects last year, but I didn't have enough money saved up. He loaned me the difference and I've been paying him back. And then a family problem came up."

His mother was the only relative he'd ever mentioned. Given his childhood, Lei assumed he never saw her. "I'm sorry. I hope it's nothing serious."

"My mother's husband is fighting cancer. He's had a grueling year. The medical bills are covered and he gets some disability, but it's not enough to live on. My mother was going crazy trying to work enough hours to cover their expenses and still take care of him, so I offered to help out. He's been doing much better lately. He hopes to return to work by the end of the year."

It was a moment before Lei answered. She was too moved. "Did anyone ever tell you what a fine man you are? After the awful childhood you had ... after the way he used you—"

"I made my peace with them years ago. My mother did the best she could—both of them did. I don't have much in common with them, but they're the only family I've got. Besides, I admire his courage." He paused. "About the tiki, sweetheart ... If you should change your mind—"

"It's a wonderful work of art, but if I were going to ask for a gift, it wouldn't be that."

"I know." He held her very tightly. "I don't want to leave you, either—not ever. Will you come to San Francisco with me when my job here is done?"

It wasn't a proposal, but even if it had been, she couldn't have accepted. She'd thought he understood that. "I can't, Paul. Hawaii is my home."

"And San Francisco is mine. The things I've struggled for all my life are there. I can't leave them, Lei." He smoothed her hair. "I'll find you a good job and a place to live. We'll get used to being a family. When it's right for us and the kids, we'll get married."

It was everything she'd ever wanted except for one thing, but the gap was unbreachable. She couldn't expect a man who'd scratched his way up from nothing and had heavy financial responsibilities to start all over again.

She swallowed back the lump in her throat. "Hawaii isn't just where I live, Paul. It's my homeland. The islands are a part of me—in my blood and in my soul. I could never leave them. Even as much as I love you, I'd long for them every moment."

"And if I left and you stayed behind? Wouldn't you long for me just as much?"

"Yes." Her eyes filled up.

"Then one of us will have to change our mind." He cupped her chin. "Don't cry, sweetheart. I'm not going anywhere yet."

"But you will. The vision in Liliha's glass-she said we'd be lovers, not husband and wife." Tears rolled down her cheeks. "Oh, Paul ... I can't bear it...."

"Listen to me."

His tone was gentle but firm. She sniffed and stared at him.

"The vision was wrong. Or incomplete. Or meant something else. We're going to be together forever."

"Do you really believe that?"

"I don't just believe it. I know it." He smiled confidently. "I know lots of things. You want to make love again, you're hungry and you miss your kids. So let's make love, and then you can call Mrs. Keala and tell her to put the twins on a plane tomorrow morning, and then we'll have dinner. Okay?"

She was stunned. There was no way he could have known all that—no rational way. Overwhelmed by the power of his *mana*, she murmured her agreement, then sought his lips.

Chapter Sixteen

Paul had assumed Lei was hungry because she'd eaten lunch early, and he'd known she missed the twins because she smiled at every child she saw. As for making love, she was so passionate and responsive that she never *didn't* want to make love. It was all perfectly logical—expect for one thing. He hadn't stopped to think; he'd simply known, just as he knew they were going to spend their lives together.

In his more rational moments he told himself it was wishful thinking. He couldn't give up the success he'd achieved and the security he'd finally attained and start all over again in Hawaii, but Lei would be lost anywhere else. She was rooted to this volcanic soil as surely as the Ohia trees near the volcano. She needed air suffused with magic in order to breathe.

Besides, there were the children. He didn't want to be like his own stepfather, an overbearing, humorless disciplinarian. Good fathers were wise and patient. They worked fewer hours than he did without counting the cost, and gave up golf in favor of trips to the zoo and days at the beach without resenting it. It was a tall order.

His elderly carpenter friend had a couple of favorite sayings he was always quoting: "You learn by doing" and "Begin as you mean to go on." Along with another old chestnut that probably came from some ancient Hollywood romance, "Listen to your heart," he figured it was the best advice he was likely to get. Unfortunately, trying to follow it turned his weekend into a total yo-yo.

Sometimes fatherhood was a breeze, like when he snorkeled with the twins or hit golf balls with Jason and felt as if he'd been a parent all his life. You did learn by doing, he'd thought in amazement. There was nothing to it.

Other times it was damn hard, like when Jessie kept teasing Jason at dinner even after Lei scolded her and he'd agonized about whether to get involved. "Begin as you mean to go on," he'd told himself. Your heart says you're going to marry the child's mother, even though your brain keeps listing the obstacles, so act like a father from the start.

So he'd had the effrontery to tell Jessie he'd take her upstairs if she didn't behave, and predictably, she'd replied that he wasn't her father and couldn't tell her what to do. It was as much a question as a challenge. He and Lei had been discreet that day, but obviously the kids had picked up on the change in their relationship and wondered what was going on.

Lei had thought for a moment, then come to a decision. The twins were to mind what Paul said, she'd announced. Naturally they'd asked her why. Was she going to marry him or something?

Paul was sorry he'd opened his mouth by then and relieved to have Lei do the talking. She explained with quiet eloquence that they loved each other and wanted to marry but had a problem about where to live. The kids had a dozen questions after that. She answered them all honestly, even the final one from the frighteningly precocious Jessie about whether Lei and Paul would share a bed that night the way Rachel's mommy and her boyfriend did.

Paul had been curious about that himself. Most of the single mothers he'd known over the years hadn't batted an eye at having their steady lovers over, but Lei was a lot more proper. He was disappointed but not surprised when she said no. Although he accepted it as cheerfully as he could, sleeping alone that night didn't do much for his mood.

He was tense and tired by the time they got back to Oahu. The kids, especially Jessie, seemed torn between wanting a father and wishing he would drop off the face of the earth. For two straight days he'd struggled to say and do the right thing, and he wasn't sure he'd succeeded. He drove everyone home, took a rain check on Lei's offer of dinner and returned to the apartment.

He immediately called Everett, who told him that Marshall had been released from the ICU on Friday and phoned California the same day. He'd sounded like his old self again, Everett said, remarking that staring death in the face for the third time in less than two months had finally convinced him of how foolish he'd been to worry so much about money. He wanted to enjoy the time he had left and return something to the state that had been so good to him.

Giving life to Kapakala's design was one way to do that. He was even willing to waive his profits and donate the *heiau* to the state if it would help. His only worry was his partners. Their investments had to be protected.

Paul held a news conference the next morning to announce Marshall's offer, then initiated a new series of meetings. As Everett had guessed, a couple of weeks with no activity had made the politicians realize they might lose the housing project entirely if they didn't come up with something more than sympathy. The latest developments added to the pressure. Between meetings about Waikane, frequent visits with Marshall to keep him informed and daily trips to the shopping center, Paul was seldom in the office during the day.

His evenings were spent with Lei and the kids. His reward for enduring sibling squabbles and helping them with their homework was the joy of receiving his first two kisses good-night and the satisfaction of seeing As on their next few tests. They seemed to enjoy having him around as long as he didn't take their mother away from them.

He certainly would have liked to, if only for an evening now and then, but Lei worried it might upset them. Since she wouldn't sleep with him in the house, they grabbed whatever time they could in the apartment, rushing there every day or two for a hurried half hour in bed. Instead of playing golf that weekend, he went to a luau at Lei's neighbor's, an exhibition at Jason's karate school and services at Kawaiahao Church, where Lei also taught Sunday school. Many of the hymns and prayers were in Hawaiian, which he could barely follow, much less sing. In general, he felt as if he'd been dropped into an alien sea. He had to struggle just to keep his head above water.

His patience wore thinner with each passing day. Finally, after they'd put the kids to bed on Tuesday, he told Lei he wanted to go out to dinner the next night—just the two of them. He needed an evening alone with her, he said.

"But the kids are still getting used to you," she replied. "They need another few weeks to accept you first."

He sighed. "Try to understand, sweetheart. I expected a breakthrough on Waikane by now, but all I've gotten are sympathetic noises and empty promises. It's damn frustrating. And then I come here—"

"But you said things were going well." She gave him a disapproving look. "You weren't totally honest with me, were you? For heaven's sake, Paul, if you can't tell *me*..."

"When am I supposed to tell you? During dinner, when the kids are clamoring for our attention? After they go to bed, when you're dead tired?" He slumped back on the couch. "I'd like to make love to you for more than half an hour at a time. I'd like to sleep with you in my arms. Let me spend the night."

She tensed and looked away. He knew there was no point pressing her. "I'm sorry. I guess I'm just tired." He kissed her and got up. "I'll see you in the morning."

"You're leaving? You're not going to tell me what happened?"

He shook his head. "I'm tired of thinking about it. I don't want to talk about it." He trudged to the door, telling himself he'd feel better after a good night's sleep.

Lei winced as he closed the door. He hadn't slammed it, but there had been something cold and final about the sound. Obviously things weren't going as well as she'd thought, but how could she have known?

She'd never had to juggle a lover and motherhood before; she'd always put the children first. Paul was so helpful and patient that it hadn't occurred to her that he might feel slighted. Besides, he'd seemed to enjoy himself last week. She wanted more time alone as much as he did, but it would have to wait. In another few weeks the kids would be secure enough to accept being excluded once in a while.

In another few weeks, though, he might be totally fed up. Hadn't more than one friend remarked that if you wanted to keep a man happy, you had to pamper him a bit? Torn and uncertain, she walked slowly into her bedroom to think.

Paul took a cool shower, then scanned the bookcase for something to take his mind off his troubles—something about Hawaiian mysticism, maybe. The subject was important to Lei, so it wouldn't hurt to read up on it.

He started with a study by Creighton Howe, *The Role of Kahuna Magic in Hawaiian Culture and Thought*. Maybe because it was so dark and quiet in the apartment, the book gave him the willies. Its accounts of magical powers and mystical deeds were eerily convincing. The creepiest chapter of all concerned the feats of a *kahuna nui* on Niihau named Liliha Kamaka—Howe's mother-in-law and Lei's grandmother. Her enemies seemed to have an inordinate amount of bad luck. He told himself he didn't believe a

single word, but he wouldn't have crossed the old woman
for anything in the world.

He stayed up late to finish the book and didn't get the
sleep he'd needed, but he still felt more optimistic the next
morning. He didn't know why, but a breakthrough seemed
closer somehow. When he saw Lei that afternoon, he apologized for being so moody the night before and filled her in
on Waikane.

The state had decided to reconstruct the *heiau* and in-
clude it in the new state park, and the city council had
agreed to expedite approval of David Kapakala's design, but
funding was still a stumbling block. He'd asked the county
to pay for more of the infrastructure and pressed the state
to subsidize the cost of the apartments with federal grant
money, but so far, neither had happened.

"The legislature is halfway through its session already,
and doing nothing out at Waikane day after day is costing
Marshall a bundle," he said. "I've tried every argument I
can think of, but I just can't pin them down."

"You've accomplished a tremendous amount so far. You
still have more than a month. I know you'll be able to put
something together." Lei paused, thinking he'd have a nervous breakdown unless it was soon. Thank God she'd come
to her senses last night. "I finally realized that you were
right about us needing some time alone. Mrs. Keala can stay
as late as we want tonight." She smiled teasingly. "How
does ordering a pizza and eating it naked together in bed
sound?"

He smiled and said it sounded terrific, then described in
great detail how to enjoy tomato sauce and pepperoni to
their fullest. She thought he was kidding, but he wasn't.

They went out every few evenings after that, always
stopping by the house first to spend some time with the kids.
Lei loved being with Paul—the long, quiet dinners and the
passionate hours in bed—but she hated leaving the twins.
She could never escape without a chorus of pleas, especially from Jessie: "Do you have to go?" "It's boring

without you." "If you stay we promise not to bother you." "Can't you just go to dinner and then come home and put us to bed?" Paul told Lei not to feel guilty, that they would stop begging once they realized it never worked, but she couldn't help herself.

Still, it was only a few nights a week and it did Paul a world of good. He was more optimistic about work and more relaxed with the kids. Before, he'd done his damnedest to be a model father. Now he roughhoused and joked with them, genuinely enjoying the role.

Because of that, she was reluctant to cancel their dinner plans when they got home on Thursday and learned that Jessie was sick with a cold. "She was tired when she got home from school," Mrs. Keala said. "Sniffling a little, too. I got a little soup and toast down her and put her to bed. She's been sleeping on and off all afternoon."

Lei went into Jessie's room and felt the small of her back. If she had a fever, it was very slight. She read to Jessie until she dozed off again, then kissed her good-night and left. Paul was in Jason's room, playing a computer game. Much to his disgust, he was losing badly.

Mrs. Keala had raised four children and seen them through a lot worse than colds, so there was no reason not to go out. Still, Lei was worried. She called twice during dinner, but Jessie was sleeping peacefully both times.

As they left the restaurant, Paul put his arm around her and smiled. "Why do I have the feeling it would be a waste of my time to try to seduce you tonight?"

"I know I'm overreacting, but Jessie is used to having me home when she's sick. If she wakes and I'm gone—"

"I know. It's okay." They got into the car. "To be honest, I'm worried about her myself. There's a lot of flu going around. People have been pretty sick with it. Let's rent the most mindless movie we can find and go home."

Lei gave him a hug, silently thanking him for being so understanding. They stopped at a video place in Manoa and picked out a comedy, then drove to the house. She felt a little foolish by then. Things were probably fine.

But they weren't. They heard Jessie's screams even before they opened the door. Lei ran into the living room. Jessie was sitting on Mrs. Keala's lap, rocking and holding her head, sobbing and yelling that it hurt. Jason was sitting beside them on the couch, looking tense and upset.

Lei took Jessie into her arms.

"Thank God you're home," Mrs. Keala said. "I called the restaurant but you'd left, so I tried the apartment, but you weren't there, either. She woke about ten minutes ago, screaming this way. She has a fever now, don't you think?"

Lei nodded. Jessie was much warmer than before. "I'm taking her to the ER. She's never acted this way before."

Mrs. Keala offered to stay with Jason while Paul drove Lei and Jessie to the hospital, but she wound up going home because Jason refused to be left behind. He huddled close to Paul in front, while Lei held Jessie in back and tried desperately to soothe her.

She'd never known what fear was until that car ride. Jessie got hotter and less coherent, whimpering as though she was too weak to sob. Lei was terrified she was going to slip into a coma—or worse.

The admitting nurse at the ER asked a few questions and then put them at the head of the line. That and the rash Jessie suddenly developed frightened Lei even more, but she tried not to show it. Jason was scared enough as it was. Paul's calmness and strength were the only things that kept the boy from getting hysterical.

Within minutes, Lei and Jessie were led to the examining area. Jessie was lethargic and delirious by the time the doctor came in, only fighting him when he manipulated her neck, which seemed to be painful and stiff.

"All the symptoms point to meningococcal meningitis," he said, "but we'll run some tests just to make sure. She'll have to be admitted to the ICU, but you can stay with her if you want to."

The words "meningitis" and "ICU" struck terror into Lei's heart. Meningitis could kill people. The ICU was only for the dreadfully ill. She was only slightly reassured when the doctor explained that most patients improved rapidly after treatment began and recovered completely. She didn't care how most patients did. This was her beloved daughter.

She was asked to leave at that point so that intravenous antibiotics could be started and blood and spinal fluid drawn. Jessie was too dazed and incoherent to know who was or wasn't in the room, so Lei didn't argue. At least they wouldn't be separated for long.

She paused outside the waiting room to get a grip on herself. Jason was on the couch with Paul, listening with sleepy awe to whatever he was saying. Jason had never looked at *her* that way.

Having Paul as a father would be wonderful for him, she thought. Paul had to stay here. Jessie had to get well. A feeling of icy dread enveloped her, almost suffocating her. Suppose neither one happened?

She forced down her panic and walked inside, somehow explaining the situation in a reasonably calm voice.

Paul drew her down beside him and put his arm around her. "Jessie'll be fine. Don't ask me how I know. I just do."

She bit her lip and nodded. "I'm sure you're right. It's a good hospital." She took Jason onto her lap and cuddled him. Thank God *he* wasn't ill.

He yawned and clung to her. "I want Paul to stay with me," he mumbled. "Not Mrs. Keala."

"But, sweetie, Paul has—"

"Of course I'm going to stay with you," Paul said. "Us guys have to stick together at times like this."

Satisfied, Jason nodded and closed his eyes. He was asleep within seconds.

"I don't want to be alone any more than he does," Paul added softly. "We'll keep each other company."

"Then thank you." Lei paused. "I saw the way he was looking at you. He's beginning to idolize you."

"I was telling him about a run-in I had with a grizzly when I was hiking in Glacier National Park. He's a great kid. Both of them are." He hugged her close. "Just look after Jessie until she's better and don't worry about Jason. He'll be fine."

"It's just that he's getting so attached to you . . ."

"Children *should* be attached to their father." He smiled gently. "I've been reading up on Hawaiian mysticism. I can't say I'm a believer yet, but lately I've been sure of things I have no reason to be sure of—that we'll be together, that things'll work out with the kids, that we needed to go home before . . . I was thinking about your grandmother's prophecy just now. Fear and anguish, she said. She sure hit the nail on the head, didn't she?"

Lei felt a little faint. The vision *had* come true, but she'd been too worried about Jessie to realize it. "You're right. I'm so afraid, Paul, and I can't stop thinking that if only we hadn't gone out—if only I'd been there when Jessie woke up . . ."

"We'd have gotten to the ER five minutes sooner. It wouldn't have made a difference. Anyway, maybe it was fated. I don't know what to think anymore."

The doctor came in a moment later, telling them that the spinal fluid had been very cloudy, another characteristic of meningitis. In fact, he was so sure of the diagnosis that he wanted everyone who'd had close contact with Jessie to start on precautionary antibiotics immediately. Paul took prescriptions for himself, Jason and Mrs. Keala, arranged to meet Lei at nine the next morning to find out how things were going and hugged her goodbye.

They went to a pharmacy, then stopped by Mrs. Keala's house and gave her a bottle of pills. Paul promised to call her if he needed help, but nothing could have made him leave Jason. He identified with the boy. At eight, he'd had the same earnest hunger for a father's love and attention as Jason did.

Back at home, he tucked Jason into bed and told him a story, then settled down in Lei's room with a magazine. Within minutes, a small, solemn figure appeared in the doorway. Paul smiled and beckoned him inside.

"It's tough to sleep in a strange bed," Paul said. "You want to keep me company?"

"Okay." Jason crawled in beside him. "Sometimes my sister and I keep Mommy company. My original mom and dad used to sleep here, too. It was better having two parents. At least I think it was. I don't remember them too well."

The innocent longing in Jason's voice melted Paul's heart. "You think I would do? As a father, that is?"

"Yup. Jessie does, too. She's afraid you're going to leave, though. That's why she's such a pain sometimes." He paused. "Are you?"

"Not without you, your sister and your mother. We have few problems, but we'll work them out. I promise."

"Is my sister going to be okay?"

"Yes. They know what's wrong and they know how to cure it." At least he prayed to God they did.

"And I won't get sick 'cause I'm taking the pills."

"Right."

Reassured, Jason asked, "When you were hiking, did you ever meet anything besides a bear? A lion or tiger, maybe?"

Paul told him about a marmoset that had eaten out of his hand and a shy lady moose that had retreated whenever he got too close. By the time Jason fell asleep, Paul's heart was aching with love. The thought that he could give this boy and his sister all the things he'd never had as a child filled him with joy and humility. Since Lei would be miserable on the mainland, he would just have to move to Hawaii.

The next morning, he canceled all his appointments and kept Jason home with him. Being together seemed more important than business or schoolwork.

Lei looked exhausted but calm when they met her in the hospital. Jessie did have meningitis, but she'd already begun to improve. She was more coherent and more demanding, wanting Lei every moment and complaining loudly whenever she left. Paul offered to drive Lei home for a few hours' sleep, but she refused. She felt Jessie needed her.

He and Jason spent the day in Sea Life Park. On the surface, they were looking at marine life and learning about the ocean, but deep down, they were becoming a father and son. During lunch, Jason mumbled guiltily that it wasn't right to be having so much fun without Jessie, but Paul assured him that she would be well again soon. The fact that they were twins didn't mean they had to do everything together, he explained. Sometimes he or Lei would do things just with Jessie.

It was nearly five by the time they got back to the hospital. Jessie was still improving, so this time Paul didn't just offer to take Lei home, he insisted on it. The Ala Moana Center was only a few blocks away, so he picked up some dinner on the way. Lei went straight to bed after she ate, sleeping until ten. Then she showered and returned to the hospital.

There were tears of relief in her eyes when she greeted Paul and Jason the next morning. She told them that Jessie had no sooner awoken that morning than she'd begun to pepper her with questions. It was as though the past two awful days had never happened. She'd been moved to a regular room and would remain in the hospital for another week or so, until her treatment was finished.

"You two guys seem to be doing great on your own, so I thought I'd stay here most of the weekend," she added.

Paul lifted Jason up and settled him on his hip. "How would you like to go on a trip? It'll get us out of your mom's hair so she can concentrate on your sister."

The boy's eyes shone with excitement. "Can we go to Disneyland?"

"I had someplace closer in mind—one of the neighbor islands, maybe. We can go to Disneyland after your sister gets better." He smiled at Lei. "We could take our honeymoon there, all four of us. Will you marry me now even though we'd have to live apart at first?" He knew she would, but he still added soberly, "It might be two or three years before I can afford to move here."

He expected her to smile and embrace him, but instead she replied in a very serious voice, "Of course I will. I've been waiting for you for centuries. Another couple of years is nothing."

Lei knew it wasn't true, though. They could write, phone and visit, but she still would miss him terribly. So would the twins, who would go from childhood to preadolescence in the time he was gone. But good things were worth waiting for, and Paul Lindstrom was a very good thing, indeed—for her, for Jessie and Jason, and for her beloved islands.

She put her arms around him, the three of them making a tight little huddle in the middle of the lobby. "There's a phone in Jessie's room. Call me when you decide where you're going." She pecked Jason on the cheek. "Have a good time. And be good for Paul."

"He already is," Paul said. "And so are you."

"I'm so glad. I love you so much." She kissed him goodbye, then walked to the elevator.

Paul put Jason down and led him outside. "Maybe we should go to Maui," he remarked. "Your mom told me you have some cousins there. We could visit them." He would have liked to visit the Hawaiian side of the family even more, but that was impossible. You couldn't go to Niihau without an invitation from the owners.

It was as though Jason had read his mind. "I'd rather visit my real family. You know—Mommy's mother and grandma."

It spoke well for them, Paul thought, that Jason thought of them as his real family. After all, they weren't related by blood. "But they're on Niihau," he said. "Your mom has

enough to worry about without getting us permission to go
there.''

He was a little taken aback when Jason answered matter-
of-factly that he would make the arrangements himself
''I've known the owners all my life. I've even had dinner at
their ranch on Kauai.''

''They might not let me come. I mean, I'm a *haole* from
the mainland, I'm not related to anyone there—''

''But you will be. You're going to marry my mom
Everyone'll want to meet you, especially Liliha.''

Paul hadn't known that an eight-year-old child could
radiate such unholy amusement.

''Everyone does what she wants,'' Jason went on. ''If you
value your life, you'd better, too.''

Paul grinned at him. ''You can count on it. I've read
about the lady.''

Jason was as good as his word, making the call as soon as
they got home. He explained the situation in a very adult
way, then asked if he and Paul could visit. The answer was
yes. Paul made the specific arrangements, thinking that the
man he spoke with was warm, helpful and not the least bit
mysterious.

Afterward he called Lei, who was thrilled that he wanted
to meet her family but disappointed she wouldn't be there
to see it. Her grandmother, she said with a giggle, would
make mincemeat out of him. From what he'd read, he could
well believe it.

Niihau was anything but easily accessible. While tourists
could take helicopter flights to uninhabited areas of the
island, people going to visit their families in Niihau's sole
village, Puuwai, had to sail on an old landing craft that the
owners had leased from the navy. It would be leaving their
private dock early the next morning.

Paul and Jason took the first available flight to Kauai
spending the night in Lihue, the county seat. Makaweli
Landing was about half an hour away. They arrived to find
they'd be sharing the craft with various types of freight and

two other passengers, a Niihauan returning from his lady friend's house on Kauai and a vet going to Niihau to examine some sick sheep on Niihau Ranch.

The seventeen-mile trip to Kii Landing on Niihau was choppy enough that Paul got queasy, but Jason airily insisted it was usually far worse. A pickup from the ranch took them into town on a well-graded dirt road that ran through a hot, dry expanse of red dust and thorny kiawe trees.

Finally the sea came into view, and then the tidy little village of Puuwai. They were dropped in front of a small wooden house surrounded by a low stone wall that looked like every other home in the town. Jason pointed out the church and school buildings a short distance beyond, then led Paul onto the veranda and opened the front door.

He called out something in Hawaiian, and an elderly woman with snow-white hair, nut-brown skin and perfect posture walked slowly into the hall. She was dressed in the sort of muumuu you saw everywhere in Hawaii, and looked frail enough to collapse in a stiff breeze. Paul felt a strong urge to bow to her, but resisted it.

She crooked her finger at Jason, then bent to offer her cheek. The boy rushed up to kiss her. For all her regal formality, there was a definite sparkle of affection in her eyes. She murmured something in Hawaiian, and Jason nodded and turned around. "She says I should find my grandma. She's already at church." He scampered out the door.

The old lady looked Paul up and down. "So you came to Niihau," she said in heavily accented English. "Why?"

Jason hadn't said a word about Paul, but somehow Liliha knew who he was. It was a little spooky. "Do you recognize me from your—your crystal ball?" he asked.

"I ask the questions. You answer." Her tones brooked no argument. "Why did you come?"

"Jason suggested it. He wanted to visit you."

"If you say so." She motioned him forward. "Come."

He followed her into the kitchen and sat where he was told to, at an old wooden table. She took a can of Coke out of a cabinet and set it in front of him. There was no indoor plumbing or electricity here, but the modern world still intruded in certain ways. "The road is dusty," she said. "Maybe you're thirsty."

"Yes. Thank you." He took a sip. The soda was warm, but at least it was wet.

She sat down across from him. "So. Little Jessie. She's better now?"

He almost choked on his drink. There was no way she could have known about Jessie. There were no phones here. There hadn't been time for Lei to write.

She tapped the table to get his attention. "Are you deaf, *haole*? The fever is gone, and the pain in her head?"

The blood drained from his face. He was dying to question her but didn't dare. "Yes. She's doing very well."

"But you're not." She cackled with delight. "Leilani was very afraid. She wanted me to pray. I got a message on the radio. You didn't know there was a radio, did you?"

"No," he said, relieved she had a sense of humor, however mordant it might be.

"From Kauai to Niihau. For emergencies." She chuckled again. "Fear and anguish ... The vision was right, but I saw the wrong meaning. Doesn't happen often. Now you..." She studied him for several seconds. "Yellow hair and blue eyes, just like in my glass. You're good to my granddaughter? You please her in bed? You teach her to please you?"

Paul went from white to crimson. He'd never been cross-examined about his sex life by an ancient native priestess before. "I love her very much," he managed. "We're going to get married soon."

"Sure. Otherwise you couldn't visit here. You're good to her, but blind. You question and doubt. A little less now. You're learning. Anyway, you're young and strong and handsome. You could doubt forever and she would still want you. The pleasure is so great, how can she help it?"

Disrespectful or not, he couldn't hold his tongue. "There's no way you could have known all that. She wrote to you. She must have."

Her eyes mocked him. "Sure. Your name, your history, your job here. That was all. She said you were smart."

"And you say I'm not."

"Dumb as a chicken," she said with a cackle. "You're a mainland *haole*. You all doubt, but you all learn. Leilani swore she wanted a *kanaka*, but she chose you. She must be crazy for you. You must make her crazy. Even a chicken could figure that out, no?"

"Yes. Even a chicken." Chagrined, he sipped his Coke. "Do you toy with everyone, or just with dumb *haoles* from the mainland?"

"So you're not afraid of me, eh?"

"The truth? I'm terrified of you. I've read your son-in-law's book. You don't like *haoles* very much. If you want to, maybe you can ruin my life. Maybe. I don't know."

"I love my granddaughter. She loves you. You have problems. *Haole* or not, maybe I'll help you."

Paul didn't see how she could, but he wasn't about to refuse. "Right about now, I'll take all the help I can get." He risked a smile. "You probably know all about Waikane."

She chuckled. "Sure I know. Leilani goes on and on about it. So I snapped the rope, I sent the rain, I crashed the plane..."

He stared at her. He was beginning to think she really might have.

"What, no argument?" Eyes twinkling, she got up from the table. "I'll tell you the truth. I prayed. So did many others. Things happened. I wasn't surprised."

She poured a glass of water, cut a slice of ginger root and brought them to the table. Paul tensed as she scraped some ginger into the glass with her thumbnail. He could tell himself from now till next year that this was nothing but a pagan ritual, but the accuracy of her visions said otherwise. Besides, his instincts had told him that the incidents at Waikane weren't accidental. Something intangible had beckoned him to these islands when logically he should have wanted to stay at home. The world was suddenly a lot more complicated than it had been two and a half months before.

"We'll see what my glass has to say. Then I'll decide what to do." There was a long silence. The ginger settled to the bottom of the glass. Liliha stared intently.

Suddenly she shuddered. "Leilani... She's in pain. You're beside her. Her face—it's so pale, so hot ... The vision is dividing, breaking up. I see three images ..."

Paul felt dizzy with horror. He'd hurt Lei once. He couldn't do it again. He just couldn't. "Tell me what it means," he said. "There must be some way to change it."

Liliha ignored him. Another few seconds went by. Finally she sighed in relief. "I see now. It's a good pain. You'll give me three great-grandchildren." She straightened; her eyes narrowed. "Big, strong babies. They'll come slowly. She'll need you with her."

Five children, he thought. *God help me.* "I won't be able to move to Hawaii for a few years, but once I do, I'll never leave her. I promise I'll take good care of her."

Liliha frowned at that. "A few years is too long. You'll stay."

Paul explained the situation, but the old woman wasn't impressed. Leilani would pine for him every moment, she said. He couldn't leave her for that long. He wouldn't.

"I don't want to, but I have no choice," he replied. "I can't walk out on my responsibilities, and since I can't earn the kind of money in Hawaii that I do in—" He stopped abruptly. Maybe he could. In his particular line of work, a big enough success could make an enormous difference. All he had to do was pull off the seemingly impossible—put together a deal on Waikane.

He leaned back in his chair. "I've heard everyone in Hawaii is terrified of you."

She shrugged. "Could be."

"Even the politicians?"

"Them most of all. Look how much they have to lose."

He smiled at her tart tone. "Then come to Oahu with me. Speak to them. Tell them you'll send them bad luck unless they help me with Waikane. If I can get the project built, I might be offered a good job here. Then I could afford to stay."

"But I never leave Niihau," she said.

"You will for this. Both of us know it."

"Oh? And what makes you so sure, *haole*?"

Paul shook his head. "I don't know. I just am. That's been happening to me a lot lately."

To his utter astonishment, she took his hand and held it in both of hers. "You belong in these islands. They're your destiny. You have great *mana*. It's what led you to Niihau—and to me. You came here to seek my help. You'll have it. But never doubt that you could have succeeded by yourself. It would have taken you longer, that's all."

Paul felt as if he were floating outside of normal time and space. None of this seemed real. "But I'm not like you. I'm an ordinary person."

"You're exactly like me. Just younger and less sure of your powers. You come from a different world, so they take a different form, that's all." She released his hand. "You've had great success. Do you think it's just luck or cleverness?"

Maybe it wasn't. People were always using words like "uncanny" and "incredible" to describe the things he did. He shook his head, unable to take it in. "I don't know."

"But you do, my son. You do."

He stared at her. "Yes. Maybe you're right."

She nodded, then smiled broadly. "What children you and Leilani will have! In the old days, they could have ruled these islands!"

It was the most terrifying thing she'd said all day.

Epilogue

Oahu. Two Years Later.

Liliha had sworn she would never again leave Niihau, but events had conspired to change her mind. The housing project at Waikane had been named for her, the Liliha Kamaka Village. The governor himself had begged her to come to Oahu to bless it, and also to resanctify the burial ground and *heiau*, now known as Waikane State Historic Park. The owners of Niihau had even put their helicopter at her disposal, just as they had two years before.

Paul watched admiringly as she marched toward the reconstructed *heiau*. A local minister was at her side, the two of them leading a large crowd of people *mauka*. Liliha had been magnificent with the politicians two years ago. A penetrating stare and a few soft but stern words and she'd had them quaking in their shoes. They'd made the usual noises about supporting the project and working to get it built, but this time, they'd really meant it. Things had moved so quickly and favorably after that that even Paul was astonished. In the end, Marshall had actually made a small profit on the deal.

Marshall was here today with Grace, his wife of eighteen months, a living testimonial to the healing power of love and the miracles of modern medicine. After bypass surgery, he'd retired from the day-to-day running of his business in order to devote his considerable energies to his duties as a Bishop trustee. Paul ran Canning Enterprises now, and with remarkably little interference from his boss. It was a constant challenge to balance the desire for economic growth with the need to protect the environment, but one that made his successes here doubly rewarding.

It hadn't been easy to leave Everett, of course, but Everett had found excellent replacements in John and Amy Davis, who'd moved to San Francisco and now ran his office there. Everett and his wife and the Davises had flown in for today's ceremony, John looking worried that Amy might deliver their first child at any moment even though her due date was four weeks away.

Paul identified completely with the nervous father-to-be. Fifteen months before, when Lei was expecting their daughter, Lily, he'd been the same way. As Liliha had predicted, it hadn't been an easy birth. Although he'd coached Lei through her breathing and rubbed her back, he'd felt useless and helpless in the face of her pain. As much as he loved being a father, he didn't like the idea of allowing her to go through that again.

She wanted more children, though, so he had no choice. He'd recently asked David Kapakala to design a house for them—a very large house. David seldom had time for private homes anymore—he'd been offered one major project after another after Waikane—but he'd agreed at once. He was here today, as well, savoring his triumph.

So was Lei's mother Ella, who was walking between the twins, holding little Lily. A sprightly strawberry blonde with a strong will and perfect health, Lily was a joy to everyone. All of them spoiled her rotten, even Jessie and Jason, whom

Paul had adopted the previous year. Of course, she wasn't big enough to barge into their rooms and get into their most cherished possessions yet.

At the moment, Lily was looking around in wonder as Ella carried her toward the *heiau*. She and Liliha had a special bond, but that was only to be expected. Lily had been named for Liliha, who'd taken the honor as her due.

Lei, who was walking beside Paul, slipped her hand into his and smiled. "What a perfect day! You should feel very, very proud of all this."

Every day was perfect with Lei. So many things united them—their family, their work, their love for Hawaii. Paul had long ago accepted that there was something magical about it.

"Pleased, maybe, but not proud," he replied. "I had too much help for that. Your own love and support, Marshall's generosity, Everett's good advice, David's brilliant design...." He looked at Liliha. "And your grandmother, of course. You think she'd help me with the South Point project if I flattered her hard enough?"

Lei thought that was typical of Paul. As Hawaiian as he'd become in his outlook, he still didn't know how special he was. Friend and lover, anchor and soul mate—in all of Hawaii *nei*, there wasn't a better husband and father.

"She'd only say you could do it on your own. And she'd be right." She grinned at him. "Just use your powers, *haole*. None of us can resist you."

He squeezed her hand. "Just as long as you can't."

Liliha climbed onto the *heiau*, and everyone gathered around. She began to chant softly in Hawaiian, a prayer of purification, rededication and peace. Despite her age and frailty, her voice grew stronger and more passionate with each passing moment. Ever so slowly, the chant built into a joyful, triumphant proclamation that made the air reverberate with emotion. Some trembled; others wept.

Then, with stunning abruptness, it was over. No one made a sound. No one moved. They couldn't.

The silence was broken by little Lily, who pointed excitedly toward the middle of the *heiau* and giggled in delight. Liliha glanced around, then looked at the child. Far from minding, the old woman was smiling approvingly.

"It's the warriors," she said in English. "She sees the warriors. I thought she might. After all, she bears my name."

Lei and Paul looked at each other. The ceremony had moved them deeply, but neither had seen any warriors on the *heiau*. Their little girl, it seemed, was even more gifted than they were. Lord only knew what she'd get up to in her life.

Fortunately, they had each other. Together, they could face anything. They exchanged a smile of perfect understanding and walked forward to help Liliha down from the *heiau*.

Glossary

ali'i—a chief, royalty
aloha—welcome, farewell, love
anana—the death prayer
ehu—a red-haired Hawaiian
ewa—in the direction of Ewa plantation, west of Honolulu
haole—a Caucasian
hapa—part or half
heiau—an ancient Hawaiian temple
hookipa—hospitality
hui—a group, club or association; in business, a financial or
    investment group
kahuna—a priest or priestess, healer, expert
kama'aina—native-born; also, one who has lived in Hawaii
    for a long time
kanaka—a Hawaiian or part-Hawaiian man
kapu—off limits, forbidden
kokua—help
kupuna—ancestors
lanai—a porch or veranda
lei—a wreath or garland;

lani—means heaven, so the name
Leilani literally means "wreath of heaven"
mahalo—thank you
makai—toward the ocean
malihini—a newcomer, stranger
mana—vital force
mauka—toward the mountains
nani—beautiful
ne'i—this place
nene—Hawaiian goose, the state bird
nui—high, big, large
ohana—family
paniolo—cowboy
pilikia—trouble
pupule—crazy
pu'uhonua—place of refuge
unihipili—low self, unconscious

* * * * *

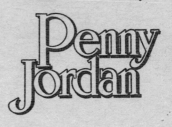